HIGH SEA SEDUCTION

ZARA COX

Boldwood

First published in 2015 as *Freefall*. This edition published in Great Britain in 2025 by Boldwood Books Ltd.

Copyright © Zara Cox, 2015

Cover Design by Head Design Ltd

Cover Images: Shutterstock

Every effort has been made to obtain the necessary permissions with reference to copyright material, both illustrative and quoted. We apologise for any omissions in this respect and will be pleased to make the appropriate acknowledgements in any future edition.

A CIP catalogue record for this book is available from the British Library.

Paperback ISBN 978-1-83678-937-6

Large Print ISBN 978-1-83678-936-9

Hardback ISBN 978-1-83678-935-2

Ebook ISBN 978-1-83678-938-3

Kindle ISBN 978-1-83678-939-0

Audio CD ISBN 978-1-83678-930-7

MP3 CD ISBN 978-1-83678-931-4

Digital audio download ISBN 978-1-83678-933-8

This book is printed on certified sustainable paper. Boldwood Books is dedicated to putting sustainability at the heart of our business. For more information please visit https://www.boldwoodbooks.com/about-us/sustainability/

Boldwood Books Ltd, 23 Bowerdean Street, London, SW6 3TN

www.boldwoodbooks.com

LETTER TO MY SIXTEEN-YEAR-OLD SELF

Dear Crazy You,

It's ten years from now, and this is what I've learned.

Don't be afraid to stand up to the bullies who tease you for having big boobs at fifteen. Trust me, big boobs are badass. They'll be even better at twenty-five when you've learned to use them to your better advantage.

It's okay to be a nerd. Nerds rule the fucking world.

Don't get in the elevator with that old man at Bloomingdales on your seventeenth birthday. If you do, you'll never use tweezers again!

When Mom tells you it's time to get on the Pill, please, please, PLEASE don't fight her on it. I can't stress this enough, Keely Nina Benson. JUST DON'T!

Now listen very carefully because this one's important. Nineteen is going to be rough. Way rougher than you think you'll be able to cope with. Hang in there. The pain may not go away. There may be times when you'll want to end it all. Times when putting one foot in front of the other, or just breathing, will seem like a task too far.

Hang in there.

Because there will be moments of acute, ceaseless joy. They may be fleeting, but... fuck it (yeah, you've taken up swearing. A lot).

Hang in there.

I love you, even though you may not feel it right now.

I. LOVE. YOU.

K Benson xxx

PS—that pink streak in your hair may look cool now, but you'll hate it in a month. Do yourself a favor. Go with the purple. I'm older. I may not be a whole lot wiser, but listen to me anyway.

1

KEELY

Orion's Belt. Cassiopeia. Ursa Minor—

I feel him approach, but I keep my gaze trained upward on the piercing stars flung carelessly on a blanket of velvet in the night sky. I search feverishly for patterns I learned a lifetime ago, before a time when I needed something celestial to ground me in the darkness. Something to connect me to the universe, so I won't feel so uselessly untethered.

His footsteps draw closer. I keep my head up, refusing to let the consternation and bewilderment take over.

I am above that. I am woman. *I am strong.*

Yeah, maybe not that last part.

The blush grows from my neck and covers my cheeks, my face. Awareness engulfs me as he hovers behind me, his presence an entity I can't deny.

I squint harder at the cold, bright stars, but my attention begins to waver. Nothing connects.

Damn it.

"What the hell do you want?"

"It's thirty-six degrees out here, without the wind chill. I figure you can use a blanket," his deep, growly voice says behind me.

As if reminded that I'm barefoot on a beach in Montauk in late February, goosebumps pile upon goosebumps, and my body screams distress signals to my brain. I shiver so hard, despite my determination to ignore my body's pain, that I nearly upend myself. My discomfort isn't enough to make me retrieve my shoes and go back inside though.

He steps closer.

"I don't need a damn blanket. If I wanted one, I'd have brought one with me." I lift the chilled, open bottle of vintage Dom Perignon Oenotheque clutched in my right hand and take a huge, bracing gulp.

Fuck yeah.

My best friend, Bethany Green, just got officially engaged to the catch of the century and the love of her life. Personally, Zachary Savage isn't my type—all that caveman, possessive shit just gets on my nerves. But they are ecstatically happy. He worships the ground she walks on, and after the year she's endured and the snippets of his past I've become privy to, they deserve a little—no, make that *a lot*—of happiness.

And if a small part of me is jealous of all that happiness, I intend to drown it dead with a little help from Dom P.

As soon as this intruder, the reason for me blushing like a damn schoolgirl virgin, goes away.

"I came out here, *Einstein*, because I want to be alone. So if you don't mind...?" I dangle the question, seeing if he'll take the bait. If not, it'll be my pleasure to shove it down his throat.

"Take the blanket. Then I'll leave," he says again. This time I'm not sure if my shiver is to do with the ridiculously low temperatures or his low, husky voice. Whatever.

"Fine." I sigh and reach behind me, without taking my gaze off the constellations. I don't want to turn around. I don't want to see his face. Not after the freak-out episode he just witnessed.

It wasn't the things I said ten minutes ago in Bethany's kitchen that were embarrassing in and of themselves. Hell, I talk about my vagina all the time. I feel zero embarrassment for that part.

It was the desolation, the fear, the neediness as I clung to my best friend while prattling nonsense that makes me not want to face the man behind me now. I'm okay with feeling desperately sorry for myself. Not so cool with complete strangers seeing beneath my skin.

The last time I felt like this was six years and one day ago. After what my parents refer to as my *Unfortunate Episode*.

The date is engraved in my mind, since it was my nineteenth birthday. Valentine's Day, for fuck's sake.

It was the day I set out to end it all. And failed.

All of that same insecure fucking panic was in my voice as I stood in Bethany's kitchen and talked about my clit, my neglected and lonely pussy and my need for a man with a big cock. Except they were meant just as euphemisms. A cry for help, which my self-aware mind contrived. I know this because I have above average intelligence. Some Stephen Hawking-type person with thick, super-nerdy bifocals told me so when I was sixteen.

At the time, having what I already knew confirmed made me smug and superior for all of five seconds.

Gradually, I've come to see that news as a curse. It means that most of the time I know what's wrong with me but often don't have the tools to fix it. I especially hate that this ball of anguish, which I carry around inside me, will never go away because I don't know *how* to fix myself.

Because I tried again yesterday. Tried to end it all. And failed.

Another shiver races through me along with the realization that the blanket isn't in my hand.

I snap my fingers, impatient to get on with my new and highly enlightened *get-drunk-and-freeze-to-death* plan. A moment later, the weight of a fleece blanket drapes over my shoulders, enveloping me in unwanted warmth.

Manners dictate I should say thank you, but I don't want to engage this man. He's seen me at my most vulnerable. Besides Beth and my parents, no one else has seen that side of me.

So I walk away, just a few feet to where a large rock juts out of the water. The tide has receded a little, so I can sit on it without getting my feet wet. I perch and take another swig of champagne.

Then I hear him. He's moving closer. Mr. Rusty Social Skills, as he called himself when I snarled at his eavesdropping in the kitchen, is clearly not into getting messages, even when they are spelled loud and clear.

"Are we really doing this?" I ask after a few more satisfying, but less than bracing, gulps.

"Looking at the stars? Yep. The Plough is particularly bright tonight."

I hang my head, my soul weary and my body chilled to the bone. "Please. Don't," I whisper, my voice barely audible above the sound of crashing waves.

"We don't have to talk about the stars. We can talk about the Pygmies in Africa. Do you know they fuck every day for the month of May, then don't have sex for the rest of the year?" he imparts.

My head whips around. "That's not true—" I realize, too late, what he's done, snap my head back around and raise the bottle to my lips. "Fuck off. Seriously," I growl. But that quick look has sparked a tiny curiosity. One I'm determined to hide.

"Can I at least apologize for the accidental eavesdropping?" he presses.

"Why is it important to you? You won't see me again after tonight. You really don't need to apologize for being inadvertently privy to the sorry state of my vagina. Go back to the party. Hell, you have my permission to share the gossip. With any luck, you can get my clit trending."

He remains silent for several minutes, and I don't know if he's digesting the information or is stunned by my direct talk. I know most men find my brazen mouth a little off-putting. I've given up caring. I've given up caring about a lot of things lately.

"I don't like parties. And the state of your vagina doesn't interest me in the least," he says finally.

My mouth drops open and I start to turn, increasingly intrigued against my will. I stop myself at the last moment and glare at the black, roiling sea.

"Then what do you want?"

"Maybe I'm curious to know why a beautiful, intelligent woman is determined to freeze to death during her best friend's engagement party. And please don't make crude references to your female parts. We both know this has nothing to do with sex."

The certainty and confidence with which he says all this throws me for a second. A particularly brisk wind slashes across my face, bringing me back to myself.

"Since you don't know me well enough to judge my intelligence, how about I just thank you for the *beautiful* comment and the blanket, and let's be done with this conversation?" I stand, ready to move off again.

I sense him rise to his feet, hear him brush sand from his pants. "Is there any reason you won't look at me, Keely?"

My breath catches slightly at the way my name sounds on his lips, then I steel my spine. This has gone on long enough. "Because I don't want to talk to you. Nothing personal, but I really want to be alone. Even a guy with rusty social skills can surely compute such a simple request?" My voice is growing exasperated, and I resent him for that.

"I could leave, but then Zach would cut off vital parts of my anatomy I prefer to hang on to should anything happen to you. Bethany too, I'm guessing, although I don't know her well enough to judge."

A reluctant smile tugs at my lips as I think of my friend and her fiancé. But then I sober up. "What if I promise to just sit on this rock and enjoy my champagne?"

"Then I hope you won't mind some silent company. We don't need to talk. Hell, I won't even ask how you know the mating habits of African pygmies, although I have a feeling it has something to do with the intelligent part."

"Or maybe I'm addicted to the Discovery Channel?" I don't bother to hide the snark in my voice. "I'm disappointed it takes so little to impress you."

I gulp some more champagne and am heartened to see that half of it is gone. Great, maybe I'll freeze to death quicker with three thousand dollars' worth of champagne swishing around inside me.

"I didn't say I was impressed." The cadence of his voice tells me he's smiling.

Fucker.

"I don't care what you are, Rusty. All I care about right now is being left in peace."

"Rusty?"

I remain silent. I drink. Finally, I begin to feel a buzz. It's not strong enough to drown out my thoughts, or the unsettling presence of my unwelcome beach companion. But it's definitely a buzz.

Raising my head, I stare at the stars again, a little pleased to see them weave in and out. I make out Ursa Minor, but just barely. Yes, definitely a buzz.

"You know there are over—"

"What the fuck are you doing?"

"Making conversation?"

I surge to my feet and face him, anger bubbling through my veins. That's when I see him, really see him, for the first time. Back in the kitchen, I was too embarrassed and rage-y to really take him in. Now, for the first few seconds, while losing a few billion brain cells, I'm taken aback by his intense, attractive looks.

Even with the full beard and unruly hair, he's breathtaking in a way that few men can pull off. My eyes drift over his thick folded arms and the cross-legged stance he's adopting as he perches on his own rock.

There isn't enough light out here to determine the color of his eyes, but he stares back at me with a directness that's unsettling, despite the layer of sadness in the dark depths. Then his gaze drifts over the blanket, as if he can see my body through the thick wool.

My bare feet seem to intrigue him the most, and I can almost feel him touching each digit. My toes curl into the cold sand, prompting a quirked brow from him that finally frees me from my stupid tongue-tied-ness.

"You're not making conversation. You're making specific conversation. About stars."

"That's probably because I know a little about them. No,

actually, that's not true. I know a lot about stars. And a whole range of other things, too. Pick a subject."

"I see you're not the humble type."

"Is that the type that interests you?" he fires back, raising a hand to drag his fingers through his thick facial hair.

I find that oddly distracting. Enough to fire up my anger another few notches. "God, if all of Savage's friends are like you, then I'm glad I never let him set me up with one of them like he wanted to."

Something gleams in his eyes, but it's gone too quickly for me to hammer down what it is. But I get the feeling he didn't like my reference to Zach's friends.

I toss my hair and settle back on my rock, but I continue to look at him. "How are you on the subject of silence? And practicing it?"

He doesn't respond. He merely smiles, showing perfect white teeth, which for some reason I can imagine biting my clit. I suppress a shudder, and after a few minutes, I turn around and face the churning waves again.

The silence holds. But whatever peace I hoped to find is gone forever. His presence is too distracting. Too overpowering. Now I want to engage him. That realization alone makes me drink some more, thus increasing my buzz.

My bottle is getting lighter. Soon it'll be empty. The thought makes me incredibly sad. Maybe when I'm done, I'll shed the blanket and walk into the ocean, try again to do what I failed to manage in my bath last night.

"Keely?"

God, he's relentless. "*What?*"

Was that my voice? That bleak but eager response, desperate for some sort of tether to a world I no longer want to be in?

"You know when I said I wasn't the least bit interested in

your vagina?" he enquires in that low, dark, increasingly alluring voice.

Suddenly, I'm not feeling so cold anymore. I'm alert. And I'm holding my breath. "Yeah?"

"I lied."

2

KEELY

I get up from my rock, drop the blanket and bottle. My feet crunch through cold, packed sand as I run into the icy, white waves.

"Jesus!"

Freezing water closes over my calves and rushes up my thighs. My silk skirt is soaked in seconds, but I keep going. Before I can throw myself headlong into the Atlantic, strong, implacable arms seize my waist.

"Let me go!" I grab his wrists, desperately trying to dislodge his hold.

"Fuck no. What the hell is wrong with you?" He raises me clear of the water as a strong wave hurls into us. He curses and struggles to keep his footing and me from landing in the water.

Still clutching me in his arms, he walks us backward toward dry land.

Tears prickle my eyes, fill them and begin to spill down my cheeks. I keep my head bent. I don't want him to see my despair and shame.

He doesn't. He's too busy cursing and striding to the outdoor shower near the steps leading up to Zach and Beth's house.

I'm not exactly lightweight, but he carries me as if I weigh nothing, his steps sure and confident in the sand. He reaches the shower and places me on my feet, one hand clamped around my waist to keep me there while he switches on the jets and waits for the water to warm up.

I can feel him staring at me, but I keep my head down, for the first time in my life almost afraid to look another human being in the eye.

God, what's wrong with me?

That's what he asked me, and what I've asked myself most of my life.

Foolish question, really. I know exactly what's wrong with me.

I did the unforgivable six years ago. And unlike the fairy tales expound, time doesn't heal all wounds. It makes it worse. Time bloats the pain, feeds it until you're one huge walking piece of agony.

"You react like this every time a guy tells you he's interested in you?" Gone is the amusement in Rusty's tone. Instead his voice is hard, almost sinister. I feel the bite in it slash over my skin, as if his voice is a living abrasive brush.

"I told you to leave me alone."

"So what, you could drown yourself? A little selfish on your part, don't you think?" he snarls.

My head snaps up, tears forgotten. "Excuse me?"

"You pick today of all days, at your supposed best friend's engagement party, to drown yourself?"

I breathe in slowly, not sure whether the emotion moving through me is anger or humiliation or a combination of both. "I don't know who the hell you think you are but—"

"It doesn't really matter who I am. What matters is that you understand that if you want to pull a shitty stunt like this, you can fucking wait until tomorrow to do it. There are two people up there who've been through hell and back—one of whom is supposed to be your goddamn friend—who deserve not to have their night fucked up because you're drunk and a little sad that your poor sex life is in the toilet."

Anger. Definitely anger. "Who the fuck do you think—"

"Get in." He cuts across me, dropping his right hand to his side after testing the water temperature.

"No," I return coldly, reminded all over again why I detest domineering men.

He doesn't say a word. In the next second, I'm lifted off my feet and placed beneath the hot spray. Welcoming warmth cascades over me, and I realize how cold I am. But I'm too angry to appreciate the heat.

Hell, I'm incandescent.

Before I can say a word, he steps in with me and crowds me against the marble tiles. I gasp and raise my head to find his eyes —a deep hazel that appears almost dark gold in the soft lights placed around the shower—narrowed, his gaze daring me to do anything other than what he wants.

I push his chest. Hard.

He doesn't budge. Just stares at me like I'm a puny fly and he's a fucking mountain. Which, I guess, he is. It dawns on me how big he is. Well over six foot three to my five six. Normally, my heels lend me a good four inches of confidence. But I came out here barefoot. And I have a giant in front of me.

A giant with a chest built to stop tornados in their tracks. Or a stupid woman intent on ruining his friend's engagement party. That's what his gaze tells me.

I push harder.

His hands capture mine, holding them prisoner against his chest. I blink at him through the water cascading down my face and glare harder.

"Get the fuck out of my way."

"Anyone tell you that you have a very dirty mouth?"

"Do I look like I care what anyone has to say about my mouth?"

His gaze drops to my lips. The water running over them intensifies the sudden tingle of awareness at this stare. I have to fight the impulse to lick them. Just as I fight the urge to stare at his mouth in return.

"No, you don't. It's still no excuse to talk like a goddamn sailor," he says.

"I believe in getting to the point as quickly as possible. Equivocating isn't really my thing."

"I hear you fine without the extra filth."

"I don't think you do. Because here you are, still in my fucking way."

Something dark and dangerous gleams in his eyes, and a residual shiver crawls up my spine. His chest expands beneath my palms and he slowly exhales.

"If you were mine, I'd spank that dirty mouth right out of you," he murmurs, his tone once again that deep and mesmerizing quality, which makes me want to stand on tiptoe and strain closer so I can hear more of his voice.

"Well, I'm not *yours*, Rusty. And FYI, I hate being spanked."

"Probably because it hasn't been done in the right way. But I could teach you to love it," he replies, his eyes raking my face with an intense intimacy that fires up a spark in my belly. "I can teach you to love a whole lot of things, Keely."

That spark turns into a flame.

For a moment, I can't define what the feeling is. Then I

realize it's arousal. I'm at once sad and elated. Sad because it's been so long that I've forgotten what arousal feels like. Elated because... well, I'm not dead below the waist, after all.

But this arousal isn't the kind I normally feel for a guy I want to sleep with. This feeling is different. It's sharper, more intense, as if it could actually cause damage if ignored.

Which is ridiculous.

I pull my hands away, and he lets me go. But he doesn't move from his guardian position. I turn around, let the water cascade down my back. My silk Donna Karan outfit is ruined, but what the hell. It feels good to be warm. Despite the guilt and pain clawing through me, it feels good to be alive.

"You can go now. I promise I won't try to drown myself," I mutter loud enough for him to hear.

He doesn't move.

I sigh. "I wasn't really going to drown myself. I was just trying to clear my head a little."

"With a bottle of champagne inside you? You have to do better than that."

"Look, Rusty—"

"My name is Mason. Mason Sinclair. You can call me Mason or Sinclair. Rusty doesn't work for me." There's a hard command in his voice that impresses the seriousness of his dislike for the nickname.

"Okay, Mason. If you knew me better, you'd know I'll never do that to Beth, especially not by drowning myself. She... she has a history with water..." I stop, knowing I am verging on being indiscreet about my best friend's past.

"I know," Mason says.

I turn my head, meet his eyes. "You know?"

He nods. "Zach asked for my help last year, in how to assist Bethany to tackle her fear of water."

My eyes widen. "Are you some sort of doctor?"

His eyes gleam again, and he sluices the water from his face and beard. "I'm a lot of things. Are you warm enough?" he asks.

I nod absently, and he reaches out to shut off the water. There are stacks of towels on a shelf next to the shower. He grabs two and hands me one. I quickly mop up the water in my hair and slide the towel over my wet clothes. But it's no use. I'm still dripping and getting chillier by the second.

He grabs two more and tugs one around my shoulders. "Let's get you changed before you catch pneumonia."

He steps back and indicates the house.

Still reeling from the fact that he knows about Bethany's near drowning and the fear she has of water, I start walking before I realize that he's still commanding and I'm obeying.

We reach the steps leading to the house, and I stop.

"What?"

"My room is upstairs."

There are only two ways to get to my room—the kitchen and the front entrance. Both will be filled with guests, and I don't want anyone to see me like this. Like Mason, I don't want anything to ruin Bethany and Zach's night.

"Come on, I'm staying in the pool house. You can use my bathroom," Mason says.

I hesitate. Because, *hello*, I'm from Brooklyn. Only stupid-ass women in B-movies accept invitations like these. "No, thanks."

He inhales. "If I wanted to harm you, I'd have done it on the beach, where I was less likely to be discovered."

"Maybe you like toying with your victims first," I challenge.

"You see yourself as a victim?" he asks with a touch of amusement.

"Only one way to find out. Try something," I dare him.

He tunnels his fingers through his hair in exasperation.

"This is why I hate these things," he mutters beneath his breath. There's a genuine bitterness in his tone that fans my interest higher.

"What things?" I ask, in spite of myself.

He shakes his head and starts to walk up the steps. "I'm sure you know where the pool house is. If you're interested in getting out of those wet clothes, feel free to come inside. If not, it's been... interesting meeting you." He walks off and leaves me standing in the sand.

I swear I'm not going to follow him. That I'll find a way to sneak inside the house and go up to my room without alerting anyone to my wet, disheveled state, or the frightening turmoil in my soul.

But then I look up and see Bethany and Zach standing at the kitchen window, their eyes devouring each other, the sheer depth of their love a living thing I can almost reach out and touch. And I know I can't wreck their night with even a hint of my own personal drama.

For one thing, I suspect Bethany already knows there's something up with me. She just hasn't taken the time to tackle me about it because she's been busy getting things ready for the party. If I show even the smallest hint of distress, she'll be on me in a flash. I can't let that happen. My emotions are too close to the surface for me to hide them adequately enough to fool her.

So I retrieve my shoes from the steps and trudge after Mason Sinclair.

I reach the pool house door and knock. For several minutes, he doesn't answer. I curse under my breath and start to turn away.

The door opens, and he fills the space. Larger than life and wearing only a pair of boxer briefs. In the brighter light I see that his hair is a dark chocolate brown, and his eyes are indeed a golden hazel. His mouth is both sensual and cruel, as if he's seen things in life he's loved and hated at the same time.

And his body. God, I don't even bother to hide my interest in his body.

Lean but muscular in a way only a seasoned athlete can achieve, there's a tensile strength in him, a latent energy pulsing through him that reeks of danger and the not-so-civilized.

My scrutiny reaches his very masculine feet, and I try not to smirk at the size of them. But my gaze travels back up and lingers at his groin. The thickness outlined against the black cotton is impressive, but I wish I have X-ray vision right now. I want to see the real thing. I want—

"If you're looking for the bathroom, it's this way." He interrupts my porny thoughts, and a flush crawls up my face as I lift my gaze from his crotch.

"I... Thanks." I avoid his probing stare as I slide past him and enter the large living room.

As with the main house, the pool house has been designed with luxurious comfort in mind. Heated floors warm my feet as I walk through the cream and black decorated room. Expensive landscapes adorn the walls, and a couple of sculptures on pedestals complement the thick sofas and entertainment center arranged in front of a large, already lit stone fireplace.

I go past the two master bedrooms to the bathroom at the end of the hallway. Shutting the door on the intense gaze I can feel boring into my back, I breathe a sigh of relief.

I quickly disrobe and shrug on the smaller of the two guest bathrobes hanging at the back of the door. Opening a drawer in the vanity, I find a new hairbrush and run it through my shoulder-length hair, all without meeting my eyes in the mirror. I know what I'll see. Weariness. Bitterness. Guilt. But I'm too exhausted to deal with it tonight.

So I put away the hairbrush, tighten the robe belt and open the door.

Mason is leaning against the wall right outside the bathroom. He's dressed in jeans and a black T-shirt, but he's barefoot. And his gaze is locked on me.

The dark and dangerous hunger lurking in his eyes is unmistakable.

My breath catches.

"So... what now?" I ask.

"You come and have a drink with me. You can tell me what's wrong with you or we discuss how quickly we dance around each other before you let me fuck you."

3

MASON

With remote fascination, I watch the battle on her face. She's debating whether to come at me all guns blazing or pretend I don't exist.

I don't really mind which option she chooses. She can walk out of here, and all I'll feel is a modicum of disappointment. Maybe more than a modicum. There's something... compelling about her. Something I should probably walk away from. Maybe I'm drawn to her turmoil because I have the same storm raging inside me. The need to smash, destroy, roar is a never-ending buzz beneath my skin.

I've learned the mechanics of letting it out.

The Amazon jungle has heard it a few times in the last six months. It was in the rage-soaked sweat from my skin that mixed with the straw and mud as I built the school and shelters in Roraima.

And I let it bleed out through the asphalt of the Pacific Coast Highway when the demons get too loud at 2 a.m., and I slide behind the wheel of my Koenigsegg. Or in the converted basement of my L.A. house.

When all else fails... I fuck.

Normally, it takes about a year for the guilt and rage to come to a head. This time, I've barely lasted six months. I can feel the tempest gathering ever closer. Hani, my facilitator at the exclusive service I use, was put on standby earlier this evening. All it'll take is a single phone call, and I can calm the storm. But I choose not to.

Not just yet.

I watch the woman in front of me in silence.

She has a brash strength about her that almost camouflages the gaping vortex of pain flowing from her. Her goddess-like beauty perfects that disguise, until you choose to look beneath the surface. I'm certainly finding it a little challenging to not gape at the wet tumble of caramel-blond hair that hangs in ropes about her face and shoulders, or the wide, sensual mouth that vacillates between a pout and a typical New Yorker's sneer.

She's stunning enough to stop any clear-thinking man in his tracks. For murkier-minded men like me, the allure and intrigue that shrouds her is a siren call, which howls its rapturous destruction.

And yet, I cannot look away. Not yet.

"I'll take a drink minus the talking," Keely finally responds, her chin raised in pointed defiance that I almost find amusing.

I nod and head to the kitchen. Her soft footsteps follow. "Hot or cold?" I ask when I walk past the center island.

She pauses. "Excuse me?"

"Coffee, water or club soda?" I look over my shoulder and that glare is back.

"I don't want coffee," she growls, and I'm once again fascinated by the rich, dominatrix quality of her voice, the no-nonsense way she ends every sentence, like she's impatient with the words coming out of her mouth. "Or water," she adds.

I open the fully stocked double fridge and take out two cans of soda. "Soda it is then."

She watches the can I slide across the island like it's an IED. I suppress laughter as she snaps, "Is this a joke?"

"What's wrong? Did you think I was going to top up your already high alcohol intake with more booze?"

"What are you, the fucking booze monitor?" she throws back at me.

As I lift my own can to take a long swig, my hands itch with the need to teach her a lesson about her foul mouth. I don't plan to stick around after my meeting with Zach tomorrow. But between now and then, if she continues to pique my interest, I might just grant her the spanking she richly deserves.

"I don't keep any booze here."

One sleekly outlined brow lifts. "Afraid you'll fall off the wagon?" she taunts.

"Yes," I answer truthfully.

Again, surprise and intrigue slide across her face. "Oh... okay." Slowly, she reaches out and picks up the soda. One perfectly manicured finger toys with the rim, and something awakens inside me as I watch that finger.

"How long have you been sober?" she asks after a few minutes of silence.

"Ten years, two months, three weeks and five days."

Her forehead creases for all of three seconds. "You stopped drinking on Christmas Day?" she says, confirming my initial impression of her quick wit. Why she chooses to hide her intelligence behind foul language and an abrasive manner isn't a subject that particularly interests me. But I find the whole package intriguing nonetheless.

"Yes."

Her lips twitch, and I can tell she's dying to ask me more.

The phone I left on the island earlier buzzes, and I step closer as her gaze drops. We both see the message clearly displayed on the screen.

> Welcome back, Mr. S. Your usual selection is available when you are.

"Let me guess, that's your dealer?" she jibes, without excusing herself for reading my message.

I shrug. "Of sorts."

Her sea-green eyes widen, and I'm thrilled to have surprised her again. She doesn't seem the sort to be easily shocked. "You don't drink, but you do drugs?" she asks, condemnation brimming her tone. "Isn't that swapping one addiction for another?"

"It is if you consider sex an addiction."

Her mouth drops open, and she flicks a glance at the now dark screen. "So that was your... your..."

"It's a service I use, yes." I drain the last of the soda, my eyes tracing the color washing up her neck. "You're blushing. Does that embarrass you?"

She cracks the top of the soda and pulls back the lid. "That you get your sex through an escort service? Hell, no. Maybe I'm a little embarrassed *for* you." She gulps the soda slightly too fast, and several drops trickle down the side of her mouth. She wipes it with the back of her hand and her color rises higher.

I smile. "Save your sympathy, Keely. I use the service for expediency. And because I detest the mindless games that society has imposed on an act that should have no frivolities."

Her head tilts to one side, and she slams me with a speaking look. "That your fancy way of saying you don't want to buy a girl dinner before you fuck her?"

"She can have all the dinner she wants. I just don't see the need for tedious mores or the need to display false affection before the act."

"So why not just club her over the head and drag her to your cave?"

"Why do it myself when my service more than meets those particular urges?"

She studies my face to see if I mean it literally. When she looks away, I can't decide whether she's satisfied with what she reads in my expression or not.

"So you gonna call them back?" she asks after another minute of thick silence.

"Do you want me to?" I ask.

Her breath catches. "Why the hell should I care?"

My gaze drops to the escalated rise and fall of her chest, then the belt of the robe that emphasizes her trim waist. Her excitement is as obvious as the condensation dripping down the soda can.

A touch of ennui seeps into my blood. "And you wonder why I find all this tedious?"

She frowns. "Perhaps if you took your time to make yourself clearer—"

I crush my empty soda can in my fist, and she jumps at the sound. "You're intelligent enough to know what's going on between us, and yet you want me to spell out my feelings before you feel comfortable with admitting you want what you want. Isn't that right?"

"Umm, no, wrong. I don't give a rat's ass about your feelings. And just because two people happen to find each other mildly attractive doesn't mean they have to strip and fuck on the nearest flat surface."

"Why not?" I counter.

"Because that would make them nothing more than base animals."

"But I am a base animal. And so are you."

"Keep your fucking insults to yourself, Rusty." She glares hard enough to drill holes in me.

I take a deep breath to reel myself in. I remind myself that I've been out of the land of meaningless conversation and talking just for the sake of talking for over a year. She's ironically right in calling me *Rusty*. I'm rusty when it comes to fitting back into society. But I still want to teach her a lesson for that dirty mouth. For making me want to see more of that saucy body she's hiding under the robe.

And as long as I remain this close to her, exchanging *words* when I want to do something else entirely, that temptation will only grow.

I stalk toward the living room. "I need to get out of here."

"You're going back to the party?" she asks, trailing after me.

"God, no. If I have to smile and answer another question about my status on social media, I won't be responsible for my actions," I snarl.

"Wow, someone really went to town on your social skills, didn't they?"

I don't answer. I've reached the limit of my tolerance. I need to get out into some clean, clear air before it's too late. I grab my leather jacket and punch my arms into it, wishing for the dead silence and the simple existence of Roraima.

My loafers are by the front entrance, and I shove my feet into them before I yank open the door.

"What the hell's so urgent?" Keely asks, still following. "It can't be your escort service situation since you left your phone back there."

I suck in a breath and tunnel my fingers through my hair. "I just need to get some air, okay?" I step out and start to shut the door.

"Can I come with?"

I turn slowly, catch her gaze. "Are you sure you want to?" I don't disguise the echoes of my turmoil.

She licks her lips and slowly nods. "Yes."

My breath shudders out. I take in the short robe she's wearing and the V-shaped gap at the front that shows a hint of her breasts. "I don't have time to wait for you to change." My gaze drops to her feet. "Or put on shoes."

She replies with a shrug. "We're not going far, are we?"

I don't answer. I turn and skirt the pool. After a moment, I hear her behind me. The ennui evaporates from my veins, replaced by another equally dangerous drug.

Lust.

The unsettling kind. The kind that means I have to pay Hani double when I'm done with one of her girls. I quicken my steps and round the back of Zach's house. Or the front, depending on how you view the property. I key in the code and the quadruple garage doors roll upward.

"You're going out?" Keely asks.

I head for the indigo and black McLaren P1 GTR and slide behind the wheel. Throwing open the passenger door, I start counting silently. I reach eight before she slides into the seat.

I almost wish she didn't. The moment she shuts the door and her scent engulfs me, I know I'm going to fuck her.

"Seatbelt," I growl.

She complies.

I step on the gas, reversing in an expert arc that throws her against me.

"Whoa, easy there, Rusty," she admonishes as she rights herself.

My jaw clenches, and my fingers curl around the cold steering wheel. "I'm keeping tally, Keely. For every time you call me that name."

She laughs and fiddles with the climate control until warm air flows into the car. "And how exactly do you intend to get me back, seeing as you're leaving tomorrow?"

The smile barely twitches on my lips. "The night is still young."

"Umm, no, it kinda isn't. It's almost 1 a.m." Her voice holds a cautious delivery, as if she's realizing just what she's let herself in for.

I don't respond as I quickly navigate the quiet streets on the outskirts of Montauk, letting the powerful engine beneath me growl and fly. I drive fast and aggressively, and every now and then I hear her breath catch when I take a corner too quickly. After about ten miles, the turmoil in my chest starts to calm.

In direct proportion, the turbulence in my pants is growing. My cock has been hardening since she slid in barefoot beside me. Seeing one fist clenched around the door handle and the other gripping the center console is not doing my libido any good either. Nor is the rapid rise and fall of her chest, and the very visible outline of one breast playing peekaboo with the gaping robe.

A glance at the GPS shows a mile-long road, leading to a dead end coming up on the left.

I take the turn and floor the accelerator.

She slams back against her seat. "God, slow the fuck down, would you?"

"I'm keeping a tally of that, too."

The needle rises to a hundred, then one-twenty. One-forty. Her breath shudders out. "You can keep all the goddamn tallies you want. If you make me dead just one day into my twenty-fifth year, I swear you'll never have a moment of peace. I'll haunt you until you beg me to kill you."

My foot doesn't lift from the pedal, but I glance at her. "Yesterday was your birthday?"

She visibly shakes as she sees the row of white oak trees that marks the end of the road. "Jesus, slow down, Rusty!"

"Answer my question."

"What question? God! Yes, yesterday was my birthday."

"What did you wish for?"

"Not to fucking die in a psycho's car today!" Her fingers have turned white and her face is ashen with fright. One nipple is fully exposed and I feel the blood rushing through my veins.

"*Please!*" The word explodes from her lips. "Slow down," she whispers. "Slow down, slow down, *slow down!*" The words trip over themselves.

"What about your foul language?" I ask, returning my eyes to the road.

"Fine. I won't swear again!" She starts shaking her head frantically as the trees rush toward us. "God, no!" Her right hand clutches my thigh, digging in with a tight, nail-biting grip.

I narrow my eyes, scan the dashboard, then the tree line. After exactly three seconds, I transfer my foot from gas to brake.

The McLaren skids to a stop at the exact point where the road ends.

For several seconds, her breath gusts out in loud gulping heaves, her eyes frozen in wide-eyed fear.

Then she explodes at me. I easily block her blows, my arms gripping her as fear turns to anger.

"You are a FUCKING ASSHOLE!"

4

MASON

I throw open the door and drag her out through my side, making sure her feet don't touch the frozen ground.

"Get your hands off me!" She flails against me.

I don't stop until I round the hood and set her down on it. When she tries to stand, I stay her by inserting myself between her thighs. She's too high on adrenaline to notice how amped up I am on my own adrenaline. And also by her state of undress.

"What the hell is wrong with you? An hour ago you bit my head off because you thought I wanted to kill myself, and what, now you're helping me achieve the same goal?"

"I've no intention of killing us," I reply. The car's interior lights and bright headlights bathe her in a soft glow. Her near-dry hair is wild from her antics, and my attention is riveted to the pulse racing at her throat. "We were doing two hundred and ten on a mile and a half stretch of road. I calculated the distance and horsepower and knew the exact moment to apply the brakes. Of course, I didn't calculate your nails digging into my thigh. Good thing I can control my urges, or we'd be wrapped around that white oak tree behind me by now."

She gapes up at me, not sure what to make of my calm, matter-of-fact tone. Then she inhales sharply and shakes her head. "God, you're crazy!"

"Am I?" I move closer, sliding my hands up from her covered arms to her shoulders. Her soft, silky hair caresses my fingers as I massage the tension from her rigid muscles. "Your blood is pumping and your heart is racing and right now, all you can think about is how glad you are to be alive. And in about a minute, your body will begin finding ways to disperse all that adrenaline." I move a hand down her throat, pausing to feel her pulse hammer beneath my fingers, then I travel lower, between her warm breasts and heaving chest to where her robe is still secured by the belt. With a firm tug, I release the belt and her robe falls open.

"What the hell are you doing?"

She starts to close the gap, but I quickly capture her hands in one of mine. I press her back against the hood of the still-running engine and lean over her. Her eyes widen, but I'm satisfied to see it's not with fear. Although a touch of fear would be welcome at this point. This woman is far too cocky for her own good.

"You promised me you wouldn't swear. Or call me Rusty. You failed on both accounts."

She struggles against my hold, but she's no match for me. Not that it stops her getting in my face though. "You were trying to kill me, you bastard! I would've said anything to make sure that didn't happen."

I lean in closer, until our mouths are a scant inch apart, until I can feel her breath mingle with mine. "So you lied?" I say softly.

"Look... Mason, I don't know what kind of trip you're on, but I'm freezing. You wanted to get some air, I'm guessing with a side order of death-wish driving. You've done that, so can we go back now?"

"Not until we find a way to deal with your excess adrenaline. And address your foul mouth in the bargain."

She swallows. I watch the movement of her slender throat, my own pulse nowhere near settled. Somewhere between yanking her from death by freezing and her turning up at the pool house, my interest has dialed up from zero to infinite. I want her with a craving that is unnerving.

I look back up and see the moment she senses the change in me. I almost feel sorry for her. She twists away and tries to dislodge me from between her thighs.

That's when I look down. And freeze.

I knew she wasn't wearing a bra, but I'm unprepared for her total nakedness beneath the robe.

"You got into the car with me, not wearing any fucking panties?" I croak, not sure whether the sight of her stunning body makes me crazier or angrier.

"Who's got a dirty mouth now?"

I can't pull my gaze away from the sight of her pussy to admonish her for that tart reply. Her skin is flawlessly golden, as if she's spent some time in the sun recently. And from the looks of it, she likes to sunbathe nude. Her body flows in a perfect symmetry of full, heavy breasts, a lean and shapely torso, to a thin strip of pubic hair, which arrows to the hood covering her clit. My eyes stay riveted on that part of her body, my cock going from urgent twitch to full-bloodied throbbing, until she begins to squirm.

I look back up. "My swearing is justified. Yours isn't."

She squirms harder, and her nipples begin to tighten when my eyes are drawn to the perfect globes of her breasts. My mouth waters and the need to fuck builds in my groin.

"Okay, fine. I'm sorry for my potty mouth. Can we go now?"

There's a breathless quality to her voice, and I allow myself a smile.

"Does this usually work for you? You get yourself out of trouble by throwing out empty promises and apologies like confetti?"

She closes her eyes for a couple of seconds. "God, why did I think it was a good idea to get into your damned car?"

"I don't know. Why did you?" I transfer both of her wrists to one hand and trail my fingers down the middle of her chest. Her skin quivers beneath my touch. I reach her navel and circle the cute button, my gaze rising up to capture hers again. Her green eyes are a touch darker now, and her mouth is parted.

"Because you looked like... I don't know, like you shouldn't be alone?" she whispers.

"You don't sound sure. But let's leave that for the moment. Did you think it was a good idea to come out without your panties, Keely?" I ask. My fingers drift to the top of her pussy, and I swear I can feel her heat beckoning my hand.

Her breath catches. "I didn't think I'd find myself in a position where I'd have to explain my lack of underwear to anyone."

My jaw tightens. "Anyone?"

"Fine. To you."

"And?" My thumb is itching to stroke her, to feel if she is as wet and hot as I crave her to be. "Are you in a habit of going out without underwear?"

"My panties were wet and uncomfortable. And I thought we were going for a walk, not dicing with death in a sports car."

I smile. "You made a choice right before you got into the car with me. You knew this would happen. But you got into the car anyway. So what shall I do with you now?"

Her breath shudders out, and her nipples tighten harder.

"Why are you bothering to ask? You seem to think you know what I'm feeling and thinking."

"I'm only going with the evidence before me." I'm unable to hold back any longer, and my thumb grazes her clit.

A small sound jerks from her, and her hips twitch upward, seeking more of my touch.

"Is this what you want?" I ask, my voice thick with the lust ripping through my insides. "Shall I give you the release you're so desperate for?" My touch is firmer this time, and I watch her try and stifle a moan.

"You think I'm desperate just because of what you overheard at the party?" she taunts, but she's still squirming and she's no longer fighting to get free.

"Are you always this stubborn?"

"Only when I'm dealing with insufferable bastards," she replies.

I lower my head and suck one nipple into my mouth. I bite with a lack of gentleness that makes her cry out. She starts to struggle, and I soothe the ache with the tip of my tongue while my thumb continues to flick over her clit. Her cry morphs into a moan and her gasp washes over my ear. I roll her nipple in my mouth, warming her, teasing and sucking until I earn another moan.

When I transfer my attention to her other nipple, I dip my finger lower into her pussy and am rewarded with another jerk of her hips. I test her hole, feel its tight wetness and groan.

Need claws through me. I want to devour this woman with a hunger and possessiveness that is almost alien to me.

I look up and see the stark hunger burning in her green eyes, and I know I have her. I release her wrists and seize her nape. Freeing her nipple, I kiss my way up her throat, her jaw, then capture her mouth with mine. Unlike her attitude, her kiss is surprisingly timid. She barely parts her mouth to let me in, and her tongue is almost hesitant in seeking my own.

The idea that she isn't used to kissing fires my blood, makes me want her even more. I flick my tongue against hers and she shudders. Angling her face to suit my needs, I go deeper, harder, and slide one finger inside her. Her pussy is slick and hot and so damn intoxicating, I can barely think straight to slide out and back in again.

She makes a sound—a cross between a whimper and a growl —that sets me off. I press her backward until she's flat on her back against the hot hood and the running engine vibrates through her body. I prop myself up so as not to crush her and finger-fuck her pussy while feasting on her delectable mouth. Against her naked thigh, my cock is throbbing with an urgency that could become an embarrassment very soon.

But contrary to my decision when she got into the car, I decide not to fuck her. My needs are too great and too specific to be satisfied with a quick fuck in near-freezing temperatures. Fucking her right here, right now, would barely scratch the surface of my problem. And I don't have any condoms with me. The reminder cools my temperature a little, lending me the focus I need to pleasure her.

Her frantic noises alert me that she needs to breathe, so I release her mouth but latch on to her breasts again. Her eyes roll shut, and she bucks against my finger as her breath pants out. As I slide another finger inside, her eyes pop open.

She raises her head, and her gaze meets mine. Whatever she reads in my face makes her wilder. I lift my mouth from one tight nipple.

"Are you ready to come, baby?" I slur, almost as intoxicated with what I'm doing to her as she is with receiving it.

Her face twists in a sexy grimace, and she nods frantically. I increase the piston of my fingers and return my thumb to her clit. Her hands fly up to my shoulders and dig in as her hips lift off the hood to meet my thrusts.

I cup one breast and squeeze her nipple, unwilling to lower my head because I'm hungry to see her face when she falls off the edge into ecstasy.

"Oh God!" Her nails dig in harder, and her back arches off the hood as her insides begin to clench around my fingers.

She's so tight I have to twist my fingers to go deeper. The recollection that she hasn't been fucked in months slashes across my mind, nearly pushing me into abandoning my resolve not to fuck her.

Color rushes up her chest and neck, and I curl my fingers, stroking her sweet spot. I watch her explode, her moans guttural and deliciously helpless as she thrashes on the hood. I continue to tease her clit and finger-fuck her until her legs start to close.

"Stop. Please." She sounds nothing like the mouthy Brooklyn girl intent on driving me nuts with her stubborn streak. She's pliant and soft in a way that really isn't safe for me to be around. Because this is how I like my women. In a position where I can bend them to my will, get them to agree to almost anything I want from them.

But I'm unable to move. Unable to stop watching Keely come down from her sensual high. I continue to slide in and out of her. She moans and moves her fingers from my shoulders to my hair. Her eyes open, and she looks at me. She seems to want to fight it, but then her legs fall open again and her breathing changes. I stroke her pleasure until she's panting again, then remove my fingers. I silence her groan of protest by placing my soaked fingers against her mouth.

"Lick," I instruct harshly.

The spark in her eyes confirms something I've been suspecting. Keely is used to calling the shots when it comes to her lovers. A tinge of regret goes through me. In another time, I would take pleasure in challenging that dominant streak, in honing her fire until she accepts my leash without question.

"Do as I say, Keely."

Another spark of green fire. But slowly she parts her lips, and her tongue licks between my fingers. I groan. The sound seems to please her, enough for her to lap faster, her eyes locked on mine as she licks her juices off the inside of my fingers. When she starts to turn her head to get at my knuckles, I turn them and spread the moisture over her lips.

Then I seal my mouth over hers, crushing her sweetness between our lips. Fire burns through my veins, and once again I debate the decision to hold back. I slide my hand between the robe and her body and cup her plump ass. Pulling her closer, I rub my aching erection against her wet pussy, every cell in my body screaming with the need to fuck.

When she starts whimpering again, I pull back. I grip her thighs and spread them. The sight of her exposed pussy on the expensive car almost undoes me. I should put her in the car, drive us back to Zach's and walk away from her. But the need to make her come again overwhelms me.

Knowing I'm toying with danger, I trail my hands down her inner thighs, seeking a distraction but finding none from the wonder of her glistening pussy.

Her hands reach for me. "Please," she moans.

I grit my teeth. "You like the stars, baby?" I ask.

Confusion clouds her face, but then she nods. "Yes."

"Good. Recite the constellations, clockwise from Pegasus. Not all of them, but generally."

"What? Why?"

"Because otherwise, I'm going to throw my good judgment

away and fuck you. So do as I say and distract me while I eat your sweet pussy. You want to come again, don't you?" I ask.

I can see her fight it, but she nods after several seconds. "Yes."

I grip her thighs, unable to stop my eyes from appreciating her beautiful pussy. My mouth waters and again I have to pull myself back from the brink. From temptation. "Start now. If you stop, I stop. If you get it wrong, I stop and we go back minus another orgasm for you. Deal?"

5

KEELY

Having grown up in a tough neighborhood in Brooklyn, there are very few things that surprise me anymore. And yet, tonight I've been hit by one surprise after another. Most of them shocking enough to almost flatten me.

I stare up at Mason Sinclair, knowing my mouth is hanging open like a dead fish, but unable to do more than grapple with the fact that I'm naked on the hood of a half-a-million-dollar sports car, my only protection a thigh-length cotton robe, my body exposed to the elements and the avid gaze of the powerful man looming over me.

A man who just asked me to recite the constellations while he goes down on me.

I want to laugh. I want to snap at him for stealing my line, that I'm the one who normally demands nerdy morsels with my sex. Most of all, I want to get up off that hot hood, throw some snarky quip in his face and walk off into the night. Because he's seriously crazy.

I can see it in his eyes. I can feel it in his voice when he speaks to me. I think I have issues. But this man has them by the barrel-load. And for whatever reason, tonight they're straining at the leash of his control.

I should put a stop to this madness before it goes any further. But I don't.

Because I want to experience another orgasm like the one he just gave me. Again and again. I lie here, the heavens shining above me, and decide to chalk it up to the insane rush of a near-death experience firing up my blood.

"Deal," I find myself responding.

My reward is a twisty-wicked smile followed by a less-than-gentle trail of his fingers down my inner thigh. That alone is enough to set my body on fire.

He lowers his body until he's crouched in front of the low-slung car, his shoulders, neck and face the only visible parts of his body.

"Start now."

Another curt instruction that would normally put my back up immediately. But that orgasm was beyond this world, and as a woman who's made it a mission to only chase the best, most satisfying ones, I know the difference between mediocre and platinum standard.

Mason Sinclair's are definitely double platinum.

I let that growly dominance slide. Especially as I can feel his warm breath caressing my sex.

"Pegasus." I gasp when the rough edge of his beard whispers over my outer lips. "Andromeda, Cassiopeia, Camelopardalis, Leo." I struggle to keep my gaze fixed upward, not to glance down at what he's doing to me. His tongue flicks my clit and I groan. God, he's so good. "Ursa Major, Venatici." The broad side of his tongue licks me from hole to hood before he buries his face in an open-mouthed kiss of my sex. My whole body shudders and my hands slam against the expensive paintwork. "Coma Berenice, Virgo— Oh!" My hips jerk as he opens me up and goes to town on my pussy, eating me with an expertise that makes my world tilt sideways.

"Keep going," he growls against me after a long pull on my clit.

I shut my eyes and recite from memory. "Serpens Caput, Ophiuchus, Libra, Serpens Cauda." I recite them slower now, because I'm drowning in sensation and my brain can barely remember my own name. "Scutum..." My hands lift off the hood and I grab my breasts, pulling on my nipples as my hips roll against Mason's mouth.

"God, that's so hot, baby," he croons. I don't know whether it's because of what I'm doing to my own body or the names spilling out of my mouth.

All I know is, this is the hottest non-penetrative sex I've ever experienced. And I don't want it to end. But I feel myself cresting the edge. "Aquila, Vulpecula..." He increases the intensity of his mouth and tongue, then slides two fingers inside me. "God, yes," I gasp, squeezing harder on my breasts.

Strong fingers brush mine away and my breasts are cupped in warm, expert hands. He sucks my clit into his mouth the same time as he twists my nipples. I explode and feel myself bounce on the hood of the car as pleasure rips through me.

He laps me up in greedy licks, his own groans deep and guttural.

I disconnect with reality and just exist in pure, mind-blowing sensation. I'm not sure how much time passes, but I slowly open my eyes to find him leaning over me.

He's not smiling, and his brooding gaze rakes over my face with an intensity that raises the hairs on my neck.

When I manage to pull my gaze from his, I look down. My

robe is done up and tucked around my thighs, and my belt is secured around my waist.

Disappointment and relief twist through me, and I school my features as I raise my eyes to his. While a large part of me wants the next step to be Mason fucking me, a part of me is reticent about ending my months-long dry spell with a one-night stand.

Having the decision firmly made for me isn't one I foresaw, however, and I feel a little flustered as I lie on the car, with the stars I've just named winking above me.

"Time to go," he says. He straightens and holds out his hand.

I place mine in his, but before I can stand, he scoops me up, much like he did before, and places me back in the car via the driver's side. I secure my seatbelt in silence, and a second later, he's throwing the car in reverse.

He drives back with much the same speed and intensity as the outward journey, and I suspect that whatever demons are chasing him were nowhere near quietened on our little danger-laden jaunt.

There are fewer lights on at the house, and I guess the party has wound down.

Mason parks the car in the garage, and once he turns off the engine, the silence becomes almost impossibly deafening. I stay in my seat, unsure what to do next.

Me, the woman who's never lost for words and always ready with a snappy comeback, according to my family and best friend, is stumped as to how the next minutes will play out.

Mason thrusts open his door and steps out. Striding round the car, he opens mine and stands back, his arm thrown over the edge of the door, as if he doesn't want to stand too close.

I get out of the car. My legs feel weak from the depleted

adrenaline and from the two powerful orgasms, which continue to ripple residual tremors through me when I move.

My eyes meet his, and a small smile plays about his lips.

"Shall we dispense with the awkward goodbyes? I have a cold shower to get intimately acquainted with."

My gaze drops to his crotch, and sure enough his cock is still hard and thick behind the fly of his jeans. My pussy clenches with renewed need, and the temptation to offer him relief hovers on my lips.

I stop myself before it spills out, frown at my disconcerting emotions around this man and try to think of one of my famous, but now oddly elusive, comebacks.

"Sure. Umm... have fun with that."

God. Really?

A corner of his mouth crooks upward, but his eyes reflect a solemnity that cracks at something inside me. He watches me in silence and I can't help fidgeting again.

The man has given me two mind-blowing orgasms, and I can't find one word to say to him? "Thank you" seems odd and flippant. And despite the craziness with which our meeting started, I can't flip him off either, no matter how richly deserving I think it is for him scaring me to death on our drive out.

So I stand here, my eyes locked on his.

Slowly, he comes toward me and stops. He traces a finger down my cheek, and I catch a faint scent of my sex on his hand.

"I wish I'd met you in another time," he says with that strange look still lurking in his eyes.

"I'm not sure I can say the same."

He looks at me for a long moment, then he nods. "Fair enough."

He leans in close, brushes his mouth against my cheek. "But

just so you know, your pussy is the sweetest thing I've tasted in a very long time," he says in my ear. "I'm going to miss it."

He walks away before I can draw breath, his long, lean body disappearing around the house.

I stay there, stunned, for almost five minutes before the sound of voices drifting from upstairs forces me to move.

Luckily, I don't encounter anyone as I hurry to my room. As I disrobe, I see clear imprints of fingers on my breasts and thighs.

Blushing, I slip on my nightie and hurry into bed. I fall asleep with my hand resting between my thighs, a sudden fear that unless I keep it there, the memory of what happened on that dead end road in Montauk will disappear forever.

I wake to brilliant sunshine and my best friend's curious stare.

"We missed you last night. Where did you disappear to?" Bethany asks, her blue eyes full of curiosity as she steps forward and holds out the mug of coffee in her hand.

I take my time sitting up and arranging the pillows behind me to buy myself time to respond. Bethany and I used to share everything, but since she became one-half of the powerful Savage couple, I've begun to feel as if burdening her with my mundane life and problems isn't fair on her. Plus, the man behind my disappearance from the party last night happens to be a good friend of Zach Savage's. Which makes this whole thing a little tricky.

I accept the coffee and blow on it before sipping.

Bethany perches on the edge of the bed and eyes me. "I know that look. You're thinking of how much to tell me, aren't you?" she accuses with a narrowed gaze. "What the hell happened after you stormed out of the kitchen? You made me really worried."

I shrug and try to smile my way through it. "Well, your Neanderthal friend found me."

She frowns a little. "I don't know him that well. I only met him one time before last night."

"So you know nothing about him?" I ask nonchalantly, even though my stomach knots with more than a little tension.

"Very little, but Zach says he's been through some issues. I only asked because I didn't want him to come after you without..." She stops, and I muster a grin.

"Without knowing that he'd return alive?"

She grins. "Yeah, you were pretty pissed when you stormed out of the kitchen. Anyway, Zach said whatever he's been through has made him a little... eccentric, but he wasn't unpleasant to you, was he?"

I stifle a hysterical laugh. "No, he wasn't unpleasant. A little judgmental, sure, but nothing I couldn't handle."

Liar, the hard throbbing between my thighs seems to echo. I shift in the bed and sip my drink as Bethany continues to eye me.

"You sure?"

I nod. "Seriously, he came to find me on the beach and apologized for his rudeness."

"That's all?"

"Pretty much." I cringe inside at the barefaced lie and quickly change the subject. "How did the rest of the party go?"

She shrugs. "Okay. Everyone left happy, which is the most important thing, I guess. But"—she bounces on the bed, her eyes shining with happiness—"Zach and I finally agreed on a date for the wedding."

"Oh?" I heave an inner sigh of relief that she's dropped the subject of Mason and me. "And is Aunt Keely helping with the organization?" I ask with a genuine smile this time.

"Of course you are. The date's April thirtieth."

"Wow, I thought for sure Savage would want to get you hitched by next weekend."

She rolls her beautiful eyes. "He tried, believe me. But he's learning he can't always have his way." I hide a smile and raise an eyebrow when she bites her lip, a worried look crossing her heart-stoppingly beautiful face. "You think you can help me organize the wedding on top of the Indigo Lounge project?"

I send her a speaking glance. "You kidding? Have you forgotten what I do for a living?"

She laughs. "No, I know you can juggle projects in your sleep, but Zach can be demanding."

"Girl, please, he may rule your world with thunder and lightning, but Zach Savage doesn't scare me. Besides, I've hammered down most of the project details and expect everything to be done by the end of March, so that leaves me a clear month to help you with your wedding once I'm back from the IL trip. I'll be able to devote a full month to helping you, babe. Don't sweat it at all."

Her face lights up with a smile so radiant, I can't help but smile in return. But again, I feel that sharp ache in my chest that makes me feel like a bitch.

We talk wedding shop for another fifteen minutes before she leaves me alone to get dressed. I know she has a relaxing day of entertaining her remaining guests, but I've already made the excuse to return to New York under the pretext of work pressures. For a moment, I feel bad, but then I'm glad I'm not staying, because I don't think I can face running into Mason Sinclair this morning, in case he hasn't already left.

In the clarity of day, my behavior last night seems even more shocking. I've enjoyed one-night stands before, those which I've initiated, and those I've gone along with just for the hell of it.

Last night was different. The intensity of the whole thing is not something I'm familiar with. I want to think it's my uncharacteristically long abstinence that made me react like I did, but I know it's not true.

Something about his intensity drew a response from me that still makes me reel.

I sit in bed, sipping my coffee, then feel my face heat up as I recall his parting words.

Your pussy is the sweetest thing I've tasted in a long time... So why didn't he go a step further? I'm not ashamed to say that I wanted him to. That I would've let him fuck me right there on top of his car.

He certainly wanted to. So why didn't I push?

I set my cup down and slowly absorb the answer I've known for a while. Because I like being in control. Every single one of the men I've slept with was carefully hand-picked because I like my sex one way—by being the one in control.

From the moment I set eyes on him, I knew Mason wasn't that sort of guy. I called him a Neanderthal just now. Deep down, I know it isn't far from the truth. Behind all the demons lurking in his eyes is a deeply primitive guy who will push all the wrong buttons in me. Buttons I haven't let anyone push since I was nineteen.

No matter how hot the sex, I'll never give up control in bed. Or in any other aspect of my life.

Never again.

6

KEELY

Two weeks later

I step from the private jet in Nice, France, and immediately smile at the warmer climate, glad to have left the sub-zero temperatures of New York far behind me. I love my birth city, but even I am tired of the wet snow and constant freezing temperatures. A little warm sunshine is very welcome.

"I hope you have a pleasant stay, Miss Benson."

I smile at the sharply dressed pilot. "Thanks, Grant."

Breathing in deep, I send a silent thanks to Bethany for securing the ride on the Indigo Lounge plane. Due to her help, I've been able to finish my last assignment for Rubio Events, the PR company that I worked for right up until an hour ago. I grin from the sheer high of quitting my job while cruising in a private jet at thirty-thousand feet.

There is an unfettered thrill in the knowledge that I no longer have to account to anyone for my time, that I can come and go as I please. Zachary Savage has tried to hire me full-time, but I prefer to come on board his latest Indigo Lounge project as a freelancer. Until I weigh all my options and decide what I want to do with my life, I don't intend to tie myself down to another company, no matter how huge or reputable.

Nevertheless, whatever I decide to do next, having a successful Indigo Lounge event on my résumé will be a huge feather in my cap. Especially an IL event that is the first of its kind. I was more than excited to discover that the latest Savages Inc. launch was to be on a super yacht and not another jumbo jet.

I don't have anything against planes, but I find yachts much sexier, and I can't wait to get started on planning the events for the maiden voyage of the *IL Indulgence*.

The ten-day trip will start in Monte Carlo and stop in Mallorca, Sicily and then Valetta in Malta, before terminating at a private island in Greece.

"This way, Mademoiselle Benson." I smile as another uniformed crew member, this time a helicopter pilot, points me toward a six-seater Mercedes chopper sitting about a hundred feet away. "The flight to Monaco shouldn't take more than ten minutes," he imparts with a sexy French accent. "Your luggage will be delivered by car to your hotel within the hour."

"*Merci*," I say in my best high school French, and I watch his appreciative smile as his gaze drifts over me.

I pin my smile in place but feel a touch disconcerted. His tall leanness and intelligent eyes are just my type, but the normal twinge of attraction I experience when a hot guy shows interest in me is absurdly missing.

That perfectly healthy twinge has been AWOL since that chilly night in Montauk two weeks ago, specifically after my toe-curling orgasms on top of a certain hot sports car. In contrast, the face of the man who gave me those orgasms has plagued my every unguarded moment, starting from the instant I opened my door that next morning to find my Blahnik heeled pumps placed neatly outside my door with a note that read, *Feet as sexy as yours should only go bare for someone special.*

Mason Sinclair has occupied an irritatingly large portion of my thoughts. Once I returned to New York City, I even went as far as to google him—and had every single suspicion confirmed.

Hailing from seriously old New York money, he attended all the nauseatingly good schools, held all the right roles during his college years and graduated with reams of accolades. Benedict Mason Sinclair III, great-grandson of an Irish immigrant who arrived penniless on Ellis Island, but owned half of New York City by the time he died, is every bit the entitled, unapologetic alpha male I met.

The evidence was clear to see in each photo I came across, especially in the way he eyed the women on his arm with a heavy dose of distaste. To him they were pieces of meat he meant to devour at the earliest opportunity, but much to my annoyance, I wasn't able to stop the slice of electricity that sizzled through me each time I found myself staring into his long-lashed hazel eyes.

Regardless of the social setting, Mason's eyes held a deep allure, a bottomless intensity that seemed to see right into my soul. After the bewildering realization that I couldn't stare into his eyes without feeling the need to lower my gaze, I slammed down my laptop lid and attempted to do something useful.

But those eyes stayed with me. Followed me into my dreams and haunted me.

Dammit.

My smile falters as the chopper lifts off, and I force myself to activate my phone.

My heart twists and drops into my stomach as I see the app I acquired specially to hold my secret—one I don't trust to remain floating in my inbox.

Out of the corners of my eyes, the picturesque aqua-watered Cote d'Azur passes in a blur as we follow the craggy coastline and head into Monte Carlo.

My hands shake as I stare down at the app. I want to delete the email, just as I deleted the first one. But each time my finger hovers over the bin icon, the rush of fear makes me hesitate. I'm intelligent enough to know that ignoring a problem won't make it go away. And normally I thrive on problem-solving.

But not this one. This one I want to seal in the vault, without knowing whether it's a hoax or real. I want to pretend it doesn't exist, that I've never seen it.

Because if it is real...

My heart hammers, climbs from my chest into my throat, and stays there, clogging my breathing until my vision hazes.

"Mademoiselle, are you all right?" A voice disturbs me.

I turn my head and meet the young pilot's concerned stare. When his gaze drops to my hand, I realize I'm gripping the plush armrest with white-knuckled fingers.

"I'm fine," I reply and consciously relax my grip, but this time I can't summon a smile.

"We will be landing in less than sixty seconds."

I nod. Let him assume it's a fear of flying that's causing my distress and not an unknown ghost from the past come back to haunt me.

I quickly press the home button, drop my phone into my handbag, and force air into my lungs as the aircraft hovers over the helipad at the Indigo Hermitage Hotel.

As the rotors wind down, my gaze drifts over the stunning views of the Prince's Palace, the streets below that will be converted into a Formula 1 circuit in a little over six weeks and the dozens of multi-million-dollar yachts slotted into the marina.

The *IL Indulgence* is easy enough to pick out. Even if it wasn't already the largest vessel out there, the bold indigo and silver colors gracing its stunning lines would've made it easy to spot.

With five stories, two helipads, ten master suites, two restaurants and six entertainment areas, this ship is easily the jewel in the Indigo Lounge crown. For the last month since the latest event was announced, I've fielded calls from A-listers whose eagerness to get on the guest list for the inaugural launch has made me grin like an idiot. If I were the bribes-for-favors type, I'd be sitting pretty and laughing all the way to the bank.

But I'm the sort of girl who respects her client's wishes, and Zach has been specific with the type of guests he wants on his yacht.

So far I've vetted and double-vetted nine of the ten guest groups who will be sailing on the maiden voyage. The tenth slot has been left open, a practice I'm familiar with since I know the mercurial temperaments of the rich and famous. The slot will be used for last-minute guests or on an ad-hoc basis for guests who can't take the full trip.

The chopper door opens, and my pilot holds out his hand. I smile and let him help me out, not protesting when his hand lingers on mine for a few seconds longer than necessary.

"I hope mademoiselle wasn't too disturbed by the flight?" he asks.

My gaze drops to the name stitched into his uniform before I look back up into his deep blue eyes. "No, Henri, it was great, thank you."

I indulge in his pleased smile and let my eyes linger on his until he drops his gaze. A pulse of satisfaction pounds through me, and I feel my world right itself again.

"Enjoy your stay, mademoiselle," he says before he reaches into his pocket and extracts a card. "And if you need anything to make your stay more pleasant, please do not hesitate to call me."

I take the black card. There's only a phone number printed in gold on the embossed surface. I hide a smile and thank him, not in the least bit insulted that my pilot also moonlights as a gigolo and is interested in me.

Different strokes for different folks. Plus, he's cute enough, should I get desperate during my stay or thoughts of Mason Sinclair's mouth and fingers drive me to the edge of distraction.

"Where's a good place for cocktails around here in case a girl gets lonely?" I ask, even though I've done my homework thoroughly and know which places are up to Indigo Lounge standards and which aren't.

His smile widens. "Jimmy'z is a good place, but also La Rascasse."

"Which one do you prefer?"

"Jimmy'z. I'm there most nights."

I nod. "Great, I might see you there then." It's one of the places I planned to check out.

His eager nod makes me feel a touch better.

Whatever is headed my way, I'll deal with it.

Two weeks ago when I stood on the beach in Montauk, I was a little shaky about my options, but then it was to be expected. This time of year always gets to me. The memories become too overpowering, and sometimes I buckle under.

Did I want to die when I threw myself into the icy waves after having drunk almost a full bottle of champagne? Possibly.

If Bethany didn't call me when I was about to get in the bathtub, would I have gone through with taking the bottle of pills the day before? Probably.

But I'm used to it, the push and pull of these suicidal

thoughts, especially around my birthday. If I put a little more effort into it, I don't doubt that one day I might succeed.

The idea doesn't fill me with dread. Or fear. Because the end result is I'll either be alive. Or I'll be dead.

"You're welcome, *mademoiselle*."

I jerk a little and realize I've spaced out again.

Seriously. Time to get yourself under control, Benson. I look beyond Henri and see a member of the hotel staff heading my way.

I send Henri another smile, making a mental note to look him up if I get bored while in Monaco, and head toward the concierge.

I'm whisked to my penthouse suite in minutes and offered a welcoming glass of champagne, which I decline. Kicking off my shoes, I'm drawn to the sweeping floor-to-ceiling windows that overlook the marina. Once again, a thrill ignites upon seeing the yacht.

For the next few days, I'll be interviewing chefs, wait staff and personal valets, while working with the specially contracted designer to provide specific amenities for the guests.

Since the sex lounge specifications are Zach Savage's remit, I haven't been made privy as to whom is responsible for that aspect of things or what will be required of me in that department. All I know is that I have to report to the yacht at four this afternoon to meet the guy in charge.

Which gives me about an hour and a half to get ready.

The moment my luggage arrives and is unpacked by the penthouse butler, I undress and take a shower. The concierge informed me that a car will be available to take me to the marina when I'm ready, and as I dress for the high-fifties sunshine in a cream fitted linen dress and dark brown heeled boots, I try to ground myself, but my mind slides to my phone and the contents of the email again.

Why now after all this time? Why sit on the secret for six years before making threats? And is it even a threat?

Dammit!

I shut off the endless loop of questions and finish dressing with a long, camel-colored cashmere sweater and a Hermes scarf. I leave my blonde hair loose, insert small gold loops into my ears, and finish applying a light makeup before I grab my Gucci clutch and head out the door.

The ride from the hotel down Rue Grimaldi to the marina is embarrassingly brief, and I decide to make the return journey on foot. Dismissing the driver, I turn to where the launch boat is moored.

My phone rings as we approach the breathtaking super yacht aptly named *IL Indulgence,* and I can't suppress my awe as I stare at the vessel. The indigo theme runs throughout everything owned by Zachary Savage, and this yacht is no different. I reach for my phone and grin when I see Bethany's smiling face.

"Tell your husband for me that I'm seriously tempted to accept his offer to work for him full-time. I haven't been on the boat yet, but I love it already."

Bethany laughs, but I hear a note in her voice that makes a tiny prickle of apprehension wash across my senses. "I'll tell him. But that'll make him even smugger than he already is at the moment. Despite it being my idea, he's taking all the credit for snapping up the boat when it became available."

That surprises me. "I thought it was built from scratch just for the Indigo Lounge?"

"He was thinking of building a boat, but this one came on the market through a private sale and he snapped it up."

"Wow, who would build a boat like this just for themselves?" I ask with an incredulous laugh.

Bethany hesitates and I frown. "Hey, is everything okay?"

"I don't know. That depends."

"On what?" I ask as the launch slows alongside the yacht. This close, the vessel looks huge, like a floating palace of pure decadence. If my hands weren't full, I'd reach out and stroke the sleek indigo lines running alongside the silvery metallic paint-work—my lady wood for the stunning vessel is that hard.

But Bethany hasn't responded, and my frown deepens. "B, what's going on?" I spot the driver waiting to help me out. "Hold on, let me get off this launch."

I tuck my clutch under my arm and step onto what I know from the vessel plans is the second floor. It's where I'll be welcoming the guests in a little over a week's time, and I'm struck dumb as I walk into the silver and indigo-trimmed reception room.

Holding the phone to my ear, I start to turn in a wide circle. "Wow, Bethany, this ship is incredible."

"Keely, there's something you should know. It may not affect how you feel about the project, but..." I stop listening as I catch a shadow from the corner of my eye. And even before I turn fully, I *know*.

My senses jump to alert as my eyes widen. The phone slips from my useless hand and clatters to the hardwood floor as I recognize the man entering the room.

"What the fuck are you doing here, Mason Sinclair?"

7

KEELY

"Hello, Keely."

I thought I exaggerated the brooding growl of his voice. But as it washes over me, I realize I've underestimated its feral power.

A shiver ripples down my spine as he stalks slowly toward me, his eyes conducting a leisurely survey over me, which does nothing to reassure me that this man isn't anything but a menace to my wellbeing. And he hasn't answered my question.

"I said what—"

"I heard you," he cuts across me without raising his voice. When he stops in front of me, I force myself not to take a step back from the raw energy vibrating from him. Perhaps it's the shock of seeing him here, or it's the setting sun behind him, bathing him in a larger-than-life aura, but an inner voice mocks my attempts to put him in a safe, comfortable box.

There's nothing safe or comfortable about Mason Sinclair. Despite the stylish black roll-neck sweater and faded jeans he's wearing, I'm not fooled into thinking there's anything civilized about him. His full beard is gone, but it's been replaced by a day-old stubble that somehow intensifies the dark, unrelenting allure I find myself getting dangerously drawn to again.

I forcefully snap my gaze from his, bending to retrieve my phone. The blank screen announces my lost connection to Bethany, and the sensation of being even more untethered irritates me.

"If you heard me, then perhaps you care to answer me?"

"I will if you attempt to ask the question again without the foul language."

A smirk plays on my lips as I tilt my head. "My dirty mouth really bothers you, doesn't it?" I tease.

"There's a time and place for it."

"Don't tell me. You're the I-like-a-lady-on-my-arm-and-a-whore-in-the-bedroom type?"

Deep hazel eyes gleam at me, and I get the feeling he's secretly amused by my question. "Doesn't every man?"

Before I can answer, he looks past my shoulder and nods. I turn to see a waiter heading our way with a tray of drinks. Mason hands a champagne-filled one to me and takes the other —soda with a wedge of lime—before dismissing the waiter.

"Shall we start this conversation again?" he asks with a sexily quirked eyebrow.

"If it'll get my question answered quickly, sure, why not? What *on earth* are you doing on this boat, Benedict Mason Sinclair the Third?" I ask in fake upper-crust tones and wide-eyed pseudo innocence. Then I immediately cringe inside because I've let slip that I know more about him than he's revealed so far.

His smile tells me he's noted the slip, and I take a hasty sip of champagne and wait for the inevitable smug comeback. "I'm setting up the entertainment lounges for Zach."

My champagne threatens to go down the wrong way. I

hastily clear my throat. "*You're* the designer I'm meeting?" Nothing in his online profile mentioned he was a designer. Then again, it hadn't said anything specific about what Mason does for a living.

"I am. And bravo," he murmurs, watching my lips as I frown.

"Excuse me?" I ask.

"You just expressed yourself succinctly without swearing."

Jesus effing Christ. "Okay, fine, cool your jets, mister. I can actually speak without swearing."

"Then why do you choose not to with me?"

"Because..." I stop, then kick myself for floundering. No way am I going to tell him he brings out the flustered, awkward teenager I used to be. Or that I secretly hate that he's seen me at my lowest. So I shrug. "I don't know. You seem to bring out the worst in me."

That twitch at the corner of his mouth again, the one that makes me even more irritated, and even more attracted to him. We watch the sun heading for the blue horizon for a few minutes, until the silence becomes too uncomfortable for me.

"So, your first name is Benedict?"

His gaze slides to mine, but again he doesn't respond, only tilts his glass to his lips and takes a long swallow.

"Do you prefer Ben, Ned or just Dick?" I ask, my tongue firmly in my cheek.

His jaw flexes. "I told you what I prefer two weeks ago. For an intelligent woman, your continued need to aggravate strikes me as quite reckless. Or perhaps it's something else entirely?" he speculates, his voice a low, rough rumble that reminds me of all the time I've wasted trying to forget that voice, that face.

"What, it's suddenly reckless to make conversation?"

"You're not making conversation. You're goading. The question is why. Are you hoping I'll punish you again like I did out in Montauk, Keely?"

Suddenly, I'm hot. My breath strangles somewhere in my lumbar region, and I can't quite meet his gaze. If what he did to me on the hood of that car was punishment, then I shudder to think what his brand of pleasure will feel like.

"Get over yourself, my buttons aren't that easy to push," I lie.

"Really?" He turns toward me and cocks his hip against the railing. That stance should make him seem relaxed, cordial. It should make *me* relax, but it does the opposite and brings to mind an image of a cobra drawing back before it strikes, sinking its deadly venom into unsuspecting prey. "So far the evidence points to the contrary," he says, his eyes staying on mine with a ferocious intensity that makes me aware of every single vulnerable pore in my body.

I can't seem to move, or respond. He conducts another survey down my body, this time deliberately lingering on the pulse hammering at my throat and the shadowed area between my breasts, then dropping to my hips and legs, before climbing back up again.

Every inch of me tingles. I want to shut off the sensations this man seems to pull so effortlessly from me, but I can't. My usual ability to flirt and discard at will has deserted me, and all I can do is watch him watch me.

"Perhaps we should explore that," he invites with a dark undertone.

I desperately pull myself together. "Or perhaps we should get back on point and you should give me a tour of the boat, seeing as that is the purpose of this meeting?"

He blinks disgustingly long lashes, and frustration hums from his body. I recall his condemnation of basic social graces in his kitchen two weeks ago, and I can't help but wonder what he's doing in this place if mingling with society is so abhorrent to him.

Of all the places on earth, Monte Carlo is the very fleshpot of decadence and flashy luxury, a place where people specifically come to see and be seen. So far, Mason Sinclair has struck me as the very antithesis of that lifestyle.

He remains silent for the time he takes to finish his drink, and I realize another thing about him. He's not a man who feels inclined to fill silences with conversation.

Whereas I'm the opposite. Silences terrify me. I can't help but wonder what another person sees and thinks of me when they're not talking to me.

The moment he sets his glass down, I turn away from the breathtaking view. "Shall we?"

"In good time." He folds muscle-roped arms across his broad chest and my attention is reluctantly drawn to his shoulders. "You want to tell me something about yourself?" he asks lazily.

I bristle at his indifferent tone. "Why would I want to do that?"

"Since you've gone to some effort to find out about me, I thought I'd make an effort to extend the courtesy."

The implication that he'd rather not be asking makes my teeth grind. "I know how basic etiquette bores you. You needn't feign interest on my behalf."

"My interest in you isn't feigned. I think I made that clear on our first meeting."

"And I think we also drew a firm line under our meeting that night?"

His head cocks to one side. "Did we? That's funny. I remember walking away feeling distinctly... unresolved."

I shake my head, exasperation seeping through my tight hold on composure. "Heads up, I'm going to use a dirty word in a

minute, so you might want to hang on to your fluffy cravat. Your
blue balls are your problem. I have no interest in fucking you.
Before I fuck someone I have to like them. And I don't like you,
Mason Sinclair."

He studies me for almost a minute before a blinding smile
spreads over his face. The transformation in his features makes
me eternally grateful to be holding on to the rail when I feel the
power of that smile move through me like a potent burst of electricity.

I remain in place as he drops his arms and closes the
distance between us. "Why don't you like me?" he asks. The
smile is gone, but his voice remains darkly amused.

"Do I have to have a reason?" I ask, denying myself the urge
to breathe deeply and take in more of that earthy scent pulsing
off his body. I want to bury my nose in that scent. Roll around in
it like a goddamn bitch in heat.

He reaches up and toys with a strand of my hair, moving it
through his fingers like it's his divine right. Like I'm his
possession.

"No, you don't. Same way I don't have to have a reason for the
need to strip you of every stitch of clothing you're wearing—bar
those fuck-me boots—bend you over this rail right now and ram
my cock so far up inside you, you'll taste me in your mouth for
years. I just do. And unlike you, I don't intend to fight it."

I stare at him, feeling hot. And dirty. And more turned on
than I've been in my entire life.

I also feel afraid. Because that look is back, lurking in his
eyes. The one that says he's riding an edge that could take a
wrong turn at any moment. Like a tornado you think you're safe
from, only to watch it twist your way and annihilate you in the
blink of an eye.

He continues to caress my hair, the back of his fingers faintly grazing my cheek. Then he steps closer and brings his mouth to my ear. "I know how tight your abstinence has made you. Or it could be that you're naturally tight." His chest rises and falls, and he seems to be lost in his own head. "No matter. Either way, the first time will be fast and a little rough. I haven't fucked anyone in a very long time. But after that, I'll take my time... make you ready to accommodate me. But not too much time. I want to stretch you, make you feel every inch of me. To do that, I'll have to get a little rough. But you can take it, my little nerd girl. Can't you?" he breathes in my ear.

A full body shiver engulfs me. I turn my head slightly so my mouth is close to his ear. I wait a beat, make sure I have his full attention. "Maybe I can. Maybe I can't. *You* will never find out," I say.

I step back and summon a smile I'm far from feeling.

His eyes gleam with a simmering fire before his features smooth into a blank canvas I find impossible to read. "You're fucking someone else?" he bites out in a low but ferocious tone.

I laugh at the sheer audacity of him. "You think the only reason I'd refuse you is because I have someone else in my bed? It can't be that I don't want you?"

"Are you denying that you do? Or are you denying that you're involved with someone else?" he challenges, his eyes narrowing.

"What does it matter which one it is?"

He grabs my upper arms in a tight hold, and his nostrils flare in such an animalistic exhibition of rage that I swallow. "I've never quite mastered the art of sharing my things, so yes, it matters which one of those you mean."

I fight the heat dragging through my pelvis with everything I've got. Through the material of my sweater I feel the naked stamp of his touch on my skin. "There's this wonderful little thing called free will that lets me say yes or no to whatever and whomever I want."

"Answer the question, Keely. Are you fucking someone else?"

I wish with all my heart I can answer in the affirmative. But even the "mind your fucking business" that rises to my lips dies a quivering death when confronted with the dangerous vibes spiking from him.

I open my mouth to answer when a throat clears behind us. "Excuse me, sir—"

"Leave!" Mason snarls, his gaze not once moving from my face.

I gasp at the depth of his rudeness, and my head swivels to see the crew member hightailing it down the stairs. "You can't speak to the staff like that!"

He catches my chin in his hand and forces my gaze to his. "Keely." He breathes my name with a rumble that shoots straight to my belly.

"Jesus! No, I'm not screwing anyone right this minute. But I can't promise that won't change anytime soon." I pull myself forcefully from his arms and he lets me go.

"Do you have anyone specific in mind?" he enquires silkily.

"Why?" I toss back, bewildered at the path of this conversation.

"So I can ensure they meet an unfortunate end before they get anywhere near you."

Normally, a statement like that would be uttered with a smile or joviality intended to take the threat and bite out of it. Mason Sinclair says the words with a lethal bluntness that makes my eyes widen. "Did you crawl out from under some rock recently?"

"Yes," he answers, again with that deadpan look. "I've spent most of the last four years in the Amazon with a tribe cut off from the rest of civilization."

My mouth drops open. "You... Are you serious?"

His lashes sweep down in a slow blink. "Why would I lie about something like that?"

I shake my head to clear the conflicting messages bombarding me. "Regardless of that, there's no excuse for your rudeness considering who you are." His eyebrow starts to spike, and I purse my lips. "Yes, I know exactly who you are. I googled you. People do that nowadays. In fact, it's considered an insult not to google a person you meet at the first opportunity."

His mouth twitches. "Duly noted. But the facts that interest me about you won't be online. Unless you've been a very naughty girl," he drawls.

God. I can't make up my mind where my exasperation ends and my excitement begins with this man. All I know is I need to get away from him. Now. Before I lose my mind. Or throw myself at this hard wall of a body.

I drag my gaze from said body and look around to find that while we've been engaged in what can only politely be labeled as verbal intercourse, the sun has set and lights have come on aboard the other boats and along the marina.

"I'm going to find the captain of this yacht. I'm sure he'll give me a tour since you don't seem inclined to."

I hurry to the sofa where I dropped my clutch and head for the stairs, which lead God knows where. As I near the stairs, I hear him behind me.

"I'll give you your tour. But bear in mind that each hour you force me into this useless dance with you is another hour I add to your punishment board."

I hide a shiver of excitement and thread a bored tone through my voice as my heels click on the solid wooden floors down a wide hallway. "Give it up, Mason. Not every woman you meet is destined to fall at your feet in abject worship."

I come to a halt when the hallway forks into four crossroads. With all that's happened so far, I feel like this is some sort of ominous sign.

Mason stops behind me. His breath brushes the top of my head as the heat from his body engulfs mine. Every single cell in my body stands to attention at the ominous feeling that washes over me, as if the moment is an important one that I can never retrace my steps from.

I feel his touch a second before his fingers trail down my arms, eliciting a deep shudder he can't miss. "No. But *you* are. You're destined to fall at my feet and stay there. Not because I want you to, but because you'll like it. And because you won't want to be anywhere else. I promise you that, Keely."

8

MASON

My fingers trail over the delicate skin of her inner wrists, and I can feel her stiffening herself against another shudder. I want to tell her not to bother. I already know her body's reaction far better than she thinks I do. But I hesitate.

I'm not even sure who I'm hesitating for. Her, for the skittishness she's desperately trying to hide? Or me, for the line I know I shouldn't cross but can't help caressing and toying with? Everything she said on the deck is right. Well... almost everything. I have no intention of taking her fast. I already did that on top of the car in Montauk. And as much as the need pounding through me demands a fast, bough-breaking release, it won't be that way.

Not with her.

If I end up taking her.

I told her when we first met that I won't play any games with her. And I won't.

But the fact of the matter is that I still haven't picked up the phone to Hani, haven't done anything to alleviate the diabolic edge riding me. I'm playing a dangerous game of chicken with myself that could explode into a steaming shit storm if I'm not careful. I know this. And yet, I let Zach talk me into this project, knowing very well it will keep me here in an environment I detest. With people I despise even more.

But not this woman in front of me.

I don't despise her. I'm compelled by her. My intense fascination is enough to make me want to do things to her that are probably against any law in any land.

"Are you going to respond to what I said?" I ask, noting her tripping pulse with dark satisfaction.

"No. I've decided to let you exist in your deluded little bubble."

I almost smile at her tart tone. She's contrary in a way that mesmerizes me. In another time, I'd love to break her down, piece by piece, and build her up again just the way I want her. To do that with her now will need time, patience. Neither of those commodities is available to me. The strain I'm under is too much to even think about adding to it.

"Okay, princess. I'll let you keep pretending everything we're *both* feeling right here, right now, is all in my head. Which way do you want to go?" I ask, reluctantly lifting my fingers from her skin.

"I came to see the whole yacht, so it doesn't matter which way we start, does it? And please don't call me princess."

I step beside her, and she has to tilt her head up to look me in the face. My gaze trails over her vulnerable neck and the pulse beating at her throat, and I admit I like the sight of it a little bit more than is healthy. "Why not?"

Her beautiful green eyes shadow before her eyelashes sweep down, hiding her expression from me. "Because I'm about as far from a princess as you can get."

From any other person, I'd believe that statement is a coy attempt to gain my interest. From her, I believe she really means it. Just as I believe it stems from whatever pushed her into throwing herself in an icy ocean two weeks ago.

I shrug internally. I've never been the sort of guy who doles out pet names. Although, if I allow myself to think about it, she reminds me of an alley cat—all claws, sharp teeth and vulnerable underbelly just itching to be stroked.

It's that vulnerability I want nothing to do with. I don't want to know her weaknesses. The temptation to exploit them will be too great. My subtle, insidious ability to twist weakness to my advantage is the reason my mother called me a monster when I was eleven.

It's the reason my father handed me the keys to his kingdom on my eighteenth birthday, slapped me on the back and toasted to my genius when I quadrupled the family fortune by the time I was twenty-five.

It's the reason Cassie was a sitting duck the moment she entered my orbit. She never really stood a chance.

Thoughts of Cassie bring the clarity of mind I need. "Point taken," I say to Keely.

Her eyelids start to lift, and I turn away, knowing the tiniest hint of interest will tip me in the wrong direction. I head down the port hallway, away from the entertainment lounges.

I enter the first room and let her wander in. As she passes me, I smell her perfume and stem the need to breathe her in like a greedy, sick fool, regardless of the fact that it's exactly what I am.

Enough is never enough for you, is it? You have to take and take and keep taking until there's nothing left! You know what you are? You're fucking EVIL!

I block out Cassie's voice and keep my eye on Keely.

She walks down the arena-like cinema, taking in each detail of the seats and the adult accessories attached to the plush upholstery. She picks up a remote and examines the buttons before she looks at me.

"Are there no privacy settings on the seating areas?" she asks.

"What's the point? Isn't part of the thrill of being in this room the exhibitionism?"

The room is too dark and she's too far away for me to see if my response makes her color rise, but I see her shrug. "I've seen a few of the Indigo jet blueprints. I just thought clients here would be given the same options."

"Zach didn't design this boat. I did."

Her head jerks up. "You? I thought you were just refitting the adult entertainment areas? From what I recall of the initial design, this cinema was already here."

I fold my arms. "It was, from when I owned this boat."

Her mouth drops open in that adorable way that makes me have to lock my knees to keep from moving in her direction and reacquainting myself with those lush lips. "*You* owned this boat?"

I don't respond. She knows who I am. Or at least she thinks she knows enough about me. What she doesn't know is that I've ruthlessly erased about 80 percent of my past from every known, and most unknown, databases. Everything she's been exposed to so far is just online fluff pieces that gossip whores find salacious.

I hide a grim smile.

If they knew the truth... if *she* knew the truth, she wouldn't be standing here, running her hands over the velvet cushion like she wants to fuck it.

"Are we done here?" I ask tersely. Watching her hands move like that over the seat is making me a little nuts. And in my world, a little nuts isn't the same as most people measure it to be.

She glances at me for a second, and I know something in my voice has thrown her. She debates whether to heed that inkling of danger, then pulls out a mini tablet to make a few notes. "I'm done here." She throws the words out in that sexy, snappy way that makes my cock jerk to full attention again.

I walk her to the next room. She stands at the door and peers in with a look of puzzlement on her face as she glances down at her tablet. "What room is this? It's not in the blueprint Zach sent me."

"No, it's a new addition. One of many, in fact."

She frowns. "Why wasn't I told about it?"

"What you were or weren't told is none of my concern. As to what this place is..." I turn and flick on a switch. She winces a little as the room is flooded with harsh light. I adjust the mood switch to a warm indigo and flick another switch. A gentle sparkling mist—a late addition I concocted two days ago—starts to fall from the ceiling. Her mouth drops open on a soft gasp as the first cloud of mist touches her face. I watch her reaction as her tongue darts out to taste my creation.

Her eyes widen. "Wow, it tastes... incredible. Wait, it's not poisonous or anything, is it?"

"No, it's not poisonous and you can't overdose on it, but it's set on a timer."

"Really? Why?"

"Because it can get addictive."

A sultry smile spreads across her face, and she licks more of the mist from her lips. "I'll say! What exactly is it?"

I watch her face for her reaction and reply, "It's an Aphrodisiac Shower."

"*Fuck!*" She bolts out of the spray and glares at me. "You didn't think to tell me that before you doused me in that shit?"

"Two seconds ago, you thought it was incredible." I study the color in her cheeks and her dilated pupils and wonder how scarlet she'll blush when my cock is deep in her ass and my hands are wrapped around her throat.

"Fuck that. You should've told me."

She heads toward me, and I curb the urge to slam my hand across the doorway to pin her against the frame so I can test if she's as wet as she was the last time I tasted her pussy. She'd gotten so wet so fast that day that I later wondered if it was real or a fluke of my imagination.

Whatever it is, I know I should walk away, but I can't. I feel my near obsession with her reaching worrying proportions. And that terrifies me. Because she thinks she knows what lies beneath my uncivilized exterior. But really, she has no fucking clue. And I can guarantee that she won't like what's underneath when she finds out.

"Keely." My tone reminds her of our agreement.

She glares harder and the urge to test her boundaries claws through me.

"Don't give me that tone. You want me to not swear, then you tell me upfront what I'm walking into. At least tell me what you're doing before you start flicking switches. Or the deal is off." She tucks her bag under her arm and brushes her hand over her skin in an attempt to get rid of the mist.

"Fine," I reply. "Then I guess I should tell you that once imbedded in skin, the aphrodisiac's effect doesn't wear off for four hours."

Her eyes bulge. "What? Are you serious?"

"I don't joke about my inventions."

"Your *inventions*. You mean you designed this? I thought you were..." Her words taper off and she frowns.

"A what?"

Her head tilts and strands of her blond hair caress her neck and cleavage. I don't even bother to avert my gaze. She has a beautiful pair of tits. Ones my hands and mouth are itching to touch and taste. I return my gaze to her face when she keeps silent. The look in her eyes has slightly altered, and I know the effects of the aphrodisiac are in her bloodstream now.

I've never been into forced sex, but God, the *Fuck Me* look in her eyes makes me wish she's mine to do with as I please. And I wish many, many things with this woman.

She shakes her head. "It's... umm... Your online bio said you're the CEO of S3, the hedge fund company."

"Yes, that's true. But I'm also a few other things."

A corner of her mouth lifts, and she glances over her shoulder at the dissipating mist. "An aphrodisiac inventor, obviously. Where the hell do you learn to become an aphrodisiac inventor anyway?" She's pulling her wrap from her shoulders in a slow, sexy movement that makes my temperature spike.

"I can tell you, but then I'll have to fuck you. And you don't want that, do you, Keely?"

Her mouth compresses. "That's not even remotely funny. And it's the sort of thing that will see you slapped with a sexual harassment suit."

I straighten. "But I'm not your employer. We don't even work together. I'm just your tour guide. Shall we continue?"

She stares at me for another few seconds before she nods. I walk her into the next room.

"This one is pretty much self-explanatory."

She gazes warily around the spank room as if she expects one of the many whips and floggers to attack her any moment. I restrain a smile and watch her walk around the room, checking a list on her tablet.

"I have eight gadgets on my list. There are nine in here," she snaps with a touch of exasperation. "I can't start emailing clients the activity sheets if things are going to be added and taken off without my knowledge."

"I had the last addition flown in this morning."

"Which one is it?"

"This one." I lead her to a black and indigo velvet free-standing cubicle. Inside, there are two horizontal bars at the top with restraints dangling from them. I watch her face as she examines everything.

"How is this different from the bench and the bed?" she asks.

I smile. "It won't make sense until you witness it for yourself. Wanna be my guinea pig?"

She rolls her eyes. "I think you know the answer to that."

Despite her reply, the interest in her eyes is clear to see, as is the unsettled pulse at her throat that hasn't quite returned to normal.

I decide to test the true level of her interest. "I'm testing it out tomorrow. Swing by and see for yourself."

Her gaze connects with mine. "You're testing it out? Who with?"

I hide a smile at the ticked-off note in her voice I'm sure she thinks is nothing but curiosity. I recognize it for what it is. Keely Benson is territorial. She's deeply possessive to a depth I'm sure even she isn't aware of.

"Stop by after lunch. See for yourself."

Leaving it at that, we finish the tour of the deck. We bypass the middle deck, where the construction crew is putting the finishing touches to the restaurant, bar and pool areas, and head for the deck below.

"So, why the need to own a sex boat?" she asks, again in that offhanded way, which gives the false implication that she doesn't care about my answer.

"Why does any red-blooded male need one?"

"Two things spring to mind. Either you're a sex maniac or you need a penis extender?"

I smile. "If I'm a sex maniac, I'll hardly confess to it, will I? As for this being a penis extender, if you want to see the size of mine to judge for yourself, you need only ask."

Her eyes drop to my crotch instantaneously, almost a reflex action. My body responds to the flash of hunger in her expression, and I grit my teeth against the powerful arousal moving through me.

Being around her is worse now than it'd been in Montauk, and it'd been pretty fucked up then. My phone's presence in my pocket reminds me that I have a way out of this. One call to Hani and all will be well again. She is sending me two girls tomorrow, but that is different. They are just test subjects for the various additions I've made to a few sex implements on the yachts. Like everything I create, I need to make sure it's fully tested before I release it to the public.

My blood rushes a little faster through my veins at the thought of taking them through the routines. It would alleviate some of my pent-up frustrations, but it wouldn't be anywhere near the usual twelve-hour sessions I need to place my edge back under control.

My hand itches to take out my phone, but like every other time I want to take that final step toward numbing myself, I hesitate. The part of my brain that worked out my problem a long time ago knows this is yet another form of punishment, another form of self-flagellation for my sins.

I'd continue to live in this hell if I didn't know that my rage and pain will spill to an innocent bystander.

Someone who doesn't deserve it.

Someone like Keely.

I focus to find her answering her own phone. "About time

you called back," she snaps, but I catch a note of affection in her voice.

Affection, a now alien feeling that makes me cock my head and listen, the sound of it a concept punished out of my system a long time ago.

She flicks a glance at me. "Yeah, too late, B. He's already sicced himself on me." She stops and listens. "Fine. Whatever. Tell your husband that the next time he hires one of his friends to work on a project with me, he should give me a heads up. I don't like surprises." She rolls her eyes at whatever Bethany says. "No, sister, flattery will get you both nowhere. Now leave me to work, and don't forget to feed Jeigerhamster," she snaps, then her gaze softens. "Yeah, me too. Bye."

She joins me in the hallway, and we walk for a minute before I say, "You named your pet Jeigerhamster."

A smile plays on her lips before she bites it away. "Watch it. You mock, you die."

"And you think I sicced myself on you?"

She glares at me. "Didn't you? You knew I was working on this project, right?"

"Yes."

"After what happened in Montauk, I figured you'd excuse yourself or at least make sure our schedules don't clash?"

I shrug. "Why would I?"

"You don't care that I saw you freak out and try to kill us both in that car?"

"I don't really care what you think. And there are more effective ways to end one's life. Driving headlong into a tree offers no guarantee that you'll be killed instantly. You could end up with nothing but a scratch or two. Or partial paralysis. If you want death to be certain and irreversible, there are more efficient ways."

She inhales sharply. "Are you joking?"

"No."

Wariness creeps into her eyes. "You sound like you've thought about this a lot," she says.

I wonder whether to bludgeon her with the truth. Is this tough girl from Brooklyn equipped to handle the evil that stains my heart and plagues my nightmares? "I'm an inventor and an architect, amongst other things. In order to innovate, I have to know how to disinvent."

"And that includes learning how to kill?" Her voice quivers with a sick curiosity she doesn't want to admit—a curiosity I understand all too well.

"Are you sure you want to know the answer to that, Keely?" I taunt.

She stares at me for a moment before she collects herself. "If you're trying to increase your air of intrigue and mystery, save it. I'm not on the market for freaks and weirdos."

"What are you on the market for?" I parry. "A quick fuck to alleviate that ache ripping you apart inside?"

A flush rises from her neck. "Don't be an asshole. My sexual needs are none of your concern."

"So you haven't done anything about it?"

"Have you done something about yours?" she throws back at me.

"Not yet." I meet her gaze, give her a glimpse of my monstrous hunger, and am rewarded by a light shudder that accompanies her next breath.

"Damn it," she mutters before she turns away.

Her gaze lands on the sign on the double doors in front of her, and she slams to a stop.

Indigo Swinger.

She glances over her shoulder at me, and I'm even more

convinced that despite her dirty mouth and aggressive exterior, Keely Benson isn't the siren she purports to be. Granted, she's still a sex bomb. One that could detonate in my hands if I'm not careful. All the same, I feel the thrill escalate and race through my blood.

"Is this a new addition?" she asks, indicating the sign.

"No."

Her swift intake of breath makes her nostrils flutter, and all I want to do in that moment is take possession of her.

"Wow. Okay." She seems lost for a moment before she straightens her shoulders. "I think I've seen all I need to see here. I want to see the upper deck now."

We continue the tour, pretending the charged atmosphere between us doesn't exist. With each minute that passes, with each inhalation of that sexy scent, which clings to her skin, I want to flatten her to the nearest surface and take the edge off the insane need pounding through me.

By the time we finish the tour, I've made up my mind.

Fuck the consequences.

Fuck the voice of reason telling me to take the safe option and call Hani.

I've never known a hunger like this for any other woman.

Regardless of whether I risk exposing her to the monster that lives within me, by the time I escort her to the launch that will take her back to her hotel, I succumb to the inevitable.

Keely Benson will be mine.

9

KEELY

I feel too much on edge to settle when I return to my hotel suite.

Fucking Mason Sinclair has imbedded himself in my mind. I'm not sure why I'm so fascinated with him. He's part freak, part genius, part possible sociopath. The last part I'm not entirely certain of, but something in his eyes scares the crap out of me. Not enough for me to walk away from this project. Or even think about avoiding him.

On the contrary. I'm drawn to him with a singular morbid allure, which spells nothing but trouble with a capital T.

The only thing that comes fractionally close to describing what I feel for Mason is what I felt for another guy six years ago. And look how that ended.

I shiver in the cool evening air as I stand on my balcony and stare at the exquisite, unmistakable lines of the Indigo Lounge yacht. Is he on there? Did he say where he was staying? I barely remember our conversation after that charged exchange about death and killing. Something in the way he said that still makes every nerve in my body want to recoil. But at the same time, I'm fascinated beyond belief; the urge to dive beneath Mason

Sinclair's skin and discover all his dark secrets is a living thing between us.

He wants to do the same to me. I can tell.

Just like I can tell he wants to fuck me. And not just in a quickie-get-our-rocks-off-and-be-done-with-it way either. That also excites me in ways I can't explain. I shouldn't be excited. I should hate the idea of anyone dominating me. But all I can think about is the feeling he evoked when he ordered me to recite the constellations on top of his car in Montauk. The release he gave me then was out of this world.

I want that release again.

Along with insight into what lurks beneath his surface.

"For fuck's sake, Keely," I mutter under my breath.

Sometimes I hate my curious mind. It's gained me a well-paid job and a better-than-average living I'm satisfied with. But at times like these, when I know I should leave well enough alone but my brain keeps urging me to explore, I wonder whether I'll ever learn my lesson.

Because obviously those three harrowing days six years ago didn't do a good enough job.

I veer away from the view, clutching my wrap tighter around me, and return to the suite. I order room service, eat and channel surf before settling on a game I have zero interest in on ESPN. I balance my laptop on my thighs and think of working for a few hours.

Instead, I find myself googling Mason again. This time, I take my time to read his background, and I frown. Blocks of his life have been missed. Like the ages between his twenty-second and twenty-fourth birthdays, and again his twenty-seventh birthday. From twenty-seven, the details of his life grow even sketchier.

Pages and pages are dedicated to his philanthropic deeds and innovative inventions. But it's easy to donate to charities if you have a company vehicle taking care of it on your behalf. Of Mason himself, there is next to nothing in the past few years, although his company, S3, continues its staggering growth in the business sector and employs over five thousand people in the US and overseas.

My frown intensifies.

Mason isn't a recluse, at least not from what I saw of him at Bethany and Zach's engagement party. So whatever has made him suppress his past has nothing to do with a forced withdrawal from society.

How would you know?

I realize I'm trying to rationalize and humanize the man, and I impatiently shut the laptop. I know, deep in my bones, that he hides a dark secret. I have the dark, dominating Neanderthal freak and the sexy genius bit squared away. But if he's also a sociopath, I won't find out until I get to know him better.

The idea that that is exactly what I'm contemplating sends me to my feet and into the bedroom. Rifling through the clothes the butler hung in the walk-in closet, I take out a slinky, black sequined dress and my favorite silver platform shoes, which always lift my mood.

It's Friday night, and I'm in one of the sexiest, most affluent cities on earth. I may not be in the market to get laid by the first guy I come across—somehow the idea of ending my months-long dry spell as quickly as possible no longer compels my every thought—but there's no reason why I shouldn't have a good time.

I squash the voice mocking me that my need is no longer urgent because now it's found the true source of alleviation— Mason Sinclair—its search is over.

Whatever.

Until I decide where my comfort compass intends to settle

when it comes to the man, I'll be keeping my thighs firmly closed and my super dirty thoughts firmly in my head.

Hell, I'm even willing to stop dropping f-bombs around him if that's what it takes to remain remotely sane when we are in the same room together.

I sigh as I realize how much I'm thinking of giving in. How much my actions seem to be swayed by him even when he isn't around.

Impatient that I can't stop thinking about him, I drop my robe and slip the black dress on. Immediately, I feel a little more in control of my destiny.

Cut the fanciful crap, Keely. You've always been in control of your destiny.

Not always...

I freeze as my mind veers to the email waiting on my laptop. The first email consisted of only eight numbers. Eight simple numbers that form a date.

02. 21. 2009.

It's one part of three dates that are forever seared in my memory. I convinced myself that the email was spam and deleted it.

The second email convinced me it wasn't.

02. 22. 2009.

But this time it wasn't just that date. The second email came with a picture. To the casual reader, the date and picture of a dungeon-like room would mean nothing. Together, I'm in no doubt it's someone from my past.

That mansion, and its labyrinth of underground rooms, has

featured large and menacing in my nightmares for the past six years. Why the sender wants to torture me about it is something I haven't yet worked out. But I know the threat is real. Just as I know I'll receive another email with the third and final date soon.

My heart thumps wildly, and I force myself to breathe through the terror threatening to seize me. As much as my mind screams at me to confront the danger, I know I can't do anything until I have a clear demand. Only then can I form a plan of action. One that doesn't involve the police. Because to involve them will mean divulging the whole sickening truth of what I've done. And there is no way I'm about to do that.

All I can do is wait.

Continue to pretend I'm the girl everyone thinks I am. The one whose life is an endless carnival of high-flying job, partying and the occasional sexcapade. I've screwed this mask in place for six long years, not even showing a hint of what's underneath to my best friend, Bethany.

I don't doubt for a moment that she will try her best to save me if she knows of the many nights I've feared going to sleep alone, or the nightmares I deal with in my darkest moment.

But that's the reason I haven't told her.

I don't think I'm worth saving.

What happened that weekend was horrific enough. What I did next was unforgivable.

Nothing and no one will be able to wash me clean.

* * *

I arrive at Jimmy'z at ten and flash a smile at the bouncer. It's a smile I've practiced for years—the one that says *I'm sexy, I can rock your world, so you'd be a fool not to give me what I want.*

His answering smile is immediate, his manner deferring, and I don't need to flash the VIP card languishing in my clutch.

I'm not sure exactly when I decided to use my sexuality as a tool. It's a characteristic that crept on me without my knowledge or consent, but one I decided to embrace once I realized the path I'd taken. And so far, it's been the most effective tool in combating my demons. It grants me the control I need to survive.

Strobe lights assault my senses the moment I step into Jimmy'z. I squint and look around. The dance floor is a heaving mass of writhing bodies, and the scent of sweaty pheromones and alcohol fills the air.

I make my way to the bar, very much aware of lingering male interest, but not making eye contact long enough to attract singular attention. I'm more than a little bewildered as to why my libido seems to have chosen one person for its attention, so I'm beyond irritated by the time I slap my hand on the counter to attract the bartender's notice.

He looks my way with a quirked eyebrow.

"Stoli Gold. Neat."

I usually start with a cocktail and work my way to the hard stuff, but tonight I'm on edge, both from the email, whose presence is growing larger by the second, and also because I can't stop thinking about Mason Sinclair.

Maybe I should just fuck him and be done with it. Maybe that will decrease this stupid mystique I'm sure I've built up around him in my head. Sure, the fact that he has a huge brain and happens to be good with his hands is a giant-sized turn-on. I've always held a fascination for those two characteristics. Combined in one guy, along with those rough and rugged good looks, I'm bound to go a little nuts.

I also happen to know firsthand what those hands can do to my body. Which is another huge tick in his favor.

But then there are the danger signs. The ones that scream at me to keep my distance. The ones that warn me not to scratch the surface because I'll be annihilated by what I find beneath.

Danger signs I can't seem to stop myself from sliding toward...

The bartender slides the shot across. I down it in one go, and he raises the bottle and says something in French I don't understand. I nod anyway and indicate the glass. He refills and I drink, letting the sharp taste and burn slide down my throat.

When he raises the bottle again, I shake my head. I plan on getting drunk tonight but not until I've done a little recon for my project and taken a few necessary notes.

I start to turn just as someone nudges me.

I glance over my shoulder and see Henri, his charming grin trying a little too hard. "Mademoiselle Benson, I am glad you made it. I have been watching out for you." He uses hand signals as he speaks, as if I don't understand the accented English spilling from his mouth. "You look amazing!" His gaze conducts an appreciative head-to-toe assessment before he looks back up with eager puppy dog eyes.

I summon a smile I'm far from feeling. "Thank you, and call me Keely."

He leans forward, and I'm engulfed in Hugo Boss aftershave as he says into my ear, "Can I buy you a drink?"

I shake my head. One of my many rules is to never let a guy I don't know buy me drinks. "I'm good for now, thanks." I mentally roll my eyes when he doesn't move back. "I was about to go check out the VIP cubes upstairs."

He nods eagerly. "I will come with you."

I shrug. "Sure, why not?" Bringing him with me will keep

other guys from hitting on me. Plus, he's still as easy on the eyes as he'd been earlier this afternoon, despite the too-busy leather jacket he's wearing. He's also a perfect candidate for taking my mind off my problems should I decide to go ahead with using him.

He takes my hand and guides me through the throng of people. We ascend black fiberglass stairs to a set of double doors roped off with red hooks and manned by two burly bouncers. They're built like professional wrestlers, one fair-haired, the other ebony dark.

Henri rattles off a torrent of French, but the black bouncer stares at him with bored, dead eyes. Henri glances at me, a flush of embarrassment creeping up his collar. He rattles off an ever-faster torrent. The bouncer looks at me, then back at him and utters a single word. "*Non.*"

I take pity on Henri and fish the VIP card from my clutch. I wave it in front of the fair-haired one and his demeanor alters. "Welcome, Miss Benson, we've been expecting you."

They part the doors and I start walking, only to stop when I hear a scuffle behind me.

The fair-haired bouncer is restraining Henri. Sighing, I retrace my steps. "It's okay, he's with me."

"Sorry, Miss Benson. The man said you were to come in alone."

My nape tingles as I ask, "What man?"

"He's in Room 10. He said I was to bring you to him when you came up. And that you were not to be accompanied by anyone else."

"Did he?" I murmur. "We'll see about that." I tell myself it's annoyance fizzing through me, but my escalating excitement makes a mockery of my feelings. To Henri, I say, "Sorry about this. Maybe I'll find you when I come back down?" I won't, but I don't see a need to be a bitch about it.

He looks crestfallen but nods eagerly as I turn away. The second bouncer points down a left corridor and accompanies me as I start walking.

"I can find it on my own."

He gives me an apologetic shrug. "Sorry, ma'am, I have my orders."

I bristle as I march past black mirrored doors, counting off the gold numbering until I reach number 10. I'm seething. And Mason Sinclair is about to be the recipient of my temper.

10

KEELY

I slap my hand against the swing door and, as expected, it gives way to reveal Mason Sinclair. His thickly muscled arms are flung wide on the seat, his gaze on the dance floor below. Since his back is to the door, I can only see the back of his head and shoulders, but immediately my nipples tighten and my pussy clenches with a hunger so fierce, I deeply resent him for the effortless power he seems to have over me.

He doesn't turn around as I approach, although despite the music thumping from below, the room is quiet enough that he should've heard me enter.

"Next time you feel the need to summon me, take a beat and remember serfs and overlords are a thing of the past." I infuse my voice with bite, even though I'm far too enthralled with the black shirt draping his torso and the lights glinting through his vibrant black hair.

Shit, everything about this man is arresting to the point I can't tell where my interest in one feature ends and the other begins.

"Is it a summons if you were headed here anyway?" he replies in that smoky voice.

"You know very well what I mean."

"Do I?" He finally turns his head and peruses me from head to toe. The look in his eyes tells me he appreciates what he sees. Most men would tell me I look beautiful after such a scrutiny. I wait for the compliment. It never arrives. "Sit down, Keely."

"No, thanks. Oh, and I also don't appreciate you instructing the bouncers to get heavy with Henri."

I get close enough to see him drum his fingers on his ankle. The action draws my attention to the thigh straining against the material of his trousers. "You're pissed off because I sent your admirer away?"

"I'm pissed off because you exist, full stop."

His jaw flexes, and I wonder if I've gone too far. Then I immediately hate myself for caring one way or the other.

God, he drives me insane!

"Were you planning on sleeping with him?" Tension thrums through his voice, and my hackles rise higher.

"None of your business."

He turns his head and spears me with sharp hazel eyes, which are insanely effective in pinning me to the spot. "What if I decide to make it my business?"

I affect a careless shrug, despite the electricity zapping through my bloodstream. "You're welcome to do whatever the fu — the hell you want."

A tiny twitch at the corner of his mouth is the only indication that he's caught my hasty correction. The fact that I did pisses me off even more. I turn to walk out, but his voice stops me.

"Come and sit down, Keely. You'll want to hear what I have to say."

"I seriously doubt that."

He returns his attention to the dance floor, his gaze sweeping restlessly over the crowd. I sense he doesn't want to be here. "At least stay for one drink?"

I look around the room for the first time and although there's a well-stocked bar, there's no bartender or wait staff in sight as the write-up promised. Before I can ask, Mason presses a silver button near his armrest. A dull red light I didn't notice before in the upper right corner of the room turns green. A few seconds later, a side door opens and a hostess wheels in a black and chrome trolley teaming with domed platters.

"I thought we'd have some food while we talked?"

"I already ate." Hours ago, but some instinctive need to keep battling with this man spurs me on.

He says nothing, just nods to the hostess, who begins setting out the food on the low table in front of him. When she's done, she slips behind the bar and pours him a glass of sparkling water with a twist of lime, which she delivers with a far too intimate smile.

Perhaps it's that smile that makes up my mind. Perhaps I was doomed the first day I set eyes on Mason Sinclair. All I know is that my feet are rounding the seat and I'm moving toward him. I drop my clutch at the end of the wide semi-circular sofa and perch two seats away.

He doesn't acknowledge me as he begins unveiling the dishes. Delicious scents waft my way and my stomach reminds me I've only eaten a small salade nicoise hours ago. "What can I get you?" he asks.

"An explanation as to why I'm here would be nice," I reply. "And while you're at it, care to tell me how you knew I'd be here in the first place?" It reeks of the sort of mildly stalkerish shit that Zach Savage pulled with Bethany when they were dating. It put my back up then, and I'm not entirely okay with it now either. I watch him and wonder if all billionaires are prone to such behavior. "Did you follow me here?"

He picks up a delicate-looking hors d'oeuvre with his fingers, tosses it into his mouth and chews before he replies.

"No, I didn't," is all he says. "I've decided to play your game. Or an abbreviated version of it, anyway."

I open my mouth to press him more on how he knew where I'd be, but I find myself asking instead, "And what game is that?"

"The one where we dance around the fact that we want to fuck each other, because one of us doesn't know how to take what's in front of them without the song and dance."

My pulse kicks up a notch. "What the—"

His raised hand stops my response and I'm stunned I actually obey. "You want me, Keely. I sure as hell want you. Call me a bastard for seeing what I want and going after it, but I intend to fuck you very, very soon. I prefer to do it without having to treat you like a bimbo princess who needs guiding into what can be a pleasurable experience for both of us. Frankly, it's tedious and unattractive, considering you're intelligent enough to cut the bullshit and admit this is what you want, too."

My mouth drops open and I splutter, "Does this brand of crap actually work to get you laid?"

He selects an array of finger foods and places them on a plate. "You assume I've ever had to work this hard."

There's a compliment in there somewhere, but I can't see it for the red haze of anger clouding my brain and my judgment. "For someone who's obviously skilled enough to be the man you are today, you have a shockingly dense outlook on what makes a woman happy."

He continues to inspect the food on the dishes. "You're under the misapprehension that I'm in this to make you happy. I'm not.

I want to fuck you and keep fucking you until I'm satisfied. Then I have every intention of letting you go."

I look around, seeking some sort of divine revelation as to why I'm still sitting here listening to this arrogant bastard. "Are you for real?"

"I am. I promise. Eat." He holds the plate out in front of me. I look from the offering in his hand and back to his face.

Everything about this is wrong. So wrong. And yet my heart hasn't stopped racing since I entered the room. And each time he mentions fucking me, my body goes crazy hot and my insides churn with blinding excitement.

He moves closer when I don't take the plate. Long, elegant fingers pluck a sesame seed-covered morsel that he dips into a dark condiment before he holds it to my lips. "Try this. You'll enjoy it."

"Because you're an expert on the things I enjoy?" I snap.

He says nothing, just continues to hold the food a whisper away from my lips until they part of their own accord. My tongue slides out to help the morsel in, and his gaze drops to my mouth. He watches me as I chew, and I try not to moan at the sharp and spicy explosion of flavors on my tongue from the Thai food. I glance down at the dishes on the table and realize each one is comprised of delicacies from my favorite food regions—Asia and Europe.

Surprise widens my eyes, and I glance back to him to see something shift in his eyes, a hunger so wild it's almost inhuman. He feeds me another mouthful, and his fingers brush lightly and deliberately over my lips before he withdraws.

My breath catches, and his mouth twitches in a ghost of a smile. He tosses two morsels into his mouth and chews with the ruthless efficiency of a predator. My loins catch fire watching him chew and I try to tear my gaze away, but I can't look away from him.

"Drink?" he rasps.

The hostess suddenly appears beside me with a tray holding a cocktail I immediately recognize—a Studded Reverse Cowboy—my favorite cocktail. Aside from that seriously stalkerish vibe, which slams into me again, I'm also thrown by the fact that the hostess has been present the whole time. Has she overheard the exchange between Mason and me?

I look up to read her expression and find her attention once more riveted to Mason's face.

Irritation churns in my belly. I pluck the glass from the tray with a curt thanks and down half its contents. I tell myself I don't care that she's eye-fucking Mason. The admission echoes hollowly inside me.

Truth is, I care a little too fucking much.

I shake my head when he leans forward to offer me another mouthful. "I've had enough, thanks."

I mean it not just with regard to the food. Whatever this is, it's got me so unbalanced I fear if I don't claw back some control, he'll steamroller me with the sheer force of his personality.

His eyes narrow at my tone, and he watches me set down the glass.

"Was this your idea of bringing me round to your way of thinking? A few mouthfuls of my favorite food and a drink or two before I decide to happily spread my legs for you?"

His face hardens. "Isn't it what you said you wanted? Some non-sexual attention before you're comfortable with this?"

"If I want that, I'll happily pay for a gigolo, or one of those escort services you use."

He looks genuinely puzzled. "Explain."

"You're right. I'm attracted to you." His frown smooths out and his eyes gleam, but I shake my head. "Before you crow about it, let me finish. I'm not just attracted to you physically. I'm attracted to your brain. If I'm to entertain the idea of dropping my panties for you, I want to be stimulated *mentally*, not just physically."

He regards me for endless seconds before he sneers. "You mean you want something *meaningful* to slot under the banner of *relationship*? Sorry, princess, that's not going to work for me."

He dismisses me with a look and drops the half-finished plate on the table. He picks up the pristine napkin and proceeds to wipe his fingers with a bored look on his face.

Anger and some unknown charge of emotion send me to my feet.

"You know what? Fuck you, Mason. I don't know why the hell I'm so drawn to you, but fuck if I'm going to keep letting you talk to me as if I'm some piece of meat you can take or leave. I don't care if we have to work together for the next two weeks, or that you're a friend of Zach's. Come near me again, and I'll rip your fucking—"

The expletive barely leaves my lips before he grabs me. My gasp strangles in my lungs as I'm pulled forward and flung across his knees. I throw my hands out and barely catch myself from tipping forward onto my face. I try to twist away from him, but his hand wedges in the small of my back, pinning me down.

The other yanks my hem up. For a moment I'm confused when cool air hits my bare ass, then I buck, my senses reeling at what I anticipate is coming.

"Mason, don't you fucking dare— Ah!"

His left hand smacks my bare backside six times in quick succession, three on each cheek.

There's no mercy in the act. No hesitation. My eyes sting with tears, and my ass tingles with shock and pain. I'm so dizzy with the emotions tumbling through me, I can't catch my breath. The hands I braced on the floor tremble as shudders roll through my body. Moisture brims my eyes and falls off my lashes. And with it, anger surges.

"You *motherfucker!*"

I start to rise, but he easily holds me down and delivers two more smacks. I gasp in horror, and my body locks in complete shock. It occurs to me then that while I can totally take care of myself on a New York street corner or a dark alley, I'm completely out of my depth with this dark, relentless predator. My lungs threaten to burst, and I suck in a desperate breath as another tear drops onto the carpet.

His scent engulfs me as he lowers his head to my ear.

"You have till noon tomorrow, Keely. I'll be on the yacht. If you're there at midday, we take this thing to the next level. If you're one minute late, I'll know you mean this not to go any further and I'll take no for your answer. But remember, if you do turn up, we'll be doing things my way. I'll grant you your wish for mental stimulation as long as it doesn't involve personal details. I don't ask about your past, you don't ask about mine. Dirty talk outside of the bedroom or sexual scenarios will be met with punishment. You're a gorgeous and intelligent woman. It's time to start behaving like one. I won't apologize for what I just did. You've been asking for it from the moment we met. Don't even think of defying me again or what I did to you just now will seem like the tip of the iceberg, punishment wise. Are we clear?"

Tears continue to rim my eyes and rush down my cheeks, and a part of me reels in horror at this unfamiliar surge of emotion. I never let anything affect me. Not anymore.

Hell, when was the last time I cried? I can't honestly remember.

Which is why I'm too stunned to answer when Mason demands again, "Are we clear? I need an answer, Keely."

I force my vocal cords to work. "Let me go, Mason. Right now." My voice is hoarse and shakes with anger.

"Not until you answer me," he rasps in my ear.

I press my lips together and squeeze my eyes shut. A second later, the hand that delivered cruel punishment slides soothingly over my burning skin. The gentleness in his touch confuses me even more than the spanking did. I lie bowed over his knees, my thoughts churning in a chaotic jumble I can't make sense of.

His left hand continues to sooth me as his right hand eases up my back to brush away the hair curtaining my face. I turn my head away so he doesn't see my tears and quickly swipe the evidence away.

I hear him sigh. "This is what happens when I'm forced to engage on anything but a sexual level. I don't play well with others, never have. You can't put me in a box and expect me to behave. Dammit, I shouldn't even *be* here," he mutters, almost as if he's talking to himself. The raw ache in his voice catches me unawares, and I twist to see his face. A frozen mask of pain and deep, dark shadows stares back at me. My heart lurches.

What does that mean, he shouldn't be here? *Here*, in this club, or *here* in this existence? The look on his face indicates he could mean both.

My instincts urge me to move, to flee.

Now.

I shift sideways, but he catches me back, his eyes flaring as he stares first at my ass, then at my face. "I can show you untold pleasure, Keely. Everything you can possibly imagine can be yours and more, if you're willing to drop the charade of needing to attach social strings to what we can have."

My throat is too choked with everything that's happened in

the last five minutes to deal with what he's saying. But I can't lie here like some fucking sacrificial lamb about to be slaughtered, regardless of the fact that his hand on my butt is doing things to my insides I've never felt before.

"Wanting a little verbal stimulation is too much to ask? How about speaking at all? If I decide to let you do what you want with me, am I expected to lie there and count sheep? Or assume a blow-up doll position until you finish?"

"We can iron out the finer details tomorrow, if you agree to this," he says.

It strikes me then what it is about Mason that unsettles me so much. Every guy I've met has a basic, civilized veneer no matter how outrageous they may pretend to be.

Mason Sinclair has none, and he doesn't try to hide the fact. Civility means nothing to him. When he deigns to respond to normal conversation, the words that fall from his mouth make my nerves jangle.

"Take your hands off me," I say again, my voice much stronger this time around.

He pulls my dress down to cover my ass and the moment he takes his hands off me, I scramble upright. A movement catches the corner of my eye, and I swing round to meet the hostess's gaze. Humiliation engulfs me with the realization he just spanked me in full view of another person.

Everything inside me wants to slap the hell out of his face, but my fists don't move from beside my thighs. I've lost too much control in front of this man. I won't give him the satisfaction of making me react out of turn again.

"I don't know who the *fuck* you think you are or what you think you can give me. I made a mistake in not believing you when you said you crawled out from under a rock. I suggest you crawl back under it and stay there because if you come

anywhere near me or put your hands on me like that again, I'll
rip your balls off."

One corner of his mouth lifts. "I'll see you at noon tomorrow,
Keely."

Every filthy insult I've picked up since I was ten years old
trips on my tongue as I watch him sit there, smug in his Neanderthal charisma and mouth-watering body.

I've never detested anything as much as I detest him right
now. I also know I can't be in the same room as him.

So I snatch my clutch off the chair and stalk to the door,
determined to put tonight and Mason Sinclair very quickly and
very firmly out of my mind.

I'm not going. I'm not going. Hell, I am so not going.

My eyes dart to the clock for what feels like the hundredth time, and I congratulate myself when the clock hand moves from 12.59 to 1 p.m.

Fuck yeah.

I've not only flipped the bird at Mason's insane never-gonna-happen noon deadline, I've managed to stay put in my suite for another hour.

Extremely pleased with myself, and sure he's finally got the message through his brilliant, but *obviously* thick, skull that I don't intend to participate in, or be, any form of a sexual puppet to his skewed proclivities, I grab my purse containing my tablet and work stuff and head for the door.

I'm a little irritated that I've had to shift my morning appointments to interview two Michelin-star chefs, but there was no way I was going to board the *IL Indulgence* before noon and give Mason Sinclair the impression that I was there for him. One of the chefs expressed a touch of diva annoyance, but not enough to cancel.

Making a mental note to keep an eye out for further drama from that particular chef, I cross the gold inlaid, marble-floored atrium of the hotel and emerge into brilliant sunshine.

I breathe deep and let the warmth wash over me. I'm ready for a new day.

The sleepless night, which I've just spent kicking myself for losing control and allowing Mason to spank me—*spank me, for fuck's sake!*—in full view of the hostess, is something I'm not going to dwell on.

I've never been into kinky in the bedroom. I don't even possess a vibrator or dildo. I've never seen the point of artificial gadgets when a cock and a man who knows how to use it well is all I've needed. As the previous owner of a sex yacht and hard-core inventor of gadgets, Mason is clearly into myriad forms of sex, including BDSM. His masterful demeanor and the way he soothed me after the spanking make me suspect he'll be extremely good at it. If that were my thing.

Which it's not.

Another flush of humiliation crawls up my spine at how utterly I let him control me, and I push the feeling away. He caught me with my guard down, and I was foolish enough to underestimate the power of the insane attraction between us *before* he spanked me. Since I don't intend to place myself in a position where either of those things will affect me, I'm good.

Last night is behind me.

From here on in, my job is the center of my focus.

I quicken my stride down the hill toward the marina. In the resplendent sunlight, the yacht looks even more stunning, but now that I know who it belonged to in its previous life, my enjoyment is a little soured. My heartbeat quickens as I step into the launch and greet the pilot. All too soon, we're at the yacht. I make sure my sunglasses are in place as I step onto the deck and return the greeting of one of the many bodyguards employed to keep nosy intruders and paparazzi away. Reading the signs so I don't get lost, I make my way along the various hallways. I arrive at the restaurant on the second-floor deck where I'm to meet the two chefs. I tell myself I'm relieved when I don't run into anyone resembling Mason.

The time passes quickly as I sample the dozens of dishes we'll be providing the guests. As suspected, the chef who threw a mini tantrum at my revised schedule turns into a diva and even before he sets down his first course in front of me, I've decided to go with the other chef. But I'm a professional, so I sit through his presentation and smile my thanks when he's done.

"Great, I'll let you know my decision by tomorrow evening."

Arnaud Delacroix huffs. "I fly back to the States tomorrow morning. I only came because Monsieur Sinclair requested me personally as a favor. If I'd known I was to participate in this... this *amateur* competition, I would've declined his request."

Irritation pulses through me, and I surge from the dining table where the tasting took place. "Let me get this straight. *Mason* asked you to come?"

His eyes slide over me, and I catch his leer as he answers, "Yes, as I said. I run one of the best restaurants in Paris and New York. I do not audition for little schoolgirls."

"Excuse me?"

A second slide of his gaze lingers at my breasts this time and my skin crawls. *Sexist pig.* "Mademoiselle, I have nothing against you personally—"

"From where I'm standing, I seriously doubt that, but go on," I quip, and I don't give a shit when his lips purse at the interruption.

"*But* my time is precious," he continues. "I arrived at six this morning to prepare for the tasting. You moved the time at the last minute. I have accommodated you. But I don't intend to hang around while you twiddle your thumbs about a decision that shouldn't even be yours to make."

I swallow the ball of anger rising into my throat. "First of all, I'm glad you rose to the occasion of the time change. If you're going to be a chef on this boat—and that is looking mighty precarious at the moment—you need to know that you'll be called to cater for clients' needs at all hours. For the two weeks you'll be on this yacht, your time won't be your own. So if that's an issue for you, then by all means, feel free to leave. Secondly, and listen up because this is important. I'm no fucking schoolgirl. I've earned my right to be here, just as you've earned the right to call yourself a chef. And lastly, Mason Sinclair isn't in charge of hiring staff for this project. I am. I don't give a damn what he promised you. If you want the gig, I'll consider you and you'll hear from me *tomorrow*. If you don't, I'm sure one of the bodyguards can make sure you find your way back to the airport."

His face tightens as I speak and he erupts into a flood of French, which I'm sure is as disparaging to women as his English was a moment ago.

When he reels to a stop, I raise my eyebrow. "Sorry, was that a yes or a no?"

"Where is Sinclair? I will speak to him and him alone!"

I wave him toward the door. "Of course, but nothing he says will change what I've told you. Goodbye, Monsieur Delacroix."

He sniffs like a startled bull and strides out.

The moment the door slams behind him, my breath shudders out and I look down to see my hands shaking.

What the fuck is wrong with men?

What the fuck is wrong with Mason Sinclair?

My mind zeroes on the person responsible for these tumultuous feelings cascading through me. I toss the pen I'm holding onto the table and stride toward the door.

Whether he likes it or not, Mason Sinclair is about to get another piece of my mind, even if I have to interrupt a testosterone-bonding ceremony between him and Delacroix.

I reach the lower deck and pick a random hallway. As I pass one of the sleek square portholes, I see Delacroix getting onto one of the launches, his face still set in angry lines. I allow myself a smile before resuming my search for Mason.

After several hallways and peering into numerous adult entertainment rooms, I take the stairs to the next deck below. Again, the rooms are empty save for one where the construction crew is working. I'm beginning to think I was wrong in assuming Mason was on board when I spot one of the bodyguards.

I assume he's just patrolling the deck, but once I approach the farthest point in the aft section where the spank room is located, I realize he's blocking the door.

He glances at me and an uneasy look flicks across his face. "Hi, Miss Benson."

He can't be older than twenty-one or twenty-two, but he's built like a Sherman tank and looks like he can take down a brick wall with one kick.

"Hi, have you seen Mr. Sinclair?" I ask.

His neck reddens a little. "Umm, yes." He thumbs the door behind him. "He's in there."

I resent the small quiver of excitement that tingles through my belly. "Thanks," I say, and step toward the door, expecting him to move out of the way. He stays cross-armed and shakes his head.

"Sorry, Miss Benson. Mr. Sinclair left strict instructions not to be disturbed under any circumstances. It's why I said no to the chef when he wanted to see him, too." His face is now flushed bright red and another feeling crawls through my belly, a feeling that tastes suspiciously like jealousy.

I stare hard at the black door. "And what exactly is Mr. Sinclair doing in there?" I ask through clenched teeth, even though I don't need a crystal ball to divine the answer.

"I... umm, not sure... exactly."

I turn my glare from the door to the guard. "What's your name?"

"Umm... Daniel, Miss Benson."

"Daniel, do me a favor and step aside, please."

He swallows, and I watch him weigh the consequences of refusing my request for a few seconds before he steps aside.

"Thanks. And you don't need to stick arou—" We both freeze as a loud whoosh sounds through the door, followed by a long, ragged, *feminine* moan.

The memory of Mason's hand on my ass slams into my brain, and my hand is turning the handle to the door before another thought forms in my head.

I stumble into the room and exhale in shock at the sight before me.

There isn't just one, but *two* women with Mason. He has his back to me and his upper half is bare and dripping with sweat. The redhead next to him is naked save for the tiniest red thong I've ever seen, and her eyes flick to me as she rakes her nails down Mason's back before sliding her fingers into the backside of the tight, black leather pants he's wearing. Mason doesn't react to her touch, most likely because his attention is riveted on the other woman in the room.

My eyes swing to the woman—an Asian beauty with small breasts and a breathtaking face—and see the stark hunger and arousal in her expression. She's completely naked and standing on the platform with the three sides I asked him about during my tour the day before. It looks no different than yesterday from what I can see. The middle partition is still covered in that curious shiny black surface and the two sides that would provide privacy are standing open.

I return my gaze to the woman and see she's fully immersed in the long whip in Mason's hand. She whimpers when he lifts his free hand to her face and brushes back her jet-black hair. His knuckles caress her cheek, her jaw, the side of her neck.

Her eyes remain downcast on the whip the whole time, but her scarlet lips part. "Please, Master. Again."

"No, wait for it," he replies, his voice a ruthless blade, but it also holds a promise of rich reward. The whip twitches in his hand and her breath shivers.

"Master, please... I want to come." Her nipples turn to hard points as she whispers the words, and her whole body quivers as Mason traces a finger down to her belly button and circles the delicate hole.

"Is that disobedience I hear?" he asks softly, his voice bleeding power and menace.

She shakes her head immediately. "No, Master."

"So you'll come when I say and not before?"

Her body quivers. "Yes, Master."

"Open your legs," he instructs.

He flicks the whip and her eyes dart after the movement, anticipation almost eating her alive. When he brings it back to rest against his thigh, she lets out a broken moan.

Mason's hand leaves her face and he presses a button on the apparatus his sex slave is leaning against.

My gaze drops to her stomach and thighs, and I see bright red welts crisscrossing her skin. My stomach roils, but the nausea I expect never surfaces. I should be sickened by the sight of such brutal treatment, by the sight of a woman who's obviously being debased.

But instead, a hum rolls through my body as my eyes stay on the lazy curl of Mason's wrist as he jerks the whip. The woman also shows no signs of distress. Just... pleasure.

He presses a button on the structure and the shiny surface comes alive. It vibrates against his slave's back, then she sinks back as the material swallows her halfway. Her eyes widen in wonder, and she gasps at whatever sensation she's experiencing.

Mason presses another button and arm-like protrusions rise from the sides and curve over her body. One moves over her breasts and torso and the other slides along her thigh. The arms flow with a beauty that's hypnotic to watch.

"Oh!" Her face contorts in bliss and her breath pants out. Mason watches her for a moment before he raises the whip and brings it down between her legs.

She gasps out another moan, and her whole body shakes with the effort it takes to keep her orgasm from erupting. Her eyelashes flutter wildly and her mouth wobbles with the need to beg.

I can't be here.

I need to leave, turn away from the visceral sight.

But my feet won't move. I watch a tear slip from one eye and drip down her cheek as Mason flicks the whip again.

I want to scream at him to stop. To give her the release she needs. At the same time, acrid jealousy pours through my stomach at the pleasure she's receiving under Mason's hands.

12

KEELY

Mason whips her between the legs one more time, then growls, "Come. Now."

His voice triggers her release and full-bodied shudders cannon through her. The artificial arms keep her from falling and Mason presses another button that makes her scream with pleasure. After a minute, the arms release her, and he catches her as she falls.

My galloping heart takes in the scene before I glance at the redhead. She's watching me with narrowed, assessing eyes and her fingers are still out of sight below his waistband where she's caressing Mason's skin. As I stare, she shifts closer and rubs her C-cup breasts against his arm.

"Master, we have a visitor," she murmurs in his ear.

"Dammit, didn't I say I don't want to be disturbed?" Mason's voice is deep and rough and the woman who's just orgasmed is a dead weight in his arm.

"Mason." I attempt to say his name, but my voice is hoarse and indistinguishable.

He whirls around with the woman still in his arms, and his

eyes meet mine over her bowed head. I see his expression for the first time and my heart slides into my throat.

He looks feral, his gaze almost inhuman as it slides over me. He's primal and viscerally male, and I hate myself for being turned on by the sheer animalistic aura vibrating from him.

"Keely." The throbbing power with which he says my name sends a tremor through me. His lips curl slightly as he rasps, "What do you want?"

"I..." I stop and run my tongue over my lips. His eyes flicker and narrow a shade, but he continues to trap me in his gaze. "I wanted... I want to talk to you."

"And whatever you need to say to me can't wait?" he asks softly.

The woman in his arms lets out a little sigh. My eyes dart to her and then to the redhead before meeting Mason's gaze. Something in the hazel expression dares me, taunts me, sets my insides on fire with a tight, grasping need I can't explain.

No matter how much I try to deny it, something about him pulls at me like a black hole sucks stray objects into its orbit.

"No, it can't," I reply, trying to summon back the anger that propelled me to this room in the first place. But I can barely remember the reason for seeking him out.

All I feel is the blood rushing through my veins, the thick smell of power, sex and domination in the air—and what the dangerous cocktail is doing to me. My skin has grown taut, and a pulse hammers through my clit with enough force to vibrate through my whole body. I can barely breathe as I stare at Mason.

"Are you sure?" he asks, his voice still radiating that low, effortless power, like a spider web in the dark, growing, spinning, drawing me ever tighter into his unbreakable grip.

He continues to stare at me, and the connection between us

vibrates with the gravity of the question in his eyes. He's not asking if I'm sure I want to talk to him.

What he's really saying is, *Are you prepared for the consequences of me sending my pets away?*

My gaze slides to the one in his arms who has recovered enough to support herself. She's staring at me, albeit with hazy, just-come-harder-than-I-ever-imagined eyes. Another lance of jealousy makes my teeth grind as I move my glare to the redhead staring at me with daggers in her eyes.

"Yes, I'm sure."

Shit, I don't know what I'm letting myself in for, and part of me is terrified. But I do know that I don't want to leave this room. Not while Mason is in here with these two women, giving them pleasure I'm not even sure I want for myself.

Mason stares at me for another full minute, all the while holding on to one pet and letting the other rub herself over him.

When his lashes sweep down, my stomach lurches, certain he's about to refuse my insane request.

"Amber, Mae Ling, you heard the lady."

Amber's eyes flash deadly fire at me. "But Mason, I haven't had my turn yet."

Jesus, it's now past four. If she hasn't had her turn yet, does that mean Mason has been working on May Ling since lunch time? My stomach flips again, and my fists clench by my side as I stare him down. His mouth twitches, but his eyes are dark golden hooks, pinning me where I stand.

My feet may not want to obey me right now, but my mouth works just fine. "Let's get one thing clear. If you and I are going to do this, you need to promise me that it's going to be an exclusive thing. You." I point at Mae Ling, who's now fully awake and eyeing me with equal venom as she hangs on to Mason's waist. I take another step, ready to fully immerse myself in a bitch-off if that's what it takes. "If you want to keep those dainty little hands, get them the fuck off him right now. You too, ginger," I sneer at Amber, who's entertaining the idea of changing Mason's mind by rubbing her crotch against his hipbone.

Mason tenses at my use of the F-word, but I don't care. Whatever punishment he wants to dole out can come after I've skinned him alive for making me feel like some jealous bitch in heat.

They both look to Mason for direction, but his gaze never wavers from mine. After a tense moment, they step back warily, sensing the volatile emotions whipping through the air.

Clothes are gathered and hastily donned and heels click past me before the door shuts behind me.

The knowledge that I'm alone with Mason slams into me as he slowly advances. My eyes drop to his solid neck, his golden rock-hard shoulders and pecs, to the ridged torso that I sense didn't come from the gym but from sheer hard work. A few scars crisscross his body—sports injuries or everyday wear and tear. I don't have time to dwell on it because he moves closer, and my eyes are drawn lower, to the black leather and the evidence of his state of mind.

My hands slam out in a fiercely protective motion. "If you think you're coming anywhere near me after servicing your goddamn pets, you're seriously nuts."

He freezes, and his nostrils flare with anger. "What the hell?"

My laughter cuts him off. "You really were going to continue with me where you just left off with them, weren't you? Do you want me, Mason?"

His brows clamp together. "*Christ*, of course I do. I believe I've said so very explicitly several times."

"Okay, how about I go and rub myself all over one of the bodyguards on the upper deck? Maybe throw in a hand job, let him blow his load all over my—" A low, deadly growl rumbles from his chest and I swallow. "Then I present myself to you. Would you still want me?"

"That's not going to happen, because anyone who touches you, besides me, dies."

I roll my eyes. "Says the man who's standing in front of me, sporting a hard-on from another woman." Something squeezes in my chest as I say that, but I ignore it.

"I didn't get a hard-on until I turned and saw you," he states with a brisk snap.

"You really expect me to believe that?"

"Yes, because it's true." He continues to eye me like I'm keeping him from his meal. A meal that involves me and only me.

"You made another woman come right in front of me." I'm still not entirely sure how I feel about that.

"I was testing the equipment. I told you I would be doing that today." His voice still holds that dangerous edge that has my nerves jumpy, and his eyes are sweeping me from head to toe, as if searching for a weakness, something he can latch on to and attack. When his gaze stops on my chest and his hands twitch, I don't need to look down to know my nipples are at full attention and craving his touch. I feel every nerve in those hard buds as if he's setting fire to them.

I gulp in air and try to think my way through the muddle my emotions have made of my head. "Regardless, I'm not letting you touch me. Not tonight."

His jaw clenches hard, and he exhales. "Tomorrow morning, then. Come and have breakfast with me."

I interpret that correctly as *Come so I can have you for breakfast.*

I shake my head. "I'm interviewing all day tomorrow, no

thanks to you and your intervention with your prima donna French chef. Oh yeah, I'll thank you not to interfere with my staff hiring, please."

His head drops forward, and I'm freed from his penetrating gaze. Free to let my eyes devour his beautiful body and the tensile energy whipping around him so thickly I can almost reach out and touch it.

His erection hasn't subsided, and I start to believe that he meant it when he said whatever he was doing to Mae Ling didn't turn him on.

"Consider it done. When can I see you, then?" he breathes without looking up.

"I'll be done by six, we can have dinner at my hotel at—"

"Six-fifteen," he bites out, his voice ferocious and final. "But I pick the place."

Alarm stiffens my back, but I accept that I've already trampled on the danger signs and there's no turning back. "Okay. I'm cool with that."

He raises his head and spears me with that intense gaze again. "There will be no backtracking from you," he says as if he has direct access to my thoughts and wants to reiterate what I've just acknowledged. "Not any more. You want this. Tell me you want this."

I swallow. "I want this. After we lay down a few more ground rules."

His mouth compresses, but he exhales and jerks out a nod.

I turn toward the door and sense him take that final step. I reach for the door, but his hand slams against it, preventing it from opening. He steps closer and cages me in with both arms, although his body never touches mine. "I want to kiss you so fucking badly," he growls against my ear. "I want to lick your pussy again, find out if you taste as glorious as you did in

Montauk. Don't leave, Keely. Stay. I'll take a shower if that's what you want. Hell, I'll take a dozen showers."

I suppress a shudder as he leans even closer. The scent of sweat and arousal engulfs me. I want to say to hell with the showers, that I'll take him raw and earthy and dirty. I force my eyes shut for a heartbeat and pray for strength before I pry them back open. "Tomorrow."

He inhales and exhales slowly. Then I feel him move away. I look over my shoulder and see him shadowing my body with his hands, an intense, deviant light in his eyes. When he looks at me through his lashes, I feel a pulse of electricity fire through me.

"Tomorrow." His voice is a steely promise. He steps back and reaches for the door.

I stumble through it and have very little recollection of leaving the yacht and walking back to my hotel.

I fall into bed sometime later and finally let the afternoon's events in.

For the first time in six years, I'm risking handing over a portion of my control to someone else. One slip is all it takes. One misguided decision—especially with a man who seems to smash through my every barrier to reach a place I don't want touched— could be the end of me.

Telling myself that this time whatever I choose to give will be with my permission doesn't stop the cascade of fear pouring through my soul. Nor can I stem the flood of memories that swamps me as I lie in the dark, gripping my pillow.

13

KEELY

Six years ago

Freshman year has been an epic bust.

I arrived at UCLA believing my academic journey was going to take a U-turn from complete joke to crazy awesome. Instead, I found the cool kids still don't want to hang out with me because my brain is too big to fit into 140 characters or Instagram shots of my breasts.

Only the nerds want to hang out with me. I pretend I'm cool with that. But deep down I wonder why the cool kids *still* hate me. My body has changed a lot in the last eighteen months. I've grown a couple more inches, and the sunshine in California has done wonders for my previously pasty skin. I'll never pass for a bombshell, but with my dark blond hair and good-enough legs, I should be able to hold my own in the pretty stakes.

Instead, the moment I open my mouth, I can see the cool guys slowly recoiling. Fuck, I can virtually see the speech bubble pop out of out their ears, fanatically detailing various ways to get the hell away from me, fast.

This has bothered me to the point where I've contemplated dressing provocatively just to get some action. Which is pathetic because I'm nineteen in three weeks and as an almost adult I should know better. My parents are proud of my straight-A grades. I can be literally anything I want to be. My self-worth should be boundless. Instead, all I want is to be invited to *one* party, one trip to the beach. A movie. Anything.

Fuck my life.

"Hey, is the sci-fi newsletter ready yet?"

I jump and quickly slam shut my laptop, hiding the pictures of Leo Brummer I was ogling, as Jake Schimansky, my co-head of the debate and science-fiction society, plunks down next to me on the grass in the campus park. A quick glance at Jake doesn't show signs that he saw what I was looking at. I sigh inwardly.

Leo.

I'm one wet dream away from doodling his name on my notebook and drawing a fluffy pink heart around it. I don't even care that he's a little shallow and wears T-shirts one size too small to emphasize his amazing body. He's got it, and he makes no bones about flaunting it. And since I'm enjoying the fruits from *that* tree, I ain't complaining.

I dwell instead on the fateful way we met.

Although he's majoring in film, TV and media, he's a psychology minor, but has fallen behind because he's also an actor and missed most of last semester's classes because of shooting some action movie in Russia.

I didn't even plan on going to the coffee shop that night. I was fed up with the guy behind the counter ogling my breasts and sneering every time I ordered green tea.

But I was super thirsty. And I needed a quiet place to brush up on my psych paper before the end of term test. My dorm room was out of the question since my oh-so-considerate room-mate, Ashley, decided to invite people over for an impromptu party without telling me. Or inviting me.

Whatever. That evening, I'm deep into the dark, suggestive powers of my Id when Leo walks in and sits down at the next table.

His glance sweeps across the almost empty coffee shop, reaches me, and keeps going. Twisting in his seat, he reaches into his skintight jeans, pulls out his phone, and stabs the numbers with annoyed fingers. From where I sit, I can hear the ringing and the female voice that answers.

"Where the hell are you?" he rasps.

Yeah, don't even get me started about Leo's voice. The only way I can describe it is to think of dripping wild honey over tiny smooth pebbles and rolling them all over your skin.

Fuck.

I jump when he snaps, "What the hell do you mean you're not coming? I don't have time for this shit, Tammie. You promised you'd help me with this paper. I've already paid you five hundred for your time, goddamn it. So get your ass over here right now and earn it, or I swear to God—"

I hear a bitchy rant and a crude suggestion before the line goes dead.

I'm embarrassed for him. So embarrassed I want to hug him. Slide my fingers into those waxy blond spikes. Pet that fine body of his and make all his troubles melt away.

"Fuck! Fuck, fuck, *fuck!*" His scowl deepens as he presses the number again and listens to the endless ring tone. Another round of swearing ensues before he yanks his books off the table.

I know this is my one and only chance. So I clear my throat. Loudly. He doesn't even look my way. "Hey, umm, listen, if you need help with the paper, I can, you know... help you?"

Jesus, fuck. I'm the co-captain of the debate team, for God's sake, and I can't string three words together to form a simple sentence?

He glances up and my breath squeezes in my lungs. Shit, he looks even better wearing that adorable scowl!

"And you are?" he drawls in a couldn't-care-less tone.

I try not to be crushed by the fact that we've been in the same psyche class for a semester and a half and he hasn't noticed me.

"I'm Keely Benson. I'm in Professor Harding's class."

His face de-scowls a little, but he keeps fiddling with his phone, obviously still annoyed that his tutor has abandoned him. I mentally shake my head. Who would deliberately do that? I guess they're both stupid *and* blind.

A pinch in my pinkie and a sharp tingle on my scalp alerts me that I'm tugging on a strand of my hair, a nervous tic I've never quite been able to master. I hastily move my hand to the table as his gaze flicks from his phone back to me.

"I have a shitload to catch up on," he says, then shakes his head. "If Harding wasn't threatening to flunk me despite my agreement with the dean for time off, I'd tell him to go fuck himself."

"Yeah, I bet a few of his students would like to tell him the same thing," I reply, attempting a smile.

He smiles back and my heart jackhammers like an over-caffeinated robot. "So." He draws out the word after another glance at his phone. I pray bitch-face stays silent and doesn't call him back. "You think you'll be able to help me catch up?"

My shoulders lift in a *hey, trust me, I've got this* shrug. "Depends on whether you're a quick study or not." His blond brows shoot into the air, and I curse inwardly. "Uh, I'm sure you are. Seriously, it'll be a breeze."

His blue eyes turn speculative. "How much is this gonna cost me?" he asks.

I bite my tongue to keep my endless list of Leo-centric wants and needs from spilling forth. "We can talk about that later," I say instead. When his gaze turns skeptical, I wave him away. "It's no big deal, really."

And thus began the sure-to-lead-to-happily-ever-after story of Leo Brummer and Keely Benson.

I've tutored him for going on six weeks now and have developed something of a super-major crush on him. I tell myself it's because he's not relying on just his looks to get him through life, but I know I'm lying to myself. He's bright, not brilliant. I'm not crushing on him because of his brain, but because of his super-fuck-hot body. And because at nineteen, I'm super eager and more than ready to rid myself of my virginity and experience what sex is all about.

From the moment I set eyes on him, I knew Leo would be the recipient of said unwanted virginity. I've even written a mini thesis on ways to get him to bed. So far, I haven't been able to put theory to practice because the right opportunity hasn't presented itself.

But it needs to happen in the next three weeks because I want to head back east to New York for the Easter holidays minus my virginity. I don't know why it needs to happen, but that's the date I've set for myself, and I always meet my deadlines.

"Umm... earth to Keely!"

Heat shoots into my face as I pull myself from my erotic daydream. "What?"

"I asked if the newsletter was done, like, five minutes ago."

"It wasn't five minutes ago, and yeah, of course it's done. I said it would be, didn't I?" I reply, avoiding the quizzical glance Jake sends my way.

"Okaaay, can I see it?" he presses.

"Why? I'm the editor, don't you trust me?" I throw back sharply. I don't want to open my laptop because Leo's googled, semi-naked body will be sitting there, ogle ready.

Jake holds up his hands. "Hey, you asked for my help with what questions to use for the end-of-semester poll, remember? If you've changed your mind about wanting my help, just say so."

I remember asking for help, and I bite my lip. "Yeah, sorry, I didn't mean to snap."

Jake shrugs. "It's cool. I know Professor Harding's been riding your ass pretty hard this semester. What's his beef with you anyway? You're by miles his top student."

I turn away from Jake under the pretext of rummaging through my backpack to hide the heat crawling into my face. No one knows about my encounter with my psychology professor last semester, when I mistook his interest in me as a sexual instead of an academic one.

The whole encounter freaked me out big-time, and I don't even want to think about it.

"I dunno," I mumble. "I'm lucky, I guess," I add snarkily.

"Well, my sympathies and all, but better you than me." Jake laughs and launches into the neuropsychopharmacology of emotion and cognition module Professor Harding has asked us to memorize before our next class. Relieved to shove the subject to the back of my mind, I concentrate and counter Jake's rapid-fire argument with my own.

Before I know it, the hour is gone and Jake has left. I slowly open my laptop and stare at the picture of Leo's bronzed, ripped torso, which is my screensaver. I imagine myself running my hands down his body, licking those flat brown nipples and hearing him moan. In my imagination, he encourages me to do more and I go to town, gorging myself on that hot body until we're both sweating and panting.

I lie back on the grass, my breathing escalating as I imagine what my first real non-masturbation-assisted orgasm will feel like. My panties grow wet and I squeeze my thighs together to stop the persistent ache that throbs every time I think of Leo.

Leo will be a gentle lover the first time. After that I might allow things to get a little... risqué. I'm all for experimenting a bit. But nothing that involves bondage or gadgets or anything like that.

Ewwww. I grimace just thinking about it. I have no idea why people use those sorts of things. I've heard Ashley use a vibrator many nights and the sound alone turns me off.

No, it'll just be Leo's mouth, his fingers, his cock.

I blush again just thinking about it and reluctantly rouse myself, sitting upright as a group of four seriously good-looking guys walk past me and claim their own patch of grass a few yards away.

I pretend not to be interested in them, but my ears perk up when I hear Leo's name.

"He owns the place?" one asks.

"Who cares? It's private and it's ours from Friday to Monday. And for the five large I shelled out, I intend to party fucking hard."

"Shit, that's a bit steep just for a weekend, isn't it?" another complains.

"Not for the special stuff he's having flown in. You know what Leo's parties are like."

I angle my head and catch their knowing smirks as they reminisce in low voices I can't quite make out, although I hear the words *exclusive* and *supermodels* and my heart sinks a little, but I keep listening.

"How many people are going?"

"At last count, he said thirty. It's going to be a fucking blow-out, man." Anticipation oozes from the group and the conversation changes abruptly to how many girls they intend to fuck that weekend.

My mind veers from the lurid exchange back to the never-far-from-my-mind Leo.

So he isn't just a hot actor with a to-die-for body. He also knows how to throw the party to end all parties. God, he's just so perfect.

And he's not seeing anyone at the moment. I know because I made it my business to subtle-dig during one of our studying sessions, and he let slip that he'd been dating his Russian co-star but ended it when the movie wrapped.

I suddenly have an idea for how he can pay me for the free tutoring I've given him so far. A guy like Leo won't stay on the market for very long, and this may be my only chance to make my move.

I quickly calculate the weekly five hundred dollars he was paying Tammie and reckon he owes me about three grand. If I agree to throw in the rest of the semester for free, maybe he'll agree to what I have in mind. My heart beats rapidly as I devise a plan to make things swing my way.

In the end, I decide to take the direct route.

My fingers shake as I type the text:

Hey, we still on for 8 tonight? I'll pick up a pack of Red Bull.

They are his favorite, and little does he know I keep two cases of the stuff under my dorm bed.

I get a reply in seconds:

> Fuck, yeah. I'll need at least six fucking cans just to keep awake and focused on this fucked-up module.

I grin.

> Dude, you swear way too much.

> Oh hi there, Miss Pot, I'm Captain Kettle.

My grin stretches, and I'm sure I look like a cross between a clown and an escaped mental patient.

> Oops!

> No need to oops! I like it. Don't ever change, Benson.

My heartstrings flutter like mad and everything inside me melts. I can barely type the question I intended to ask him all along.

Taking a shaky breath, I force my fingers to work.

> Hey, you know when I said we can discuss payment for my tutoring later?

> Uh... yeah?

> How about an invite to your party this weekend?

I consciously stop myself from adding *as your date* and press send. If everything goes well, Leo Brummer will be the first notch on my bedpost come Monday. I just need to not blow it now.

My heart lurches as I wait, my gaze on the time displayed on the texts. One minute. Two.

Shit. Fuck. Have I alerted him to my pathetic feelings? My body goes from happy and relaxed to frozen and tense in seconds. I shut my eyes in mortification, then hear a ping of another text. I'm almost too scared to look down, but I do.

I read his text and my heart bursts with celestial joy.

> Sure. Remind me tonight to organize a car
> service to pick you up on Friday. Catchya later!

I type *Awesome* and immediately delete it. Only lame people say that these days. I think of something cool but classy to say. I remember a British detective show with a cute lead that I saw a while back, and I let my fingers to go work.

> Jolly good!

He might think it strange. Or he might smile. Either way, I'm going to Leo Brummer's party, where I have every intention of fulfilling my wildest fantasy of making him my first lover.

As I sit in the Californian sunshine, happy as a clam in love, little do I know that come Monday I will wake up in hospital, battered, bruised, and with no recollection of who I am, or that I'll be carrying a secret shame that will change my life forever.

14

MASON

I wait for her in the shadows, parked across from her hotel in a spot where the glitzy lights don't reach. I grimly count the seconds till she walks through the double doors.

The past twenty-four hours have been hell, knowing that she has a hold on me I can't shake very easily. Knowing the more I let that connection remain, the more inclined I'll be to punish her for it. Not that she isn't getting punished anyway. It's why I deliberately stayed away from the yacht today. I don't think I can stand to be in the same space as her without throwing her over my shoulder, or preferably onto the floor, and fucking the shit out of her.

That's how bad she's got me.

My hands shake and my cock throbs as I watch the door. I've arrived early because I can't abide my own company for another second. I've never done well with inactivity. Idle hands bring too many temptations, too many chances to be pulled back into the razor-sharp jaws of the past.

Of what I lost.

Of the spiral of hell that became my life in the months after losing Toby.

His name shudders down my spine, and I grit my teeth as pain rattles long and hard through my rigid bones. I don't fight the pain. I welcome it. It's a part of my life I never intend to let go. Letting go means forgetting. And I'll never forget what I did.

Never forget.

Never forgive.

I sit through another half a dozen shudders and try to pull myself together. Being this close to the edge isn't a great idea.

Keely Benson is a sexy contradiction that intrigues and infuriates me. But she also needs handling with care, and it won't do to scare her away before I get the chance to have my way with her. I can't afford to let her see me like this. Not yet, anyway.

Despite her agreeing to give herself to me, part of her remains wary. And while a side of me thinks her prudent for that wariness, I'm unwilling to let it stand in the way of what I want.

I switch gears and wonder if she'll turn up dressed the way I asked. I mull over the various ways I'll punish her if she doesn't. My dick jerks and my fist unclenches to cup the bulge in my pants. I breathe deep and allow anticipation to wash over me.

She emerges from the hotel at that moment and pauses on the sidewalk.

Pleasure flickers into a flame when I see she's obeyed my instructions.

Her head swings back and forth over the row of sports cars arriving at the hotel. It's a busy Friday evening in Monaco, particularly around the streets near Casino Square.

I watch her for another minute before I gun the powerful engine of the Ducati and exit the side street. The throaty engine draws her attention, and her gaze stays on me as I roll up to a stop beside her.

She takes in the black, powerful bike. "Okay, I get the request for pants and the hair now," she says.

My gaze travels over the hair she's tied back into a long silky rope as per my instructions, the cream top and jacket, black pants and knee-high boots that make her legs look fucking amazing.

"You think it was a request?"

"I sure as hell hope so. I don't respond well to commands," she snaps.

She's obviously still testy so I decide not to respond. Instead, I cup her nape and pull her close. She stumbles into me, and I steady her with one hand over her stomach as I tug her down and take her mouth in a kiss that's all about easing the flaying hunger I've suffered since I first set eyes on her.

She tenses for a moment before her mouth softens beneath mine. I go in hard and ruthless, my tongue breaching and surging past her lips to tangle with hers. A gasp, which doesn't quite make it past our meshed lips, lifts her slender torso, and my fingers curl into her waist, imprisoning her so I can satisfy even a little of that pounding need.

Her hands slide over my shoulders and push into my hair. I tense at the strange feeling. I haven't allowed a woman to touch me like this without my permission in a long time. Years, in fact.

Not since Cassie and I were together. Not since Toby was alive.

By the time I get round to fucking a woman, she's more often than not bound, or ready to submit to my commands on how she can touch me.

Keely Benson has already taken far too many liberties. The thought freezes me from the inside, and I tense harder.

Keely lifts her head. "What's wrong?"

"What makes you think something's wrong?" I reply roughly, and struggle to get a hold of myself.

"I'm not an idiot, Mason. Something spooked you just now." Her forehead creases and a tinge of self-awareness creeps into her eyes. "Was it me?"

"You?"

"If you don't like the way I kiss, just say so."

My gaze drops to her wet, slightly swollen mouth, and my cock swells and thickens, desperate for the action I've denied it for several long months. "I like the way you kiss. I very much want you to do it again. Right now."

Her pupils dilate, and I increase the pressure at her nape with the request, not really giving her a choice in the matter. A second before our lips meet, a Ferrari roars past, and she jerks back.

"Shit, I don't mind PDAs, but do we have somewhere to be? Like a reservation or something?"

"No," I growl, my focus on the mouth she's keeping from me.

"Oh, so you're not planning on feeding me tonight?"

"Oh, you'll be fed, kitten. Just probably not in the way you expect."

Her fingers, still tangled in my hair, tighten and another cold wash of reality bathes me. I grasp her hands and pull them down to her sides. Reaching into the compartment in front of me, I pull out a helmet. "Put this on and get on the bike."

She hesitates, like she wants to argue, but then she slides the helmet on. Her small, long-stringed purse goes cross-bodied over her shoulder and she swings her leg over the seat. I wait till she's fully in place and gun the engine.

"You ready?" I ask, my head turned so I can see her face.

"Yes."

"Hold on."

She nods and shifts closer. Her crotch nudges my ass. I suppress a growl and barely wait for her arms to slide around my waist before I kick the stand and dart into the slow-moving traffic.

Her hold tightens, and she leans closer against my back. My muscles flex in reaction to the touch of her firm breasts, and I breathe through my mouth while debating the wisdom of picking her up by bike instead of using the car, despite the Ducati getting us to my place quicker.

We bypass the posh restaurants and bars around Casino Square and head east. Every now and then I tilt the bike to take a fast corner, and I feel her breath on my neck before the wind whips it away. I take a particularly sharp corner and her nails claw into my skin as she grips a handful of my shirt. My jaw clenches and I fight the urge to stop the bike, spread her naked on top of it and fuck her raw for making me hurt this bad.

But I don't stop. Because then she might bolt.

Five minutes later, I pull up in front of tall wrought-iron gates and input the security code. I sense her surprise but don't give her a chance to question where I've brought her before gunning the bike through the barely adequate gap.

I skid to a stop at the end of the sweeping driveway and dismount. A glance shows her mouth gaping as she stares at the house. "Who lives here?"

"I do."

Her astonished gaze swings to me, and she stares at me for a second before her attention switches back to the house. "Okay, for my own piece of mind, I need to ask. Are you married?"

My wince is barely controlled, and I only just manage to stop my fist from balling. "Why do you need to know?" I ask calmly, keeping the punishing, volatile sickness in my soul from showing.

Her eyes widen. "You needing to ask me that seriously disturbs me. Do I come across like some bitch homewrecker to you? Or do I seem like the kind of woman who just loves being the piece you screw on the side to piss off your wife, or whatever reason you rich people use to get your rocks off?"

Despite the feelings roiling through my belly, my mouth twitches. "No, your request for exclusivity suggests you're not either of those things."

That seems to appease her. "Then answer the question."

"I'm not married. Not anymore."

I curse silently for the unnecessary additional info, but it's too late. Her eyes glow with interest. Interest that I ignore by turning and stalking to the door. I hear the exact moment she dismounts and follows, and relief pours through me.

Not that I have any intention of letting her do anything but follow me. The gates are locked. Only I have the code. Once the front door closes behind her, she's only getting out when I'm good and ready.

I enter the cavernous hallway and kick off my boots and socks. The sensation of the cool tiles beneath my feet grounds me and allows me a moment or two of rational thought before I hear her enter.

My slip needn't be a problem. My marriage and divorce aren't exactly state secrets—Cassie and I were a prominent New York couple before I put her out of her misery and ended our marriage—but an intelligent and curious person can discover things I don't want discovered.

"So... you live in this mansion on your own?"

"When I'm here, yes."

"And how often are you here?"

I whirl to face her, and she takes a single step back. "We have an agreement, remember? No personal questions?" I all but snarl.

Her eyes flash warily, but she props her hands on her hips. "Hey, you opened that door. I just peeked through it."

"Well, consider it firmly shut."

In almost perfect synchronicity, the door behind her, programmed to shut and lock after twenty seconds of no movement, clicks home.

She jumps at the small but ominous sound.

I release a breath that has been locked in my chest. The pulse at her throat flutters, and a fissure of sadistic pleasure erupts through me. I can't help it. I'm drawn to helplessness, always have been. It's why I love living in the jungle for months on end. The shark-like instinct inside me is extremely turned on by the thought of hunting prey, especially those who put up a good, worthwhile fight.

It's why, in the end, I couldn't stand the sight of Cassie. She gave up fighting and disappeared into a bottle of premium vodka.

Keely Benson is a fighter. And the hunt will be more than worth my while.

Now that I have her here, I don't need to hold back the urgency and true scale of my hunger. I allow the barely civilized façade, which I adopted so she'll feel at ease, to slide away through my extremities. My fingers tingle with the need to grab, to possess, to devour.

She sucks her lower lip into her mouth and her arms fold in a self-protective manner. But she has no protection here. Not anymore.

I open the floodgates of the ruthless alpha inside. I see the moment she recognizes the change. Her nostrils flutter and she glances at the massive door behind her.

"Are you afraid, Keely?"

Her eyes narrow and she raises her chin. "No."

My blood surges at her answer, even though I don't totally believe her. "You wanted to set some ground rules. Here's Rule Number One for me. If I ask for something that's within your power to grant, you will grant it. Without hesitation. Are we clear?"

"Hell, no. I thought we were going to discuss this like *rational* human beings?"

I take another step closer. Her scent hits me and curls around my senses like a sweet but deadly poison, one I'd gladly expire from. "Which part of that rule isn't good for you?" I ask as I reach behind me and yank my T-shirt over my head and throw it on the floor. My very skin is on fire and stretched tight with what I feel for this woman.

Her eyes bulge, and she swallows. "I..." Her eyelashes flutter as her slightly dazed gaze tracks my torso till it hits my belt.

My hands itch to release the belt and get on with what we both need, but I give her a chance to answer. "Yes?"

"I have a problem with the *without hesitation* part."

I shake my head. "That's non-negotiable. I won't let you over-think every request. Trust that I'll think about it carefully before I demand it."

"You mean like the way you requested your sex toy to not come until you were ready to let her?"

My fingers tingle and I know I'm at the edge of my endurance. "That was different. You and I aren't quite there yet."

Laughter trips from her lips and strikes me somewhere in my midriff. I rack my brain and honestly don't remember when a woman has laughed at something I said that wasn't a deliberate joke. Normally, they're either afraid I'll take it the wrong way or just afraid, period.

Keely's brazen response makes my cock harder, and the need to teach her another lesson pounds through me.

"We're *never* going to get there."

I pause in my pursuit of her. "What makes you say that?"

"Oh, I don't know, because I have more self-respect than to be treated as a *pet* or a *toy*? I don't intend to be one of your brainless minions," she snipes.

"Brainless implies you think the women aren't cognizant of what they're doing, or that only women with low self-esteem subject themselves to submission. Is that what you think?"

She blinks, and I catch a raw flash of emotion before her eyes slide away from mine. "I don't really give a damn how other women prefer to get their kicks. All I know is that sort of thing isn't for me."

"And yet you got dressed exactly as I asked you to do today," I point out softly. "What if I told you that you'd already taken the first step?"

Furious green eyes meet mine. "I'd tell you go f—" She catches herself and I try not to let the triumph surging into my body show. "I'd tell you to check yourself before you wreck yourself. Agreeing to wear pants and boots for you is a far cry from allowing me to be tied into one of your inventions, begging to be whipped."

Her back touches the door and the realization that I've been slowly stalking her lights her eyes. Her pulse is now racing like a freight train, and I'm close enough to smell her anger and arousal. Like the most potent aphrodisiac, I'm helpless to resist its lure for one second longer.

"We'll table this discussion for later. But here's your first test.

I promise it's an easy one. Do you want me to fuck you, Keely? Yes or no?"

"Yes," she answers without hesitation.

I smile and she quickly inhales.

"What?"

Green eyes, dark with swirling lust, meet mine. "You look different when you smile. Different hot," she adds, and a hint of color touches her cheeks.

I give in to the frantic urge and touch my finger to the rapidly beating pulse. Electricity zaps me from the point of connection straight to my cock. "You're hot when you smile, hot when you're not smiling. You're hot regardless of what you're doing, and I very much want to fuck you, too."

Her eyelashes flutter, and she trembles beneath my touch. "Can we... get on with it then?" Although her voice is husky with lust, it still holds that snap, like a crack of a whip across willing flesh. The sting brings more fire to my veins, and the roar in my blood is almost overwhelming.

I lean in until my mouth is almost on her neck. I savor the anticipation of tasting her skin. "Here comes the next command —unzip my pants."

Her gaze drops to my crotch and her hands start to follow, but she stops at the last moment, and a look flashes across her face.

"Tell me what you're thinking," I growl.

She gives a tight little laugh. "I'm thinking I'm alone in a strange but beautiful house with a man I barely know, who's just asked me to unzip his pants."

"But you're not afraid of me." It's not a question because I don't sense that sort of fear from her.

She confirms by shaking her head.

I move my finger from her pulse to her chin and tilt her face to mine. "I'm the same man who rescued you from the icy ocean," I cunningly remind her. Whether she wants to admit it or not, she owes me her life. I don't intend to claim it, but I'm not averse to using it to suit my needs right now.

Her eyes shadow at the reminder, but she nods. "But then he scared the living shit out of me when I got into his car."

"You wouldn't have gotten into his car if you truly thought he would harm you," I press.

She shrugs. "I'm not ashamed to admit I wasn't exactly thinking straight that night."

I let go of her chin and plant my hands on either side of her head. Her eyes widen as she stares up at me with that touch of helplessness that makes me step from the edge of the cliff into the abyss.

Because what Keely doesn't know is that I love power. A little too much, my mother once said. A sentiment wholeheartedly endorsed later in life by Cassie. I never defended the statement. I didn't see the point. Just as I never pointed out that my love of power was what kept them draped in diamonds and private jet spa trips to Switzerland. The point was redundant and beneath me.

"You're not going to leave. We both know that. So unzip my pants, take my cock out and stroke it. Or you won't get fucked."

15

KEELY

I want to refuse.

I ought to.

Something's happening here that I can't quite wrap my head around. It started the moment the door closed behind me. Almost as if the man in front of me has become another person. The ruthless edge I sense in him is heightened, even though he hasn't done or said anything to make me think I'm in danger.

But I sense something. Something that should make me refuse his command.

Yet I know I'm not going to.

I want to fuck him harder, longer, deeper, more desperately than I've ever wanted to fuck another man. The thought of being denied literally makes my heart ache, and I can't breathe around the pressure in my chest.

So I reach for his belt and release it. Then my trembling fingers unsnap the single button on his jeans. His ominously thick cock jerks against my knuckles when my fingers brush it. I catch a strangled moan and a wash of hot breath against my neck.

My breasts tingle madly and my nipples are so painfully tight, I want to beg him to touch them, pinch them, alleviate the torture. But the words choke off in my throat. Or maybe I sense that voicing them would mean breaking some rule I don't even know about.

That's how mind-fucked this whole situation is. I firmly believe everything I said a minute ago about not wanting to be a sex toy or a pet, and yet I have every intention of groveling at his feet like some pathetic, infatuated fool.

I'm almost afraid to speak, to ask him to touch me the way my body is screaming to be touched. I make my near-useless fingers grip his zipper and slowly lower it. When my hand connects with hot, naked, eager cock on the way down and I realize he's commando, I gasp.

Urgently, I grasp him with my right hand and push down his pants with my left. His insane girth makes me moan and my head automatically starts to drop in my eagerness to see him, to see the cock my fingers can barely circle.

His finger beneath my chin stops me.

"No. You can't look at me yet. Stroke me and keep your eyes on mine."

I don't argue. The command doesn't seem like a big deal to me. And also because my left hand has just cupped his heavy balls and the look on his face has me completely enthralled.

I stroke him, long and slow, flicking my wrist just a tiny bit when I get to his head.

His lips part and a strangled groan falls from them. "Yes. That's it," he mutters thickly.

There's something raw and electrifying about him forcing me to witness his pleasure. The connection is a little too much, like staring into the sun for a moment too long. I'm blinded by the emotions charging through me, but I can't look away.

His head descends. His mouth stops a whisper from mine, and his breath washes over my lips. "Faster," he commands, his eyes still locked squarely on mine.

I open my mouth again to tell him to quit with the orders, but I stop at the last moment. Again, it doesn't seem like a big deal. I obey and he groans, rewarding me with an even thicker erection. My pussy clenches and unclenches in deprived desperation, and my whole body shudders through the storm rocking my foundations.

My next stroke upward is greeted with a drop of pre-cum, and my mouth waters with the ravaging need to taste him, but the pressure on my chin prevents me from looking, never mind tasting. My tongue slides over my lower lip and my breath shudders out when I squeeze his balls and his pupils dilate.

"Open your mouth."

I open my mouth. His thumb replaces his forefinger beneath my chin, and his middle finger slides into my mouth. I don't wait for his command to suck it deep and hard.

"Fuck," he grits out as his cock jumps in my hand. "You're incredibly good at that. You're also very wet. I can smell you."

I don't bother to release his finger to answer. My panties are soaked, and I'm not even a little bit ashamed of the fact. I continue to stroke and suck, reveling in the amazing feeling of his smooth, steely cock in my hand and his finger in my mouth.

After a minute, I feel movement below. The sound of the belt hitting the floor and his widening stance tells me his jeans are off. Mason is completely naked, and I'm still fully dressed, right down to my purse dissecting my breasts.

The imbalance feels deliciously decadent, if a little unfair. I forget all about it when he starts to pump his hips, fucking himself between my fingers.

"I'm going to come in your hand. You're going to let me."

Before he's finished saying the words, he's increasing the tempo. My fingers automatically grip him harder, and I know he's right; I'm going to let him.

Fucking hell. What's wrong with me? For the first time in my life I want to give pleasure, utterly and completely without taking any for myself. And it's not because I feel I owe him for Montauk.

No, right here, right now, all I want is to please him, to satisfy that ravenous hunger in his eyes, the voracious edge that's riding him and sending tremors through his hot body.

More pre-cum coats my fingers, and I spread it over his rod, my wrist working harder as I keep up with the almost frantic rhythm of his hips and the finger fucking my mouth.

"That's it, baby," he whispers into my ear. "Do me like that. Work me harder. Faster!"

My cheeks are beginning to burn with the pressure of sucking him, but I keep at it, a part of me reeling with the fact that I don't want to disappoint him.

I flick my tongue against the pad of his finger, and he releases a deep groan. His eyelids flutter as my left hand grips his balls harder, stroking the smooth skin in tandem with my hand pumps. "Ah, Christ, I'm going to fuck you everywhere. I'm going to spend hours imprinting myself on every inch of your body. But for now, I want you to watch me come for you. See how much you please me."

With that, he pulls his finger out of my mouth and spreads saliva all over my lips before he lets go of my chin. He plants his other hand on the door and levers himself slightly away from my body.

My eager gaze drops and I gasp when I see his cock for the first time.

The thickness I already know about, but he's also long and

lightly veined, with a beautifully sculpted head I simply need to wrap my lips around.

I feel his blood surge beneath my touch and I know he's coming. My head snaps up and he's watching my face, his eyes half-shut and heavy with the pre-orgasmic wave riding him.

Slowly, his mouth parts on a long, breathy *aah,* then he says my name. "Keely."

I'm filled with a rush of power for a single, mind-blowing second as I glimpse a strange, incandescent light in his eyes. Then the power is ruthlessly snatched from me when he surges forcefully between my fingers, and an animal growl rumbles from his throat.

The first thick spurt hits my covered belly, followed by several more. Warmth seeps through the thin cotton of my top and soaks my skin. He jerks in my hold, his whole frame caught in a series of mesmeric spasms as he covers my front in cum.

His eyes are still staring into mine when his shudders die down, and I can honestly admit that it's the hottest thing I've experienced so far in my life. That is, until he leans forward and catches my lower lip in a less-than-gentle bite before sliding his tongue over the tingling ache.

"You were magnificent," he mutters against my mouth.

The silky hairs of his trim beard tickle my skin, but before I can respond, he steps away and leaves me sagging against the door. I get a load of *his* full magnificence a second later as my eyes take in his warrior-like glory for the first time.

God.

No wonder the man is arrogant and infuriating to a huge fault. With a body and face like that, not to mention his blue-blooded pedigree, Mason Sinclair has a hell of a lot to crow about.

He's sleek, smooth muscle everywhere. Powerful thighs rise

to lean hips and a short thicket of hair frames his thick cock and balls, lending his godly body a weirdly earthy roughness that makes him even hotter in my eyes.

He takes another step back and slides not-quite-steady fingers through his hair. "Come into the kitchen so we can get you cleaned up," he says, his gaze dropping to my stomach.

I look down and see the patch of wetness on my cream top. There's also a couple drops of semen on the marble floor and my body reacts heatedly to the evidence of his release.

My gaze returns to find he's watching me. He's also getting turned on again if the thickening between his legs is any indication. My mouth waters as I watch him, and he holds out his hand to me.

"Come."

I straighten from the door and thankfully my legs support me. When I reach him, he hooks his finger beneath the strap of my purse and pulls it over my head.

"Do you have your phone?" he asks.

I frown my confusion. "Umm, yes."

He nods. "Good. Bring it with you."

I take it out of my purse, and he hangs the bag on a hook as we pass a huge archway that opens into a cathedral-windowed hallway. I want to stop and gape, but the sight of Mason's ass as he strides in front of me is a way better magnet that keeps me fixated on him.

We pass through another arch and enter the sort of kitchen I've only ever seen in luxury magazines, although I recognize the designer immediately. Gordon Neiderheimer's beautiful lines and use of steel and wood grace Bethany and Zach's new house in California, and I was the one to source the designer for them. In another life, I would've stopped to stroke the grey granite surface I pass on the way to where Mason is waiting for me.

But those eyes of his hook into me, and I can't concentrate on anything else but him. He takes my phone from me when I reach him and places it on a counter. Then he reaches behind me and peels my top off much the way he did his own a lifetime ago. Next, his thumbs pass under the cups, his fingernails grazing the underside of my breasts before he unhooks my cream lace bra and pulls it off.

The cool air hits my already pearled nipples and they furl further into hard nubs of screaming nerves.

"God, you're beyond breathtaking," he mutters thickly.

I tremble and a sound rumbles from his chest. One finger traces me from throat to navel, then he swirls his digit through the damp cum sticking to my skin. "I want to come on you again. I want to spread my cum all over you, soak you in it."

"To do that we actually have to fuck," I point out with a touch of impatience. "You've tortured me long enough. I need you inside me before I go out of my damn mind."

His head snaps up, and his nostrils flare. He's pissed, but I'm fast losing the will to care. All I want is to be fucked, and he's keeping his beautiful, hard cock away from me. I reach for him but he captures my wrist in an unbreakable hold.

"Obedience brings rewards. Remember that."

I bristle. "Yeah, I've done everything you asked since I walked in. Now it's my turn. Or are you going to withhold now you've gotten yours?" The very thought makes me want to die. Or shamelessly beg.

"I've gotten nowhere near everything I want from you." He releases me and slides his finger beneath my waistband, tugs at it. "Take it off."

I comply only because I need to take it off to get fucked. But it doesn't stop me glaring at him.

He smiles as I bend to push my pants down my legs, and my

heart rattles through my chest like a pinball machine. God, he's incredible when he smiles. I am partly thankful he doesn't do it very often, because it packs a wallop that could be seriously detrimental to my mental health.

I straighten, and the smile melts off his face. I want to crow and bask in feminine power at the naked awe in his eyes when he looks at my body, but dear lord, I just want to be fucked as quickly and as thoroughly as possible.

I prepare to jump him, but he bends and grabs my clothes and starts to walk away.

"Jesus, enough with the damn suspense! I'm fucking dying here!"

I cringe and freeze the moment the swear word spills from my lips, but he doesn't react. He places my soiled clothes in a futuristic-looking chute and presses a button before he retraces his steps.

"I sent you an email earlier. Did you read it?"

"What?" I stammer the question, and I fear my head's about to explode from the tornado-speed with which he switches from sex to other things.

He picks up my phone and hands it to me. "Since you haven't brought up the issue, I'm assuming you haven't read it yet."

He's right, I haven't seen an email from him, and as I swipe my password and click onto my email account, I struggle to think why he would send me one. The only answer my brain can supply is that it's about work.

"You want to discuss work now?" I'm fast reaching the conclusion that he's a sadist and I'm his victim of choice.

He steps behind me and trails his fingers over my shoulders. "Open it and read the attachment."

I shudder helplessly and concentrate on scrolling through my unopened emails. I locate his, which came in a little over an hour ago, when I was soaking in the bubble bath, making myself clean and presentable to be tortured by a sadist.

Lust and anger war inside me as I stab the attachment and wait for the blue wheel to stop spinning in the pdf application.

I shudder when he moves my hair out of the way and replaces his mouth with his fingers. Warm kisses caress each vertebra until he reaches the small of my back. The darned blue wheel is still turning so I flick a glance over my shoulder.

Mason is on his knees behind me, his fingers hooked into my panties. He slides the cream lace over my hips and it pools at my ankles.

"Did you open it yet?" he asks, then grips my hips in a firm hold.

I look down and try to concentrate on the document filling my screen. "Umm... yes."

"Good."

I squeal as he buries his face between my ass cheeks and tongues me from front to back. My legs turn liquid, and I barely manage to catch myself on the counter before I end up in a heap on the floor.

He stops after that one lick and stands. "I'm going to get us a drink. Read it before I get back." He kisses me, and I taste my pungent need on his lips. As he walks away, I struggle to pull my attention from his fine ass to whatever the hell he's so insistent on me reading.

At first, the words are small and meaningless to me. I turn my phone to landscape position, and the words flare up and smack me between the eyes.

Still I stare at the row after row of "Negative" before I raise my head. "You sent me your medical history?"

He takes the wine out of the chiller and pours one glass before filling another with water. "Yes. And I peeked at yours."

"You did *what*?" I screech.

He comes toward me, one hand holding out the glass of wine. "I did it to save time. I thought you'd do the same by reading my email before I picked you up. I knew you hadn't seen mine since you didn't give me the hard time you're about to right now. Before you do, let me see if I can save you the time we could be using to fuck. You submitted to the mandatory test required for the IL trips. I wasn't planning to be on one till two days ago. I did mine yesterday. As you can see, I'm clean. So are you. We're free to fuck each other raw—and you can take that whichever way you want to. You have ten seconds to debate whether you want to spend another hour arguing with me or getting the fucking you've been begging for since we walked in."

I shake my head and toss my phone back on the counter. "You're fucking unbelievable. Is it just the size of your bank account that makes you think you can— What the hell are you doing?" I yelp. "Dammit, Mason, put me down!"

16

KEELY

The arms banding my waist don't free me. I'm marched across the kitchen to the breakfast island and set down before a bar stool.

His foot roughly kicks out my ankles and he pushes me forward. I land on my stomach, and my arms flail wildly before I grab hold of the stool legs to steady myself.

"Mason, I seriously hope you're not going there again!" I use the leverage on the stool to rise, but the hand on my back prevents me from straightening.

Apprehension climbs into my throat as he leans in close enough to feel his breath wash over my ear.

"You will learn to believe me when I say there'll be consequences for your foul mouth."

His palm lands a harsh, merciless slap on my bare ass. Another five follow—two for yesterday and four for the two *fucks* I've uttered since entering the kitchen.

As quickly as he bent me over the stool, he releases me, then catches me as I wobble on my feet. He walks me to the counter and hands me the wine, while his other hand pets the soreness out of my stinging ass.

"Now, where were we?" he asks as if the last sixty seconds hasn't happened.

I'm reeling at the mind-fuckedness of the whole thing. "Mason..." I stop when I hear the wobble in my voice. At the same time, I feel the increased wetness between my legs and hate myself even more for it. "I told you I hate being spanked."

The gleam in his eyes tells me he thinks I'm full of shit. "I don't think you do. Or you wouldn't keep doing what will get you punished. I don't buy that you can't help yourself. You just choose not to."

I slam the glass down. "Dammit, I'm not a child you can take over your knee whenever you feel like it."

He shrugs. "Act like an adult and I won't."

I shake with anger, arousal and a whole multitude of emotions I don't want to name.

He gulps in a few more mouthfuls of water before he sets his glass down next to mine. "Are you ready to continue?"

I open my mouth to tell him to go fuck himself, *permanently*. But he's a fucking god, with his mouth-watering body and even more spectacular cock, and I haven't had sex in so fucking long... My shallow mind and even shallower body rob me of speech, and I just stare back at him like the sex-starved idiot I've turned into.

Like a true predator sensing weakness, he reaches out and cups my breasts, squeezes my nipples with just the right amount of pressure that straddles the fine line between pleasure and pain.

He repeats the move and my knees buckle. "Oh God!"

Another step closer, and the heat of his body touches mine for the first time. His cock nudges my belly, and my hands find his hip, eager to get even closer. He tenses for a moment, but when I look up, I see only pure hunger and lust on his face.

He kisses the corner of my mouth as he continues to knead my breasts with firm, expert caresses. God, he's good. I'm getting wetter and more desperate by the second, and he's only touching my breasts. "I said, are you ready to continue?"

"Y... yes," I sigh.

"Good, but I also need to hear that you're happy with the results of the medical report. Otherwise, I need to get the condoms."

I bite my lip and try not to think about the last time I had sex without protection. Of course the details are blurry enough to not be worth the effort, but my heart lurches and a cold shiver lances down my spine all the same.

Mason's gaze sharpens, and his hands leave my breasts to capture my nape. "Keely?"

When I refuse to meet his gaze, he bends his knees until he's eye-level with me. I have no choice but to meet his probing stare.

"What?" I throw out defiantly.

"What's going on?"

I shrug. "I don't mind ex... experimenting when it comes to sex, but you've taken almost every decision out of my hands. I don't like giving up control. Especially when it comes to sex."

He frowns. "*Especially?* Why not?"

Shit. "I just don't, okay?"

His eyes narrow. "I don't buy that. Who took away your control?"

Whoa... When did the conversation take the forked road to freak-ville? I shake my head. There's no way I'm talking about *that* with him. I try to knock his hands away, but he holds firm. "It's none of your damn business." My breath strangles in my lungs as it dawns on me that I may as well have raised a red flag by giving him that answer. "You have no right to do this, Mason."

"No right to ask why two minutes ago you were okay with all of this and suddenly, you're wound tight enough to snap?"

"Yes! How did we get here anyway? You didn't want personal, remember? Well, it goes both ways. You don't ask questions of me and I don't ask them of you. If you're changing the rules, then you have to be prepared to answer a few of my questions, too."

His jaw clenches. "It's not that simple."

"Of course not. The great Mason Sinclair is so much more complicated than I am, right?"

"I didn't say that. My personal issues won't interfere with how and who I fuck. If yours do, then we have a problem."

I don't believe that for a second, but I'm not going to probe. Probing will open doors I want firmly shut. We stare at each other for a few charged seconds. Then I shake my head again. "I guess this wasn't a good idea, after all."

His fingers spear into my hair to hold me captive, and the other hand grips my hip and slams my body into his. "Like hell it wasn't. My only agenda was to make this an even more pleasurable experience for you. And yes, I do like control. But unless I'm way off base here, I haven't forced you to do anything against your will, have I?"

"That's not the point."

"Of course it is." Despite our heated argument, he's still hard as a rock and his erection nudges me, reminding me of what I'll be giving up if I walk away. He's fucking with my mind again, and I'm beginning to question why I'm fighting this at all. Truth is, I want sex with him. Really, really badly. Enough to loosen my stance on control to get what I want.

Loosen, not abandon. I can never abandon my control. But for what Mason Sinclair promises, I can let go. For one night.

He tightens his grip on my hip, his fingers digging into me with ruthless intent. "This is all that matters, Keely. Everything else is bullshit."

Everything else *isn't* bullshit... but I swallow and nod. "Okay."

He immediately shakes his head. "No, not okay."

"*Jesus*, Mason, what the hell do you want from me?" I demand in a plaintive voice I absolutely do not recognize as mine. Is this what I'm reduced to? A needy, panting *hoe* willing to pretzel herself for some sadist who can't make up his mind whether he wants to fuck or not?

"I want for you not to sound as if I'm coercing you into doing something you don't want to do. Either you want this or you don't."

I take a deep breath to sustain my withering patience. "I want this. I've wanted this for the last hour, the last day; hell, since you almost killed me on an icy road in Montauk two weeks ago. I want it enough to give you a goddamn hand job—and FYI, I've never done that before. I want you enough for me *not* to walk out after a spanking I absolutely hated. I want to be fucked, Mason. I'm dying to be fucked by you. I'm naked, and I'm soaking wet, wetter than I've ever been in my life. How else do you want me to prove it to you?"

A slow smile lights up his face. "I can think of several other ways, but this is enough for now."

I exhale in relief and start to slide my hand around his neck. He captures my arms and kisses my inner wrists. My hands start to frame his face, but he subtly pulls away. "You're on the Pill."

The statement isn't quite framed as a question, but I don't

want to start another argument by asking him how the hell he knows, so I answer, "Yes."

He nods and returns my hands to my sides before he cups and fondles my breasts once more.

I sigh in pleasure and fall into the deep kiss he bestows on my mouth. Within seconds, the fire is back. His touch turns rough and demanding, and I can't get enough of him.

"Shit, I want you so fucking bad," he groans against my breast before he sucks one nipple into his mouth. The hungry little noises he makes at the back of his throat as he feasts on me turns my bones liquid.

I'm a useless sop by the time he snatches me up in his arms and carries me to the stool he spanked me on a mere half hour ago.

He senses my tension and smiles. "We're in the punishment-free zone now, baby. It's pleasure from here on in." He slaps the surface of the leather stool. "Up."

I hop up, and he pushes me back until most of my ass is hanging off the edge. I brace my feet on the rungs, and he swivels the stool so I'm facing the counter with my back to him. Strong arms slide around me, and he enfolds me with his upper body. I'm bathed in heat and my senses jump in frenzied excitement when his cock nudges my ass.

"We're going to do things a little differently, baby. I'm going to save this"—he reaches between my thighs and taps my pussy —"for when I can take my time with it."

"What? No! God, please, Mason—"

"Shh," he whispers in my ear. "I promise my intention isn't to make you beg. I've kept you waiting long enough. I just want to prove to you as quickly as possible how great it can be between us."

"Fucking me will solve all that," I almost pant.

His answer is to nip the skin below my ear, while his thumbs flick over my nipples. "Trust me, Keely. Just for tonight?"

I close my eyes and let sensations wash over me. "Okay."

He exhales, and I know I've said the right thing. "Have you ever been ass-fucked?"

I jump a mile wide, or at least that's what it feels like. In reality, his hold tightens around me, keeping me firmly on the stool. I can feel his gaze on my heated face, awaiting my answer.

"Tried once. Didn't work out," I mumble.

"I'll make it work for you."

Jesus, this man took edging to a whole new level. My gaze meets his, and I remember his pledge from earlier—*I'm going to fuck you everywhere*. I believed him then, I just didn't think anal would be the first option. I pull in a shaky breath.

"God, I knew you were an asshole the moment I met you."

He laughs deep and low. "How about I *be* a pain in your ass? The good kind?"

My mouth twitches. The next minute I'm laughing. He tucks his head into my shoulder and kisses my jaw. "You're fucking gorgeous when you laugh." He nibbles my earlobe until my laughter turns into a strangled moan. "Is that a yes?"

I feel like a damn wilting virgin in a period drama, but I need to ask, "Will you be gentle?"

He hesitates, and my stomach knots in anxiety. "Probably not, but we'll take it slow until we can't. Is that okay with you?"

I nod, and he reaches for a box I didn't notice before, sitting in the middle of the counter. He sets a tube of lube in front of me. "Open it."

He massages my shoulders and my back as I shakily uncap the tube. Kisses trail down my spine again until he reaches my ass. His firm grip on my thighs is the only warning I get before his tongue flicks over my puckered hole.

"Oh!" I drop the tube and grip the counter as sharp pleasure shoots up my spine. He licks again, then pushes his tongue firmer against me. Tiny stars dance before my eyes, and I release a deep moan. He swirls, probes, flicks and generally makes out with my backside as if it's his new best friend. All the while, I grip the counter and try not to pass out from the pleasure overload.

When I think I can't take it anymore, that I'll come just from the attention he's paying my back channel, he pulls back and blows on me. The stars double, then triple, until a kaleidoscope fills my vision.

"God, Mason. Please, just do it."

"You're not ready," he replies.

The embarrassingly soaked feeling between my legs says otherwise. I've never been this wet. Or this desperate. I look over my shoulder, and he's staring up at me as his hands part me wider and he replaces his tongue with his thumb.

"Fuck! I need you. Please…"

"Do you want to come?" He circles me once, twice, then pushes in.

Heat erupts up my spine. "Yes!"

He stands and crouches over me. "There are condoms in the box. Grab one for me," he says.

I start to reach for the shiny black square, then hesitate. I may be crazy to contemplate it, but I want to feel everything. I want to squeeze every last drop of pleasure from this encounter, because I'm intelligent enough to know that Mason and I aren't sustainable. We disagree on too much, have serious control issues that would fuck up any chance of this being more than a one-night thing.

So why waste a perfectly good medical report that says we can fuck the way nature intended for us to fuck?

He sees my hesitation and I hear his breath catch, but he remains silent. Waiting. The only movement is his thumb, still working the screaming bundle of nerves.

Slowly, trembling, I pull my hand back and grip the counter.

"Say it," he says gruffly. "I need to hear you say it."

"Take me, Mason. Fuck me raw."

My words shudder through him and his cock jerks against my back. A touch of apprehension dribbles itself across my excitement. Mason is big, and although I'm worldly enough to know that he would probably fit back there, a part of me reels at the thought of his cock in my ass.

"You're tensing up. Don't. I won't hurt you, but I need you to relax."

"Easier said than done," I return tightly. Now that I've let the doubts in, I can't push them away, and I feel myself coiling tighter with each pass of his thumb.

"Shit, this isn't going to work if you keep tightening up." There's a bite of frustration in his voice, along with a ragged edge of hunger, which echoes inside me. He cups my breast and tugs on the nipple. My insides melt, but not enough to take my mind away from what he's doing behind me.

After another minute, he sighs. "Show me how to make you relax, baby. Tell me what gets you soft and horny. But it can't be anything to do with your pussy. I don't want you coming from me touching you there."

Well, fuck, there goes that lifesaver. I bite my lip and heat slowly fills my face as I consider his request. I don't know why the hell I'm embarrassed when he's the perfect guy to make this a mind-blowing experience. "I..."

"Don't be shy, kitten. Just say it and it's yours."

"Talk... umm, talk nerdy to me."

He stills for a moment and mortification engulfs me. He

continues to play with my nipple, but a second later I feel his breath on my ear. "So nerd talk gets you off, huh?"

"Y... yes."

"Sure, baby. I can do that. How about *Letters of Cicero to Atticus VII*? Does that work for you?"

My heart jumps and I nod eagerly.

"Latin or English version?" he asks as he continues to play with my nipple and my asshole.

Oh, God. "Latin."

Mason puts his mouth to my ear and starts whispering: "*Dederam equidem L. Saufeio litters et dederam ad the unum, quod, cum non esset temporise mini ad scribendum satis, tamen hominem tibia familiarem sine meis litters ad the venire nolebam.*"

Each whispered word is like a little morsel of decadent dessert on my senses. I close my eyes and let the low, sexy words infuse me.

"*Sed, ut philosophi ambulant, has tibi redditum iri putabam prius.*"

I moan when the tip of his thumb slips inside me. It burns, but the sensation is unlike anything I've ever experienced, and I let it saturate my senses as his words flood through me.

"*Sin aim ills accepisti, scis me Athenas venisse pr.*"

Liquid warmth touches my sensitive skin. It feels so good I melt into it and the caresses from Mason's fingers. I hardly feel any pain when his middle finger slips into my tight sheath. He slowly eases in and out and I shudder at the incredible sensation.

"Oooh."

"Does that feel good?" he whispers.

"Hmm, yes," I gasp.

He kisses my jaw, my cheek, his mouth never straying far

from my ear. "*Idus Octobres, e navi egressum in Piraeum tuas ab Acasto nostro litters accepisse, conturbatum, quod cum...*"

I'm pure liquid sensation as I moan and move my hips against his clever finger and cleverer words. He continues to serenade me in mind and body, and I give over to the pleasure welling up inside me.

I hardly feel his fingers leave me and his head nudge my opening.

But then he pushes into me and my eyes pop open. "Mason, God!"

"Shh, easy, kitten. Breathe, just breathe." One hand holds me in place on the stool and the other rolls my nipple, tugging hard enough to distract me from the probing in my backside. "*...Febre Roman venires, bono tamen animo...*"

I exhale, and he pushes deeper. Intense burning is followed by intense pleasure, the two mingling to create a surge of bliss so powerful, I scream.

The sound seems to trigger something in Mason. He lets go of my nipple and grips my hips with both hands. On my next exhale, he slams into me. Another scream rips through my throat, and my eyes brim with tears.

"Fuck!" Mason's voice is thick and rough and filled with a menacing edge that tells me he's cresting his own endurance. He pulls out slowly and slams back into me. "So hot. Incredible. I knew you would be..." he mutters almost under his breath.

After the first few thrusts, the lube is doing its work and the burning recedes a little, but not enough to completely make me forget Mason's huge cock is in my ass.

More than that, I'm being ass-fucked and I'm loving it. Hell, I don't want it to stop.

God!

"Are you okay?" he asks when I'm too hoarse to scream anymore.

"Yes," I croak.

"Tell me how you feel, baby."

"I... feel like I'm going to shatter into a zillion pieces."

"You will. Can you hold on a little longer?" he asks.

Can I? I'm a seething ball of sensation, poised on the point of detonation. "I... don't think so," I answer truthfully in a choked gasp.

One hand leaves my hip and wraps around my shoulders. He pulls me back into his chest and aligns his rough cheek against mine. "Just a few more minutes. It'll be worth it, I promise. You feel so good, kitten. Like hot, tight silk fisting my cock. Christ, I want to fuck you forever."

A red haze washes across my vision, beckoning with a promise of untold ecstasy. "Mason, I can't hold on. Please..."

"Look at me, Keely."

I twist my head and catch his dark-gold gaze. Something raw and visceral hooks between us and I stop breathing.

"You're so fucking beautiful. Come for me."

My mouth drops open and a keening starts in my lumbar region that I recognize as the calm before the most intense storm I've ever felt. A roar fills my ears, but I still hear Mason's hoarse curses as he pounds my ass. He slams into me one last time and holds me tight as convulsions rip through me.

I'm floating on a sea of fire and ice, of rocks and silk. I don't know whether I'm in one piece or a thousand pieces. I don't care about anything, or anyone, except the man whose arms shackle me, whose own hoarse cries and hot spurts flood me as we shake through our release.

17

MASON

"You don't need to be back on the boat until Monday. Stay here with me." I hear the words drop from my lips, and I immediately want to take them back. Only the ingrained poker face, which I perfected before I took my first step, keeps my expression neutral, even as my inner voice snarls, *What the fuck is wrong with you?*

Her face, fresh and make-up free from the shower we took after our sweaty session in the kitchen, twists with indecision. Ninety-five per cent of me hopes she says no. That insane five per cent leans forward eagerly, awaiting her answer.

"I don't think it's a good idea. I have a lot of work to do before Monday. Besides, I don't have a toothbrush, or a change of clothes."

I listen to the words, and I want to laugh at the pathetic excuses. The cruel freak inside wants to do just that. It wants to taunt, jibe. It doesn't like the idea of her *no*. Hell, it rejects the idea of her leaving, period.

I silence the freak, say nothing and just watch her.

She stops eating the grilled turbot I had delivered and puts her fork down. "Why do you do that?"

"What do you mean?"

A flash of irritation crosses her face. "You know what I mean. Those *silences*."

"What silences?" I let the taunt monster out a little, and I feel a touch juvenile, but what the hell...

"Don't fuck with me, Mason—"

Her eyes widen at the slip, and another dark, cruel feeling curls through me. Silence and the expectation of retribution pulses in the air. She licks her lips and stares at me across the breakfast bar. "Dammit, you can't drive me to the point of exasperation and then—" She stops and blinks those incredible eyes. "Are you going to give me a pass?" she asks.

"No."

Her face twists. "Mason—"

"No."

She worries her lip, then straightens her shoulders. "You know what... I'm a grown-ass woman. I don't have to take this shit punishment."

"But you will."

"Even if it tips the balance of my staying here to a no rather than a yes?"

"I won't be negotiated with. Not when it comes to this."

"Why is it so important to you?"

"Because outside of the bedroom, you're better than crude words."

She studies me for a few seconds, although she knows by now that I won't change my mind. She's a quick study like that. My cock still throbs from having her go down on me in the bathroom. She learned very quickly what pleases me and gave double what I demanded.

Three orgasms in three hours, and I'm still nowhere near ready to call it a night. Quite the opposite. I want to pound her, hard and relentlessly, until one of us breaks.

Slowly, she stands and walks round to my side. She's wearing my T-shirt, which covers her from neck to knee, but she's naked underneath. My gaze stays on her face, and I read anger in her eyes. But there's also anticipation. I see it in the flush of her cheeks, her soft pants and the tiny twitches in her fingers.

I smile inwardly. "You do enjoy being spanked."

Her mouth twists. "Um, that would be a definite *no* to that, sir."

My breath strangles in my lungs, but I maintain my expression and pat the surface of the counter next to my plate.

She pulls the T-shirt over her head and slides onto the cold granite top. The chill makes her nipples pucker, and my mouth waters at the sight. The edge of my hunger is as feral and insane as ever, and the urge to rip into her overwhelms me.

I stay seated as she curls her knees beneath her and positions herself on all fours, her eyes on mine and her mouth open on a noiseless pant. My heart picks up its beat and races. Thick, pulsing blood rushes through my veins, sending a roar to my head. Tingles jerk through my fingers in anticipation of contact with her firm, supple flesh. My cock doesn't seem to care that it's in danger of falling off from overuse. It's eager and hard and rearing to go.

The stool slides back as I rise and smooth my hand down her soft, graceful back. Her skin feels like warm silk and when she trembles beneath my touch, I swallow against the pressure that climbs into my head. "You take my breath away. You're so strong, so fierce." My fingers slowly trace her spine, testing the ridges down to the small of her back. "But you're also so fragile. Breakable."

She tenses and I blink, pull myself back from the edge. "Mason?"

I shake my head to clear it, then slide my hand to her ass. "Let's agree on something, okay?"

Unease lingers in her eyes. "Okay."

"No half-truths. I prefer silence to lies."

"I don't lie."

"You said you don't enjoy being spanked." My fingers glide between her ass cheeks and her wetness coats my fingers.

Her moan is jagged, as if she doesn't want to give it full life. "I don't... but I like what comes after... when you soothe me."

"Ah." I play with her clit and stop myself from diving in between her legs and gorging myself on her. "I'll always soothe you. That's a promise."

"Thank you. And Mason?"

"Yes?"

"I'll always tell you the truth, because that silence thing? It doesn't work for me."

"Understood."

She nods in return, then nudges her ass against my fingers. I suppress another smile, right before I bring my hand down hard, once on each cheek.

She jerks and almost lands on my plate. I toy with the idea of punishing her, *then* eating my dinner off her stomach, but I catch her around the waist and ease her to the ground before I cup her flesh and rub the sting away. She blinks rapidly and breathes hard for a full minute, then her eyes defiantly meet mine.

"Are you done?"

"I'm done. You okay?" I ask.

A single nod. "Yes."

She returns to her seat, and we resume eating. When I'm

done with my steak, I carry my plate to the sink. "You didn't answer me about staying over." I still want her to say *no*, take the matter out of my hands.

"I'll stay if you answer my question. Why do you use your silences like that?"

I turn and lean against the sink with my arms folded. I debate the pros and cons of granting her this morsel and mentally shrug.

"My mother once told me when I was about four that children were meant to be seen and not heard. She was annoyed with me for some slight or other. I took the suggestion a step further and hid in our mansion's attic for a week. When they found me, she was out of her mind with worry. I was somewhat appeased, but I still wanted her to pay, especially when she sealed the attic off so I couldn't hide there again. With that hiding place no longer an option, and not really efficient in the long term, I adopted silence as my recourse. I would go days at a stretch without speaking to her and I found that, in those times, she was nicer to me."

Keely's face is a picture of confused wariness. "So you're saying you were deliberately cruel so she would be nice?"

"Yes."

"And it worked for you then, so you've carried that trait into adulthood?"

"Yes."

She places her cutlery carefully on her plate before she pushes it away. "Did she... hurt you in other ways?"

This time, I don't stop my amusement from showing. "Are you trying to explain away my asshole-ness, Keely?"

"I'm trying to understand why you chose cruelty instead of, say... rebellion or the occasional brattish behavior."

"I found it more effective."

Sharp green eyes stare back at me. "Did you kick puppies too?"

"No. My puppy grew into a cherished companion who died fat, happy and of old age."

"So your mother was the sole recipient of your mind-fuckery?"

"No. My father was invited to the party when the occasion demanded it. And later, my wife. I'd say she bore the harshest brunt of it." I hear the dull roar in my head as the pressure increases, but I ignore it. I haven't loosened the chains of my past for so long, it's almost a relief to be having this conversation.

She slowly rises to her feet, but grips the edge of the counter, much like she did when I was fucking her ass. The reminder sends blood surging into my cock, but I concentrate on what she's saying with an intensity that almost scares me.

"And being cruel to them made you feel better about yourself?"

A bark of laughter rips from my throat. "Rarely."

Her face creases. "Then why? And why the hell did they stand for it?"

"Because I was the genius son who was the answer to all their problems. The proverbial golden goose who laid basketfuls of golden eggs. As long as they were bathed in gold, they didn't much care how I treated them. I held the power. They reaped the rewards of my power. A win-win situation."

"But you're divorced now, so I guess your wife decided she had enough?"

"No, enough was never enough for her. She relished being a pathological victim. She didn't leave me. I left her."

"Why?"

Why? I wonder for a second what she'll do if I tell her about Toby. That look of bewildered confusion on her face would change to horror. And then she would leave. I'm still not decided how I feel about her leaving, so I amend my answer.

"I decided to try *not* being a masochist for a change."

"So you didn't leave her for another woman?"

"That's the definition of ultimate cruelty in your book?"

Her eyelids sweep down and I straighten, not at all pleased that I can't read her expression.

"No, I'm very familiar with how cruel people can be."

The heavy ache behind the words jerks through me. I start to walk toward her, but she picks up her plate and approaches. I take it from her and toss it into the sink.

The sound of glass breaking makes her jump, but my hands capturing her wrists divert her attention to me.

"What does that mean?" I demand. I've just confessed my own cruelty, but the thought of anyone being cruel to her sends a spike of naked rage through my body. The strength of the feeling doesn't sit well with me. I don't know what to do with it, so I leave it sitting there, a large, shiny, unmistakable testament of my insanity and ask, "Who was cruel to you?"

She stares at me for almost a minute. Her mouth purses and her chin wobbles once, before she shrugs it off and shakes her head. "I don't know."

My fingers curl and I feel her pulse throb beneath my hands. "After what we agreed just now, that's how you respond? *You don't know?*"

Her gaze slides from mine and her head bows. "I know what we agreed. I'm telling you the truth. I don't know."

I stare at the top of her head and grapple with the need to probe deeper. I remind myself of the many reasons why I don't want to be pulled into her shit. Or anyone else's.

But I can't get the thought of her willingly throwing herself into the freezing ocean out of my mind. I know what she just said, and the powerfully intimate cloud of sadness building around her is the reason for her actions that night. I don't want to think about what would've happened if I wasn't there, if she succeeded. My chest starts to burn, and I heed the warning to get the fuck off the subject of her not being alive.

But I still want to know what she means.

"Keely, tell me."

"I can't," she says, and there's no apology or hesitation in her voice. "I won't."

I let it go. "Fine. Are you staying?"

She raises her head. "Do you want me to?"

I shove hard at the 95 percent. "Yes. Very much."

A single nod of acquiescence. "Then I will."

My fingers slide up her arms and into her hair, then I'm kissing her. I'm not gentle with it. I know her pain threshold now and I mean to straddle it hard. The pressure in my head decreases when she moans into my mouth and strains closer. My hand slides down her body to grip below her ass. It's all the urge she needs to jump up and curl her legs around my waist.

I stumble with her out of the kitchen and into the living room. I have a keen sense of direction and I know where the furniture is located, but I'm heady from kissing her, and I don't want to risk Keely getting hurt from one of the many bizarre sculptures Cassie left dotted around the place, so I reluctantly raise my head.

"Seven, lights please."

"*Of course, Mr. S. What mood would you prefer?*" A sultry voice fills the air.

Keely's eyes widen in the semi-darkness.

"You still have all your settings?" I ask.

"*Updated to zero one hundred, eastern standard time.*"

"Good, let's go for Fuck Mood Three Point O."

My mouth twitches at Keely's shocked gasp.

"*Right away, Mr. S.*"

A second later, the room is bathed in black and gold streams of light. They focus on the large double-wide sofa in the center of the room.

Keely's gaze swings from the sofa to my face. "You've trained a robot to provide you with mood lighting to suit you during sex?"

"Careful, you'll hurt her feelings if you call her a robot," I whisper in her ear as I carry her to the sofa and lay her down. A soft gold spotlight frames her face and she looks almost angelic. I stare for a moment longer, enthralled by her stunning beauty.

"Oh? What is she, then?"

"We've never really discussed it." I pull back, and when she eases her legs from my waist, I grip her knees and spread her wide. "I think she believes she's a cross between my physics professor and my assistant."

"And her name?"

I smile and pull the T-shirt over her head. "She's named after the sexiest *Star Trek* alien ever to grace a TV screen, of course." My dark mood evaporates as I stare at her body. The lighting isn't hitting her quite right, so I snap my fingers.

"*Yes, Mr. S?*" Seven responds.

"A dozen more gold beams around me, please."

"*Right away, sir.*"

Black light turns to gold and washes over Keely. She gasps and looks up at me with awe.

"Wow, consider me well and truly blown away, Mr. S," she says with exaggerated bats of her lashes.

I lower my head to kiss her. "Now that I know what really turns you on, I mean to impress you with my very big and very clever brain."

Her hands slip between us and she finds my cock. "Not just your big brain, I hope."

My mouth leaves hers to trail down the side of her neck. Her smell intoxicates me, makes me want to glue myself to her skin forever. "Everything big that takes your fancy is yours."

She giggles and I adore the sound. "So what else does Seven-of-Nine do?"

"Amongst other things, the usual—liaising with house-keeping services, temperature regulation, security." I debate whether to reveal the finer details of Seven's role. "She also keeps an audio file of every conversation that contains my voice."

Keely stares up at me for a few seconds before she jerks upright. "Are you saying she recorded us in the kitchen?"

"Yes. And when you stroked me off by the front door. And when we rowed. When I spanked you. When I encouraged you to suck my cock in the shower."

Adorable heat flares into her face. "Mason!"

"Calm down." I press her back onto the seat. "I won't keep the recordings."

The look in her eyes says she wants to trust me, but she doesn't. Because we're not there yet. And I don't blame her. I don't know if I want her to trust me. I certainly don't trust me.

"You want me to destroy it now?"

She sucks in her lower lip and nods.

"Okay. Seven?"

"*Yes, Mr. S?*"

"Delete audio files from 19.00 today."

"*Permanently?*"

I look into Keely's eyes. "Yes, permanently. And turn off audio until I instruct otherwise."

"*Understood. Deleting files.*"

I suck her lower lip into my mouth, then nip it with my teeth. "Happy?"

Her hands wrap around my back and her nails dig in when I transfer my attention to the pulse at her neck and lick it. "Fuck me now. Then I'll be happy."

A groan rumbles from my chest. "Take me out, baby. Stroke me with your clever, eager little hands."

She complies and pushes down my black sweatpants. My eager cock springs into her waiting palms, and she pumps me with unabashed vigor.

"Like this?"

"Yes, just like that." I take her mouth again, more desperate than I was a second ago. I can't think straight. I want to take my time with her, savor her. But something about Keely drives me wilder, leads me straight to the edge and dangles me over it. I thicken in her hands, and she gasps against my mouth.

"Fuck me, Mason. Fuck me hard."

The red haze that washes over me is all-encompassing. Despite having come three times already, my whole body is caught in a tsunami-sized wave of unexpended lust and ready to crash.

Sensation dovetails into my groin. I'm more than ready to drive into her.

I hook one arm beneath her leg and pull it high. "You ready?" I croak.

"Yes. Give it to me, please. Fill me."

I watch her gold-washed face, absorbing her every reaction as I drive my cock into her. Each sound she makes dials up my eagerness to learn more about what pleases her. I'm heavily invested in giving her what she wants.

Her mouth drops open on a soundless scream as she sucks me into her tight and hot cunt. "God, yes, just like that!"

"Fuck, Keely. *Fuck*."

I pull out and surge back in. She shudders beneath me as her back arches and eyes roll. I fuck her harder, faster. I bring my face to hers and drink in her every expression.

I'm a slave to that desperate, slightly crazed look in her eyes, the breathless panting that tells me she can't get enough of me. I want to fuel it, stoke it so it has no choice but to engulf us both.

Her nails dig into my ass and I give her more. Her delirious pleasure feeds mine and I feel the tightening in my balls.

"God, that feels so good," she moans.

"Take it, baby. All of it."

"Yes, *yes*."

One hand cups my face, and a part of my brain scrambles backwards at the intimacy. The fight it takes not to pull away cools me down long enough to prolong her pleasure. I slide my hand down her sleek back and tease her puckered hole.

I wait till she breathes out and plunge my finger inside her ass. Her insides clench hard around me. Stars explode across my vision and it's all I can do to hold on.

"Oh God, I'm coming, Mason. Oh." Her breath locks in her throat, and she begins to unravel in a series of convulsions that is spectacular to watch.

Her tight sheath milks me, and I feel the detonation from the soles of my feet.

"Shit, I'm there, baby. I'm going to fill you up."

Her broken cries release me from the precipice, and I plunge into pleasure. My cock throbs with furious spurts as I flood her insides. Her arms welcome me, and we tremble skin to skin.

When we can breathe without panting, I gather her up and climb the stairs to my suite.

Foregoing the shower, we collapse into bed.

"That was amazing. Thank you," she says in a drowsy voice.

I kiss her forehead but don't respond. A few minutes later, her sweet, heavy weight tells me she's fallen asleep.

My gaze fixes on the ceiling, and I ignore the panic flaring through me. I feel raw and exposed and I don't know how to cover myself up. I try to shut myself off, but the bolt won't connect.

I remind myself that I have nothing worth salvaging inside so it doesn't matter if the floodgates tear me wide open.

I remind myself that this is only temporary. Nothing is happening here that won't right itself when I'm back in Roraima. I breathe deep and open my mind to the dense and wild silence of the Amazon.

All I smell is Keely's warm body and intoxicating scent.

On the ceiling of my mind, big red numbers count down loudly from ninety-five. When it reaches sixty, I growl *Fuck you*, close my eyes and bury my face in Keely's hair.

18

KEELY

I jerk awake in the middle of the night. I'm disoriented for a minute in the pitch blackness. As memory hits, my eyes flash wide open.

I'm alone.

When I put my hand on his pillow, Mason's side of the king-sized bed is cold. I try not to freak out at the crazy thoughts swirling through my head. After what happened to me six years ago, I've never fallen asleep with a stranger. And although he told me a few eyebrow raising, deeply personal things last night that I suspect very few people know, he's still a near stranger. Which makes falling asleep in his bed, in his house, a stupid thing to do.

I move around in the darkness and turn on the bedside lamp, then make sure I'm really alone in the room.

There may be a perfectly good reason why Mason's not here. Maybe he woke up with a crazy idea for another contraption or sexy robot assistant, and he just had to get on it before he lost it. I get like that sometimes.

Or maybe he's an insomniac. Seriously, there could be a thousand different benign reasons why he's not in here with me.

Chill, Keely.

I sit up and look around the stylishly minimalist room. Nothing in here tells me what time it is. My purse and phone are both downstairs so there's no way to check. I slowly lie back and put my head on Mason's pillow. His scent fills my nostrils, and I smile at the delicious aches in my body.

After my five-month long dry spell and a good few years of mediocre sex, I've well and truly hit it out of the park with Mason.

He's given me the sort of sex women write in girly fonts in their diaries and brag about to their less lucky girlfriends over cocktails.

Bethany is going to get an earful the moment I'm out of earshot of Mason Sinclair and his sexy, eavesdropping robot.

Crap, the robot...

I jerk the covers over my nudity when I realize Mason only mentioned audio files earlier. I never thought to ask him about cameras. Surely he wouldn't do something so intrusive?

Reassuring myself doesn't work, especially not when my mind throws up our conversation in the kitchen. The cold and clinical testimony of his deliberate cruelty toward his family sends another shiver down my spine.

The man who fucked me so thoroughly on the sofa was the kind of man to gossip to girlfriends about. The man in the kitchen was capable of just about *anything*. Including secretly recording our sex for whatever purpose he might choose somewhere down the line.

The thought disturbs me enough to send me out of bed. Since my clothes are still in the wash, I grab a cashmere blanket from the bottom of the bed and wrap it around my shoulders.

Mason gave me a brief tour after our shower earlier, but the mansion is immense, easily big enough to accommodate five families, and I get hopelessly lost several times before I decide to give up. Making my way back to the central staircase, I hear a sound coming from a room at the end of the second-floor hallway.

I approach quietly, not wanting to disturb Mason if he's working. Lights flicker from beneath a heavy closed door, but I hear the sound of faint laughter before it stops. I bite my lip and toy with retreating back to bed. The clock I passed in one of the many hallways reads 3 a.m. It's early morning haunting hour, and I decide that whatever Mason has gotten out of bed for is none of my business.

I start to turn away, but the repeated sound of laughter stops me. A child's laughter, joyous and unfettered. A few seconds later, it cuts off again.

My heart pounds as I put my ear to the door and shamelessly eavesdrop. The irony doesn't escape me that I'm doing the same thing I ripped into Mason for doing the first time we met. When the door swings an inch inward, my heart jumps into my throat. I freeze and wait for Mason's inevitable appearance and the reciprocal ripping to follow.

Nothing happens.

Fuck it.

I refuse to cower behind the door like a naked, spineless thief. I knock lightly. "Mason?"

Nothing but silence greets my knock. I take a deep breath and push the door open wider.

The outer edges are shrouded in darkness, but the center of the room is bathed in sky-blue light reflected from the screen. My gaze skates across what turns out to be a cavernous cinema room to the single occupant in the large club chair.

Mason is seated upright, staring dead ahead at his screen, a remote clutched in his fist.

"Mason?" I try again.

He doesn't respond, but my instincts tell me this isn't one of his mind-fuck silences. He has no awareness that I'm here.

My gaze darts to the screen, and I see a freeze-frame of a boy of about five or six with dark brown hair. His head is turned away from the camera, but by the curve of his cheek and chubby chin, it's clear he's laughing.

My breath catches as Mason lifts his hand and points the remote at the screen. The picture jumps forward in jerky slow motion, and the boy's face gradually swivels toward the camera.

He's gorgeous, with warm hazel eyes, a button nose and a mischievous expression. He's missing one front tooth, but his smile is so broad it almost splits his face. My insides twist painfully as I stare at the screen.

A sound rips through the room and cuts like a knife through me, drawing my attention back to Mason. With each frame, I watch his face morph into a mask of raw agony.

But that's not the only expression on Mason's face. My heart stops as I read the other emotion: murderous, incendiary rage.

The boy's face fills the screen and Mason presses the button to hold it.

I'm not sure how long we all stay frozen. My brain tries to grapple with the myriad reasons for the naked anguish blanketing him and the tears filling his eyes. None of them are good, and I've known enough anguish of my own to accept that, in this case, Occam's razor will prevail. I'm staring into the heart of a worst-case scenario, and I die inside as I stand there, knowing I can't offer the man who saved me from an icy death anything worth a damn.

When I finally force my legs to work, I retreat silently and make my way back to the bedroom. I lie awake, torn between sneaking downstairs to hunt down my clothes so I can make a quick, cowardly getaway, and waiting for Mason to return. I'm not sure what I'll do when the latter happens, but it seems like the better thing to do. Creeping away in the middle of the night because I don't want to confront potentially heart-shredding revelations reeks of self-preservation, and I'm well within my right to do so, especially in light of actively fleeing my own secrets.

But leaving feels wrong.

I stare at the exquisite crown moldings that decorate the ceiling, my hands gripping the sheets hard enough to cause my palms and knuckles to scream out in pain. I don't let go because I don't want the pain to go away. I don't want to swap this superficial pain for the one that lies beneath the surface of my mind, seeping poison.

But it's already rising.

It's too late.

I see *his* face. The cutest nose. His tiny, perfect hands. Eyes of indeterminate color framed by the most perfectly tipped lashes. I remember the absurd thought I had looking into his eyes. How glad I was that they were nothing like mine. Because then he wouldn't see into me, wouldn't know the dark, horrific thoughts lurking in my heart, eating away at the fierce love I felt for him the brief time I held him in my arms.

He screamed as the thought grew. Loud enough to attract concerned nurses to find out if he was okay. I wanted to join in the screaming, shout that of course he wasn't okay. How could he ever be?

How could I?

Come to think of it, I may have screamed. Because that blessed pinprick took everything away to a land of fluffy clouds dripping red rain. And by the time I woke again, all was well. My mind was as empty as my arms, and the only thought causing me the briefest discomfort was deciding which shade of Jell-O to have.

Pressure builds in my head and chest and I jerk to the side. My breath explodes from my lungs in sickening gulps as I try not to cry out. But one sob emerges, followed by a dozen before I force myself to stop crying. I have no right to tears. I have no right to grief.

How can I, when I gave my own child away seconds after he was born?

* * *

Sunshine pours through half-open curtains the next time I open my eyes. My face is tight from dried tears, and I'm still alone in Mason's bedroom.

I debate whether to take this turn of events in my stride, like the tough take-no-shit Brooklyn girl I've falsely projected all these years, or curl into a pathetic ball and feel sorry for myself. I suck in a breath and opt for the former. I knew coming into this that it wouldn't be sustainable for more than one or two brief encounters, three tops.

Clearly, I didn't account for the swiftness with which we'd go from banging each other's brains out to me being huddled under the covers, eating my sobs. I erroneously believed that the electrifying connection between us was purely sexual in nature. Now I know it's our shared pain that keeps us riveted to each other.

That hellish self-loathing and murderous rage I sense in him is the yin to the yang of the twisting, helpless blackness that bloats my soul and slams on my self-destructive button whenever I lower my guard.

We may not know the minutiae of our dark and monstrous pasts, but *it* knows *us*. And as surely as I know how to bullshit my way into a first-class seat on any airplane, I know that talking myself into prolonging any further contact with Mason will end me.

As it is, the decision is taken out of my hands. The moment I flip over to rise, I see the note propped up on the bedside table. It's folded in half, and a tall black box tied with cream silk ribbon sits beneath it.

I perch on the edge of the bed and open the thick fancy paper.

A taxi will arrive half an hour after you wake.
Your clothes are washed and pressed and on the dresser.
Help yourself to breakfast. The contents of the black box
is my ~~par~~ gift to you.
I would be honored if you would accept it.
Mason.

The crossed-out word absorbs my attention. More than knowing he's left me alone in his beautiful mausoleum of a house—why the fuck else would he leave me a note?—and more than the fact that he's left me a gift with this "fucked and dumped" note, it's those three letters that I can't look away from.

~~Par~~.

Two things strike me as I stare hard at the word.

Firstly, he should've scrubbed the whole note and written a new one. It's the polite thing to do. But he deliberately left it there for me to see it. And what? Wonder what he really means?

Play pathetic word games with myself and read things into the word that I shouldn't?

And secondly, he's gone out of his way to be hurtful.

Because I'm damn sure the word he was aiming for was *parting*. He returned to the room and left me a *parting* gift without bothering to wake me and have a simple conversation.

I toss the note when I realize I'm falling for his mind-fuckery. I should know better. Sure, he is a grand master at it, I'll give him props for that. But I'm intelligent enough to know the game he's playing with me. And yet, I can't dismiss my hurt feelings as I use the bathroom, put on my clothes and head downstairs.

"Good morning, Miss Benson—"

"Fuck!" I jump and almost miss the last step. My hand flies to the banister to steady myself, and I cling there for a moment, trying to stop myself from expiring from shock. My gaze darts around even though I know there isn't a physical body attached to the voice. "Umm... can you hear me?"

"Of course. Coffee is ready in the kitchen, and the car service will be here in twenty minutes."

I curb the urge to flip a bird at the reminder that I'm to exit stage left without delay. At least Mason hasn't left me to find my own way back to the hotel. "Thank you, Seven."

I head for the kitchen to retrieve my purse and phone and grind to a halt when I'm confronted by the banquet laid out on the breakfast counter.

Next to each plate stands a tiny flag announcing its contents. Pastries and condiments, a tiny domed plate that reveals piping-hot Moroccan baked eggs, a stack of caramel pancakes. Red velvet stuffed crepes, coffee and assorted juices complete the feast.

As a fuck-off breakfast, it excels enough to make my gastric regions tingle with pleasure, and were I in the mood, I would've scoffed to my heart's content. But the events of the early hours are still too raw and lie too heavy on my heart and mind to contemplate food.

I turn away from the spread and pick up my phone. I have fifteen minutes until the car arrives, and I want to call Bethany badly. But Mason's robot is listening, and the conversation I want to have isn't one I want Mason Sinclair hearing anytime soon. Or ever.

So I make my way back to the living room, perch on an Eames armchair and avoid looking at the wide sofa where Mason fucked me to paradise and back last night.

As the minutes tick by, it occurs to me that although I've assumed he isn't in the house, he could be in another wing. And even though his note was succinct, I find myself asking, "Seven?"

"*Yes, Miss Benson?*"

"Is Mason still here... in the house?"

"*No, Miss Benson.*"

A tiny fountain of relief jets through me. I clear my throat. "Can you tell me where he is?"

"*His coordinates show he's on the Quai Rainier III.*"

He left me to return to the *IL Indulgence*. "Thank you, Seven."

"*You're welcome, Miss Benson. The car is pulling up into the driveway now. Have a good day, Miss Benson.*"

I stand on rubbery legs and smooth a hand over my head. As I turn toward the door, I spot something I didn't see in the dark and seductive lighting last night. A picture on the massive mantle framing the stone fireplace that's tucked behind two giant iron and wood sculptures.

Everything inside me screams at me to ignore it, but my feet propel me to the opposite side of the room. I take the picture down and stare at it.

Mason has his arm around a brunette with a pixie cut hairstyle and delicate, almost doll-like features. She's holding on to his hand and staring up at him with naked adoration that's almost embarrassing to witness. She's the type of woman who would look like a debutante at fifty. The kind who would most likely have men falling at her feet well into her dotage.

But it's the look on Mason's face that holds my attention.

He's staring straight into the camera with the piercing look that I'm used to. His eyes gleam with amusement, but his mouth is curved in an almost cruel line that sends shivers down my spine. The look that says, *Your soul is mine and I intend to fuck it from here to eternity.*

I slowly replace the picture and my heart pounds as I head for the door.

It opens before I touch it, and sure enough, a sleek Mercedes sedan is pulling up to the front door. The driver exits and hurries to open the door for me, and I slide into the back seat. I don't look at the house as we circle the driveway and head for the gates.

Instead, I find Bethany's number and hit dial. She answers on the second ring.

"Are you alone?"

"No, but I can be," she answers immediately. "Give me a sec."

I hear talking in the background and grit my teeth and wait for her to extricate herself from her insanely possessive fiancé.

"Okay, I'm alone now. What's up?" she asks as we drive through the gates.

The stunningly picturesque view of Monaco and the Cote d'Azur is spread beneath me, but I can barely look at it, never mind appreciate its beauty. Instead, I twirl my hair around my finger and try to find the right words.

"Uh oh, should I be worried?" Bethany says.

"What?" I say vaguely.

"You're not speaking. And you're *never* lost for words," Bethany replies.

"I..." I stop, think about my next words and throw caution to the wind. "I fucked Mason last night. I woke up this morning and he was gone."

Bethany gasps. "Whoa, really? He doesn't seem like a—"

"Hit it and quit it kinda guy? I didn't think so either," I lie, because when it comes down to it, I have very little idea what kind of guy Mason is.

"Did something happen? I mean, something besides awesome sex, because I know you're ace in that department so it can't possibly be the reason he left."

I allow myself a small smile. "Aunt Keely loves you hard for that endorsement."

A few seconds tick by. "So...?" Beth probes.

I worry my lip and wonder if I'm letting myself in for a heart-to-heart I may not like. "Maybe."

"Shit, Keel, you're freaking me out. He didn't hurt you, did he?" Worry squeaks her voice.

I think of the note with the word crossed out. "Nothing Aunt Keely can't handle. But—"

"What the fuck does *that* mean?" Beth screeches.

"It means I called because I want to find out if there's anything I need to know about Mason, you know, in case my pussy ditches every last ounce of self-respect and jumps all over his cock the next time it comes within fucking distance," I joke, even though I get the feeling that's exactly what Little Keely would do given half a chance.

"Anything like what?"

"Dammit, Bethany, do I need to spell it out? Am I in danger here?"

"*Danger!*" Her voice hits a new decibel, and I'm not surprised when she swears. "Why the fuck would you be in danger? What the hell happened, Keel? Shit, Zach just walked in. I'm sorry, but I have to tell him—"

"No, you fucking don't! I swear to God..." But I already hear a muted, heated exchange.

"Sorry, I'm calling you back on FaceTime, babe." Her voice fades for a bit. "Zach, she wants to know whether she's in danger with Mason. I sure as hell want to know, too." She rings off, still muttering.

I wait until the line beeps and I activate the app. They're standing in the kitchen, with Zach's arms around his fiancée. "Hey, Zach," I greet half-heartedly.

He nods in return. "You okay?"

"Oh sure, you ask me that now after you sicced your friend on me?" I snap.

"He's the best in the business for what I needed done. But that wasn't why you called, of course."

"No, it wasn't. So is there something I should know?" I press.

Silence greets my question. Zach clears his throat and Bethany's head snaps up to glare at him.

"Zach? Why aren't you saying something?" she shrieks.

"Peaches, calm down."

"No, I won't. If there's something Keely needs to know, tell her now."

Zach sighs and my heart drops like a fucking stone. "Shit, there is something, isn't there?"

"Yes, but you can't hear it from me."

I shut my eyes against the bright sunshine as the car winds its way down into Monte Carlo.

"Why the f—" I stop and clear my throat. "Why the *hell* not?" I amend.

Bethany's eyes widen. "Did you just stop yourself from

swearing? Are you sure you're okay, Keel?" she asks, her eyes full of questions.

"Stop asking me that," I snap, absolutely sure now that this call has been a mistake.

Zach's expression turns speculative. "Why does it matter? Do I get the impression that this is going to continue when the trip is done?"

"How about you answer the question or be guaranteed the impression of my foot up your ass the next time I see you?" I hate that I'm dying to know whether a man who's fucked me and dumped me is worth pursuing, and I don't stop my anger at myself from bleeding all over my friends.

Zach does that infuriating half-quirk thing with his eyebrow that sets my teeth on edge.

I inhale and exhale to calm myself down. "Zach, please," I beg.

Now they're both wearing the same ridiculous, stunned looks. Zach recovers first and pats his concerned fiancée when she leans closer to the screen. "Sorry, Keely. It has to come from him. But my suggestion would be to leave it alone."

"Like you wanted me to leave you alone with your baggage last year?" Bethany glares at him over her shoulder. "What the hell *is* it with you men and your shoulder-it-alone bullshit?"

"Peaches, are you ever going to let me forget that?" He leans over her and slides his fingers into her hair. I catch the slightly glazed look in her eyes even as she responds.

"Hell no—"

"Gee, I hate to come between your vomit-worthy prelude-to-sex tiff, but can we focus on me for a tiny second, please?" I snap again.

Bethany immediately looks contrite and Zach stares into the screen at me. "You know he's been away for a while?"

"Yes, somewhere in the jungle. I also know he was married and now divorced, that he owned the yacht before you bought it, that he's a genius inventor and has a brilliant, if sometimes cruel mind." I stop for a second, then plough ahead with the suspicion that's looming at the back of my mind. "I also know that he has —or had—a son?"

Zach stills, and his nostrils flare before he hides his surprise. But I've seen enough to cause my heart to shred with dread.

"He told you all this?" Zach asks.

"Some of it. The other details I found out on my own. So am I safe? Please tell me straight. The mind games I think I can deal with, but I need... other reassurances."

I shake my head at Bethany when her face creases in concern, but my eyes return to Zach.

"He's complicated. And I'm not saying that to be fucking cryptic or mysterious. You're not safe if you decide to pursue a relationship with him. But you're strong. If you choose to take him on, I get the feeling you'll handle yourself more than adequately. Worst-case scenario, if he fucks with you beyond your comfort zone, I fuck with him. Good enough?"

Despite my like/hate relationship with Zachary Savage, I feel a warm glow. I glance at Bethany, and she's wearing that sickening love glaze again as she gazes up at him.

I roll my eyes. "Good enough."

19

KEELY

Six years ago

I dress nice in my short, black leather skirt and a sexy fuchsia halter top. Ashley has grudgingly loaned me her knee-high heeled boots in exchange for doing her laundry for a week. Since I tend to do it most days or risk brain damage from the skanky smells from her gym bag, it's no biggie. I would've gone for plain black platform heels, but Ashley assured me guys go wild for leather boots, especially stilettos. And since she seems to have a hot guy on the go every other night of the week, I've decided to trust her on this crucial point.

Leo's town car arrives at eight sharp.

I try to act cool and not giggle when the chauffeur doffs his cap and calls me ma'am. A few students drifting out of the frat house across the street whistle when I expose a little thigh sliding into the back of the car. Although I blush, I'm more than a little pleased by the confidence-boost I get from their male appreciation. I settle into the back of the car and, as we exit the campus, check out my subtle make-up in the window reflection.

We head south on Westwood Plaza, then hang a right on Wiltshire. I'm dying to ask where exactly the party is, but it feels as if it's something I would know, and I don't want to appear unsophisticated. I open my small clutch and check that the seventy-five dollars I tucked in there earlier—because my mom has ingrained in me never to leave home without a means to get back—is still there, along with my phone, a packet of gum and a tube of lipstick.

I debated whether to bring my driver's license, but I decided against doing so. Since this is a private event, and I have a photo of my license on my phone that I can always access if I need to show my ID, I'm cool with not stuffing too many items into my tiny fuchsia purse.

We hit traffic, and I start twirling my hair as anxiety churns through me. I catch myself and try to play a couple of games of Bejeweled to distract myself instead. After I fail the same level five times in a row, I put my phone away. I'm too nervous to concentrate anyway. I look out the window and see that we're climbing into the Hollywood Hills. The houses are getting bigger and farther apart. Below me, L.A. is a blanket of fuzzy twinkles.

I face forward and catch the driver staring at me with a touch of jaded curiosity that immediately gets my back up. Shit, should I have asked his name? Or made conversation? I hope he doesn't mistake me for another self-absorbed rich brat. I attempt a *hey-I'm-one-of-you* smile, but his gaze shifts and refocuses on the road.

I'm wondering what to say to him when we swing off the road and stop in front of a pair of towering black gates. He keys in a code and eases the car onto a white gravel road. Sleek sports cars and limos litter the tree-lined driveway, but there's no one outside, which makes me wonder if and how late I am for the party. And also whether I need to text Leo to let him know I'm here.

I toss the idea out. It doesn't seem like a cool thing to do, and I don't want to come off as *Needy Nerd*.

When the driver stops under a super-wide portico and comes round to open my door, I attempt another smile. His face remains impassive.

"You'll need this." He hands me a flat black box, then doffs his cap again. "Enjoy your evening, ma'am."

He disappears round the side of the house, and I'm left alone on the doorstep. I open the box and stare at the computer-chipped wristband, a tiny earpiece and a mask arranged on a bed of velvet.

Right, Keels, you're definitely not in Kansas anymore.

I feel a little sick with nerves as I slide the wristband on and insert the earpiece. The mask is a bit big, but I look on the bright side—better a bigger fit than for it to be too small.

When I'm done, I look for a doorbell, but there isn't one in sight. There's no visible handle. I chew on my lip for a minute, then knock.

Five minutes later, I'm still standing on the doorstep. I check my phone on the off chance that Leo has realized I'm not by his side yet. There are no messages. I'm about to hit my home button when a Porsche roars up the driveway and skids to a halt, barely missing a column under the portico.

I pretend I'm checking my phone as a guy and girl about my age approach the door. They're wearing masks and earpieces too. The guy looks me over and smirks, before holding his wrist-band to a black box at the top right-hand corner of the door.

The box clicks and the door opens. He ushers his girlfriend in and eyes me over his shoulder.

"You coming?" he asks me.

"I... Yeah, sure."

I start to walk in, but he plants himself in front of me. "Did you forget? You need to code in." He points to the black box.

"Oh, of course. I was miles away." I raise my wrist and I hear another click.

We walk into a stunning entryway with a statement-announcing sweeping staircase that rises from the middle and curves into two wide arcs. A guy in a tux holding a clipboard and a similar earpiece to the one I'm wearing approaches. "Names?"

"Jeeves," says the guy who's just entered.

"O," his girlfriend supplies.

The guy with the clipboard traces a finger down his page and nods. "I have you both. Proceed to the east wing, please."

The couple beam, and the guy smacks his girlfriend on the ass as they skip away.

Right, so clearly the east wing was the place to be.

I paste a cool smile on my face as he turns to me. "Name."

"Keely Benson."

Startled eyes widen as he stares at me. "Umm... did you just — Fuck, I don't want your *real* name. I need your codename."

I flush a humiliating red and I think about making one up, but he only needs to look on his list to catch me out in the lie. In the end, I go with the truth. "Sorry, I wasn't given one. I'm actually here to see Leo—" I stop when I realize I'm probably not supposed to say Leo's name either. "The host of the party invited me. He's my... umm..." *Friend? Date? BFF?* I feel foolish, standing there, trying to explain a relationship that has so far only lived in my imagination. "Can you point me in the direction of where the host is, please?"

He shakes his head. "I need your name before I can grant you access to the wings."

"Okay, just give me a minute." I turn away, still drowning in humiliation, take out my phone and start tapping. The next moment, I'm texting air.

"Sorry, there are no phones allowed at the event." He depresses the button that shuts down my phone before he slips it into a Ziploc-type bag and seals it with a padlock. He hands me the key. "It'll be returned to you at 3 a.m., when the event ends. Now, about the name..."

"You've just confiscated my only means of proving to you that I'm an invited guest. How else am I supposed to—"

"Is there a problem here?"

My head snaps round at the familiar voice and my mouth drops open. "Prof—" I clamp my mouth shout at the last second, before I commit my third faux pas in three minutes.

What the hell is my psychology professor doing here? And dressed smartly in tailored slacks and a button-down shirt, unlike his normal jeans, sweater and casual jacket combo. He's wearing a mask too, but since I've recognized him immediately and he's making no attempt to deny knowing me, I'm getting the feeling the masks are a casual prop, not a serious attempt to disguise identities.

"Are we okay here?" he asks again.

"We're just straightening out this guest's identity."

"It's okay. I'll vouch for her."

Clipboard Guy frowns. "Are you sure?"

"Yes, I'll find Dorian and let him know. In the meantime, put her down as..." Professor Harding eyes me from top to toe before he smiles. "Put her down as Holly Golightly."

That earns him a frown. "You sure about this, Moriarty?"

Professor Harding nods. "I'm sure."

The other guy stares at me a moment before he scribbles my codename down. "East or west wing?"

"We'll head west first."

Another note is made before the guy heads off and leaves me alone with the man I all but accused of sexual harassment one short semester ago. A man who just saved me from getting turfed out on my ass before I get a chance to deflower myself all over Leo Brummer.

Silence reigns as Professor Harding, or Moriarty as he's named himself for tonight, stares down at me from his six-foot height. Under the lights in the hallway, his dark brown hair gleams and his slate-grey eyes pierce a little too forcefully into my psyche. I know a few of the girls in my year are a little dreamy over his young Richard Gere looks, but something about him makes me jumpy.

Nervously, I clear my throat. "Umm... thanks for vouching for me."

"No problem, Holly. Come on," he says as he steers me left. We pass through a set of double doors made of rose-etched glass, and it occurs to me that for what is supposed to be a party, the place seems a little too quiet. There's no music pumping from speakers and no voices raised in merry chatter.

If not for the dozens of cars outside, I'd assume I'm at the wrong place. I clear my throat and think of something witty to say. But I'm hopelessly tongue-tied, and my brain chooses that moment to remind me what an utter asshole Professor Harding has been to me this semester. I debate whether to apologize again to clear the air once and for all, but rebellion hardens my spine.

Despite my apology at the end of last semester, he's chosen to single me out to crap on for weeks now. Fuck if I'll let him see how much that's upset me. But he *did* vouch for me so I can't exactly ignore him.

"So... what happens in the west wing?" *And will Leo be there?*

I'm proud of myself for not asking the second question, and for not coming out with a lame line like—*do you come here often?*

"This is your first time?"

I can feel his gaze on me as we walk through another set of doors and down a long hallway. How big is this house anyway? And why the hell is it so quiet? "Yes. You?"

He stares at me for a second longer than necessary, then smiles. "No. It's not my first time."

We turn a corner and stop in front of a black panel. I start in surprise when it parts to reveal an elevator. Professor Harding enters and extracts a key from his pocket, which he slides into the slot. He spots me hovering outside and raises an eyebrow. "You coming?"

I want to shriek, *Hell no*, because my freak-out button is definitely glowing hotter than ET's finger by this time, and I want to say to heck with it and just leave. But leaving will mean returning home to New York still a stupid virgin. Am I going to turn chicken this close to the finish line?

For the first time in my life, I feel guilty for shouting at the TV screen whenever a bimbo actress pulls a stupid stunt like the one I'm contemplating right now. For the first time in my life, I know what it's like to be paralyzed with the sheer impossibility of my quandary. Go back upstairs and somehow convince Clipboard Guy to return my phone so I can call a taxi and hope I can pay the exorbitant fare back to campus, or get in the elevator to fuck knows where, where I might be successful in grabbing Leo's attention long enough to get him to seduce me away from my virginity?

"Don't waste my time, Holly." Professor Harding's sharp voice pierces my frantic contemplation.

I want to ask why he's bothering with my fake name when we're alone and he knows who I am, but I don't want to bring further brimstone down on my head in the classroom, so I make up my mind, nod briskly, and enter the elevator.

The single button below the *close door* sign plunges us downward.

The moment the doors open, a wall of noise hits me.

Contrary to the speculation by the guys on the quad that there would be only thirty people, I count more than double that, easily. And better still, there isn't a single drug-fueled orgy in sight. In fact, everyone's fully dressed and the drinks and food are flowing like at any above-average college party. Not that I've been to heaps, but still...

I smile and mentally pat myself on the back. Then jump when a hand grabs my elbow.

"This way." Professor Harding/Moriarty nods to the left.

We weave through a crush of people at the bar and head to the far side of the room. I keep my eyes peeled for any Leo-shaped bodies, but the sea of people, in what looks like a dark-ened underground ballroom, is too thick for me to single anyone out.

Dotted around the room on tall stands are wild and varied assortments of drinks. Moriarty stops in front of one and plucks an amber cocktail from the table. I have no way of knowing which drink is which, and I sure as fuck am not going to ask my professor, so I select the least harmful-looking one and take a cautious sip.

"*Ugh!*" The sharp taste hits the back of my throat and attacks my taste buds. My eyes water and I try not to splutter all over myself.

"That's 100 percent-proof premium vodka."

"How do you know?" I ask.

He grips my wrist in a tight, almost painful hold, and raises the glass so I see the tiny white sticker on the bottom. I nod and subtly pry myself from his grasp and look closely at the other glasses. They all have assorted colored stickers on them.

"What do the colors mean?"

He sends me a scathingly bored look. "I'm not your tour guide, Holly. Part of the adventure is figuring things out yourself," he replies. "You look like your cerebral cortex needs a good work out."

There is it again, that tone of voice that makes me wonder if he's coming on to me, or just making casual conversation. Again, my spine tingles a warning I'm at odds to decipher. I feel foolish experiencing an element of danger that my brain tells me is barely minimal, and yet I can't ignore it.

I set my drink down and glance around. Relief pours through me when I spot the definite figure of Leo Brummer heading my way. When he reaches us, he nods warily at Professor Harding.

"Moriarty."

"Dorian. I've delivered your guest to you. That means you owe me one for making me play nursemaid."

What the fuck? I start to hold up my hand in a *hey, I'm right here* gesture, but a look passes between the two men that freezes my hand midair.

"I already paid you back what I owe you." Leo's voice is a touch defensive and a lot pissed off.

Moriarty shrugs. "You want to stop paying, don't keep racking up the tabs. As long as you keep slipping, I'll keep collecting."

My radar is most definitely tweaked, and I watch Leo's face twist in anger. His jaw clenches as Moriarty stares him down for a full minute before Leo lowers his gaze.

"East wing. One hour." He glances at me, then back at Leo before he disappears into the crowd.

Leo grabs my hand and walks me away from the center of the room.

"What was that about?" I ask the moment we're seated at a table away from the noise.

"Nothing." He plucks a stickered drink that looks like the skin-peeling vodka I just spat out and downs it in one go without flinching.

"Oh, come on, Leo. That was most definitely *not* nothing."

"Fine, it's none of your business!" he snarls.

I suck in a hurt breath. "Whoa, no need to go all Wolverine on my ass."

He stares at with me with those impossibly gorgeous blue eyes for a full minute before he glances away with a grimace. "What the fuck are you doing here, Keely?"

My body jerks in shock as if he's thrown a bucket of cold water over me. "Umm... you invited me, remember?"

He grips the back of his neck and continues to avoid my gaze. "I... Shit, I shouldn't have. I don't know what the hell I was thinking," he mutters under his breath.

Now my whole body feels like a giant polar ice cap. "Wow. Okay. Excuse me for thinking we were friends and that we could spend some time together." I surge to my feet and dart away from the table.

Tears sting hard and fast. I blink, then bump into a body. Someone curses, but all I want to do is get the fuck away before the humiliation tsunami bearing down on me sucks me under.

"Wait! K— Shit, I don't even know your codename. Hey, wait!" Leo grabs my arm.

"Let go of me!"

He pushes up close behind me and leans into me. "I can't," he whispers. There's a peculiar note in his voice that triggers a touch of disconcertion, but my humiliation stops me from processing it.

"What does that mean? Of course you can. You just tell your brain to tell your fingers to work. It really is quite simple."

"You don't understand, Keely," he whispers, his voice darker and more ominous than before.

I turn and glare, wishing I could hate him as hard as I ought to, but one look in his eyes and I'm done for. Even now, after he's sent me back to that cave of rejects I thought I'd finally emerged from, I can't walk away. Especially not when I spot the dark suffering in his eyes that triggers a well of sympathy in me.

"What's going on?" I ask softly.

He glances at the guests swirling around us and shakes his head. "Not here."

When Leo Brummer slides his fingers through mine and walks me through an archway to a smaller, quieter room, I'm ready to forgive him anything.

On the way, I spot a few girls glancing my way with naked envy in their eyes, and I barely stop myself from openly gloating. The evening may have started bumpy, but it's just taken a turn for the awesome.

We skirt a dimly lit dancefloor to a seat—a love seat, no less —and Leo hands me a drink. I glance at it warily, and he smiles. "Don't worry, it's mineral water. See." He shows me the sticker underneath. "Aqua stands for water."

I return his smile and take the drink. I down half of it— making sure not to let go of Leo's hand—before I put it down.

He's still wearing that broken, slightly desperate expression, and I squeeze his hand. "For someone throwing the party your friends have been talking about for weeks, you don't seem to be enjoying yourself."

His mouth turns down and he shrugs. "These fucks are not

my friends. I don't know half of the people here. But they could be, if I wanted them to be. I can have everybody in the whole fucking world be my friend if I want them to be." He doesn't sound happy about that observation. In fact, he sounds down-right jaded. I can't imagine someone as rich and famous and drop-dead gorgeous as him being jaded about anything. He's the type of guy who *can* have the world at his feet if he chooses.

I look around the room and frown. "Then why are they here?"

"This is Hollywood. I don't need to have friends to throw a party."

"That makes no sense to me."

He stares at me with a mixture of sadness and resignation. "You're sweet, Keely. So fucking sweet."

I don't do my ecstatic ferret-on-hot-coals dance because he says that like it pains him to say it. I feel like I need to besmirch that observation, so he's not so pained. "I'm not that sweet. Not all the time anyway."

One corner of his sexy mouth lifts in a pseudo-smile. "Oh yeah? Tell me something bad and dirty you've done."

I search frantically for something clever. "Well, there was this one time when I slashed—"

"*Color Code Caramel. You're up.*"

"*Shit!*" I slap my hand over the earpiece and rip it out before the loud voice shatters my eardrums. "What the hell was that?"

Leo slowly rises to his feet, takes out his earpiece too. He pockets it and tugs me to my feet. "It means it's time to head to the east wing."

The image of the TV bimbo walking to her doom flares in my brain again. But this is Leo Brummer. The man of my dirty, dirty dreams.

What's the worst that can happen?

I follow him through another underground archway and down an even longer corridor. It occurs to me that I could get lost in this underground mansion and no one would find me for years.

The stupid thought sends a shiver down my spine, but I concentrate on Leo's warm hand clutching mine.

We reach a set of double doors and he keys in a long code I have no hope of remembering. He reaches for the door, but then pauses. He glances at me and his mouth opens as if he's about to say something. He shakes his head and pushes the door open.

The first thing I hear is a scream.

The first thing I see is a naked girl, tied up with white rope on a chair under the harsh spotlight in the middle of the room.

The first thing I smell is the cold, acrid stench of my own fear, right before the bimbo reaches through the TV and slaps me hard across the face.

20

MASON

"Excuse me, sir?"

I tense at the hesitant voice behind me because I know what the crew member is going to say.

"Yes?" I force the word out.

"She refused to accept it again, sir."

I sigh. Burned bridges are aptly named for a reason. It's why I took steps to ensure mine are well and truly burned by leaving Keely alone in my house with nothing but a *Dear John* note penned with a dash of senseless cruelty. At the time, I'd no doubt whatsoever that I was doing the right thing. The specially crafted gift was the full stop that should've punctuated our brief, hyper-charged association.

By her not accepting it, things feel unfinished.

I grimace at the barefaced lie I'm force-feeding myself. It feels unfinished because I'm suspended in a limbo of my own making. By sticking around, and not heading straight to the airport once my setup on the yacht was done, the hooks I ripped from what remained of my tattered life are finding me again, like parasitic magnets seeking freshly mangled iron.

"What exactly did she say? Repeat it, word for word," I demand as I stare unblinking at a far distant shoreline receding in the darkness.

I hear an uncomfortable shuffle, but I care very little for the crew member's sensibilities. I grip the railing and stare into the dark churning waters that trail the *IL Indulgence*. All I care about is finding a balm to this insane gnawing in my stomach. Even if it's through second-hand words that'll no doubt attempt to put me in my place.

"Are you sure, sir?"

I remain silent.

"Umm... she said, umm..." He clears his throat. "'Tell that motherfucking fucker to take his motherfucking parting gift and shove it up his motherfucking ass. And if he tries one more fucking time to return it, I'll personally make sure the chef serves him arsenic in his next fucking meal, so I can fucking watch him die a miserable fucking death.'"

Laughter barks out of my chest. I turn around and lean against the railing. Daniel, the guard and crew member assigned to me, is standing in my master suite's living room with the black box in his hand and a chagrined look on his face.

"Right. I guess after six attempts in three days, I should take the hint, huh?"

He looks embarrassed for me and shuffles some more. "I guess..."

I nod, despite feeling the twist of the knife. "Thanks, you can leave it on the table," I say.

He hurries to place the box on the console table near the cabin door, then pauses. "Same time tomorrow, sir?"

I shake my head. "No. I think it's time for a more... personal approach."

He nods eagerly, even though he looks puzzled. "Okay. Well, if you need anything else, sir, just let me know."

He hurries out and my gaze swings to the box Keely left behind four days ago when I all but kicked her out of my house in Monte Carlo. I burned the note after discovering it on the floor the next day, even as I reeled with a tinge of guilt for the nastiness I glazed the note with.

That lingering guilt alone should make me rethink this doomed path. That and the fact that I woke up in a cold sweat next to another human being for the first time in almost six years, and then proceeded to open myself up to the lethal cocktail of rage and grief.

I should be making a swift and decisive retreat.

Because if those reasons aren't enough, as of yesterday, there's Cassie. And my mother. Gluttons for my brand of punishment. Or architects of their own special strain of Stockholm syndrome. A fucked-up type of delusion, which makes them think that letting me—and the vileness that inhabits my soul—get close enough to them will somehow heal all of us.

It doesn't matter how many times or how many ways I demonstrate my singular lack of care for what they think, they always come back for more.

My gaze lingers over the black box as my mind focuses on the one woman who's holding fast to her decision not to come back for more.

I finger my phone with the full knowledge that I should accept her decision. But I know I'm going to ignore the warning flashing in my brain. I draw it from my pocket.

Subject: My Gift

Got your message. Shame on you. It's not polite to refuse a gift.

—Mason

I goad because I'm certain it's the only way I'll get a response. Her reply pops into my text box a few minutes later.

Subject: My Gift

It is when it's from a self-confessed asshole. Especially one who refused to see me when I returned to the boat on Monday. I got your message loud and clear. So here's my gift to you—Fuck off.

—Keely

PS—Happy to arrange for the message to be delivered in sign language for the seventh and (hopefully) final time, if words and their meaning elude you.

I lean back against the railing and consider my answer before I reply.

Subject: My Gift

Full disclosure: I wasn't in a good place on Monday. Accept my gift, and I'll consider accepting yours. I'm heavily into sign language.

—Mason

I hit send, knowing I'm exploiting that vein of compassion I glimpsed in her tough armor back in my kitchen. She may fight it, but ultimately, Keely Benson is a curious and compassionate creature. I stare at my screen until her message pops up.

Subject: My Gift

Full disclosure: I shouldn't have stayed. Being horny

made me greedy. But you were still gone when I woke up. For
both our sakes, stay gone.

   —Keely

Thoughts of Cassie and my mother recede as the challenge
of how quickly I can dominate this situation heats up my blood.

Subject: My Gift

   I can't. We're on the same yacht. Besides… you're different. Also, greedy and horny work for me. Let me make it up
to you.

   —Mason

Subject: My Gift

   We've managed to avoid one another for four days. If you
ask me, we're doing brilliantly. Also, in what way am I different? (Not that I care, of course)

   —Keely

Subject: My Gift

   In all the ways that shouldn't matter, but do. In all the
ways that matter, but shouldn't.

   —M

   PS—Happy to repeat that in Pig Latin. I hear that turns
you on.

She doesn't reply for almost five minutes, and I wonder if
she's still annoyed at my overhearing her Pig Latin confession to
Bethany back in Montauk. When she eventually replies, my eyes
narrow at her answer.

Subject: My Gift

It doesn't. I have to go. Goodbye.

—K

I let her go for a minute. Five minutes. Ten. My fingers tremble as I ponder the abruptness of the last text and fight against the screaming instinct that urges me to let this be.

My soul craves the calm wildness of Roraima. My gaping heart howls with the rage of loss that has never dimmed. I'm a walking razor blade. The odds of her not being hacked to pieces just by being around me are ludicrously low. I already know she's caught a glimpse of the seething mess beneath. She caught a glimpse, and I responded by kicking her out of my bed and my house.

Logic dictates I should let her go before I risk turning her into another Cassie. But no. Keely will never be a Cassie. She's her own unique brand of titanium-plated strength and kitten-soft weakness. Both are lethal in their own way. Both shimmer with a mesmeric compulsion that keeps me tethered to this time and place.

So I choose to fuck logic in the ass.

I call up Seven's app and get Keely's exact location. Keely probably won't be happy to learn I've known her exact location at every moment since she entered my house last Saturday, but I've never claimed sainthood.

I swap my T-shirt for a dress shirt and tug on my leather jacket. When I leave my suite, my set jaw and lack of eye contact with other guests ensures I'm left alone. Even though only a handful of the crew know I'm still on board, word has a way of getting around, and I don't intend for anyone to get in my way of reaching Keely asap. Head down, I text as I walk.

Subject: Reconsider.

I haven't spent nearly enough time taking care of your pussy.

Come be greedy all over my cock.

—M

I smile when she answers almost immediately.

Subject: Reconsider

For someone who claims to have lived under a rock for years, you're quite adept at sexting. The answer is still no, btw. And please stop contacting me. I have work to do.

—K

Subject: Reconsider

My big brain makes me a quick study. I also have a very big cock that wants very much to get to know you better. Re: Work. We're sailing. You work when we dock. Sailing time can be fucking time.

The advantage of having been the previous owner of the super yacht is that I know the quickest way to get from A to B. In this case, I need to reach the Pleasure Deck Bar three floors up without being forced into conversation by anyone I know. And from the guest list I've seen, at least half a dozen people on here will recognize me if they spot me.

I walk past the adult entertainment lounges, absently satisfied when I notice that all the rooms are in full use. Zach is certainly earning his money.

Keeping an eye on the little red dot that's my destination, I avoid the plush guest hallways and head past the crew quarters to the private elevator I installed when I first bought the yacht.

Back in the day, it'd been a good escape route for when I

needed to board my chopper and leave before anyone knew I was gone. Now I use it as the quickest way to get to Keely and try not to be ticked off that she hasn't responded to my text in five and a half minutes. Or that it's coming up to midnight and she's still in the bar.

Exiting the elevator, I immediately find her. She's leaning against the far corner of the bar, staring down at her phone. The dark blue sheath dress she's wearing molds her ass and thighs before stopping a touch too short at mid-thigh level.

Her hair is tied in an elaborate up-do. The slender line of her neck and the way she arches her body as she balances on her heels sends the blood roaring straight to my cock.

I watch her catch her lower lip between her teeth. She brings her phone closer to her face and that's when I catch her expression.

I'm close enough to see she's not in the text application, but reading an email. And whatever she's reading grips her enough that it's fully ensnared her attention from what's happening in the room.

Which is a good thing, because two couples are pile-fucking on the loungers nearest to her, and almost every other guest is in a state of near or complete nudity.

I catalogue my deeply disturbing reaction to her being in this room—hell, on this yacht—and compartmentalize it to be dealt with later. My more immediate focus is the mixture of anger and dread on her face as she stares down at her phone. As I watch, her expression crumples with abject terror, and she shakes her head and swallows hard.

What the fuck?

"Keely?"

I realize I didn't speak loud enough for her to hear and

wonder if that's my subconscious handing me another chance to get the fuck out of Dodge.

I double-fuck both logic and my subconscious, pocket my phone, and take another step toward her.

And every single impulse I've tried to push away comes revving back. When I'm a handful of steps from her, it dawns on me that this is the second time in my life I've willfully abandoned self-preservation.

I *will* pay dearly for this course of action. And I'll most likely take her down with me. But the twinge of guilt isn't enough to keep me from her. Neither is that look of utter desolation on her face.

In fact, I'm sure my last steps are propelled by that look alone. I relish the chance to focus on something else. This I can control.

On Saturday night, before the nightmare that propelled me to seek out self-flagellation, I shut myself down at 60 percent. I have a while to go before the critical mass hits. Besides, I have a feeling she knows a little of what to expect from me. She's beautiful and intelligent. She's also intuitive.

And she stood inside the door of my home cinema for six minutes and forty-four seconds.

She's seen Toby. She's seen me. I choose to find a little absolution in all of this.

A loud grunt from one of the foursome pulls her attention from her phone. She blinks, and although her face remains a shade paler than I prefer to see, she starts to turn her head.

I charge forward and fist my fingers through her hair before she gets the chance to satisfy her curiosity.

"You owe me a text," I growl in her ear, even as I close my eyes and greedily inhale the silky warmth of her skin.

She gives a tiny *ump* and tries to suppress a shudder. "You owe me the courtesy of taking no for an answer." Her voice holds an echo of whatever brought that look to her face.

Something lurches in my chest.

I push it away in favor of the thing that I need the most. Me, between her legs, pounding to forget. "How about an apology for the way I left things on Saturday?"

Her head swivels toward me, but I'm too busy breathing her in to look in her eyes.

After a few seconds, she clears her throat. "Go on." Her voice quivers slightly.

"I'm sorry for leaving things the way I did. You didn't deserve that. I apologize unreservedly," I whisper against her ear while nuzzling her neck.

This time, her shudders reverberate through her body. "Wow. Either you really want something, or civilization has finally worn you down." Her voice is stronger, sharper. She's fully in control of whatever emotions waylaid her.

Enough to meet me on a level playing field.

I raise my head and stare at her, give her another glimpse of my intentions. She returns my gaze for a handful of seconds before she swallows. "No, I guess I should take back the second part?"

I glance at her dark-screened phone. "You owe me a text," I say again.

"I would only be repeating myself."

"Do you accept my apology?"

Her gaze shifts from mine, and I can tell she wants to hold on to her anger. Finally, she sighs. "Yes."

"Then come to my suite and open your gift."

"Said the spider to the fly," she mutters under her breath. "I really don't need a parting gift, Mason. And I'm not one of those women who craves a token of her presence in a man's bed."

"That wasn't what it was. I made your gift before you agreed to fuck me. It's specially designed for you. If you refuse it, I'll have to destroy it."

Her eyes rise to meet mine. "Crap, now you've got me all intrigued," she says.

"Enough to leave this fuck-fest and come take a look?"

Her head starts to turn, and I tighten my fist.

"Your answer doesn't require a visual inspection of said fuck-fest."

"It's past midnight. I really should get to bed." She licks her lips and I suppress a groan.

"You should. After you make a detour via my suite."

She glances at her phone, and her nostrils quiver slightly before she inhales. "No. I'm sorry. I can't."

Irrational anger rattles through me. "You can't? Why not?"

She frowns at my sharp tone. "I don't need to explain myself to you."

"Does it have anything to do with that email you were reading just now?"

She tries to jerk out of my hold, but I don't let her. "What is with you and prying?" she snarls, but the edge of her voice quivers again.

That barely detectable echo opens a fissure inside me, and emotion I recognize as concern fizzles outward. It's unsettling enough to make me growl, "Answer me, Keely."

"Why?"

"Because—" I stop when the woman being double pene-trated on the lounger across the bar starts squealing like an overeager porn star. "Dammit, let's get the hell out of here."

I pull her to my side and clamp my arm around her, prepared to frog march her out of there if necessary. To her credit, she comes along willingly.

I don't stop until we reach the elevator. The moment it shuts behind us, she glares at me. "What did you see?" she demands.

Keeping her locked to my side, I press her against the wall. "Why? What does it matter?" I toss back.

"It matters a great deal that you're reading my personal correspondence! It's a huge invasion of privacy."

"Are you sure you want to talk about invasion of privacy?" I ask softly.

Her eyes widen, then cloud over as she stares up at me. "You know."

"About you standing outside the cinema room in my house at three in the morning on Sunday? Yes, I know."

I say nothing else, and questions fill her eyes. I have her on the back foot and I can't help it. I press home my advantage.

"We can talk about you invading my privacy. We can talk about what I did or didn't see on your phone. Or we can talk about you coming back to my suite to open your present. Those are your only choices, and I think you'll choose option three. You know why?"

"Enlighten me."

"Because I don't think you want this thing between us to be over. Not just yet. You enjoyed what we did too much to walk away, despite how I left things. Your feminine pride wants to make me suffer for that. Consider your punishment fulfilled." I pull her hand over my rock-hard crotch so she feels her power over me. "I've lived with this for four days, Keely. I need you to take care of it. In return, I'll give you what you need."

Her hand slowly closes over me, and stars explode across my vision. "And what exactly do you think I need?" she asks huskily.

"You need a man to own you. Completely. To make you forget whatever is on that email that you want to forget. And you want to forget, don't you, baby?"

Her eyelids flutter, and she looks away from me, but her hand keeps its grip on me. "Maybe, but—"

"Let me be that guy. I'll do an exemplary job."

The elevator door opens. We both ignore it as she lets out a slightly strained laugh. "Wow. Is this where I fall at your feet like you predicted?" Her head tilts to one side. "You probably won't believe me, but I'm falling at your feet right now... in my head. Now if only I could get my body to actually follow through—"

"It's where you stop being a smart ass for a second so we can work this out."

Her chin lifts and Titanium Keely is back. "Work it out? Why would I want to do that? Whatever it is you think I want from a man, I'll be a fool to consider you for the job. Even if I were under any illusions, your little note made things more than clear."

I lean in closer until her hand is squashed between my crotch and her pelvis. The friction is a little too much to bear. I breathe deep and try to focus. "Shut the hell up for a minute and think about what you saw in that room, Keely. Did you really expect me to carry on blithely after that?" I ask, my voice a hard bite intended to impart that the subject is only a point-making one, and not an invitation to discuss.

Her face twists with a mixture of understanding and anger. "No, but I didn't expect to be thrown out on my ass, either."

I fist her hair and make sure she's fully focused on me when I deliver the next statement. "Stop expecting me to behave like every other guy you've known. You know I'm not. Just as you're nothing like any other woman I've known. Accept me for who I'm not and for what I cannot be for you, and take what I can be."

"A Fuck God, come to rescue poor Keely from a path of sexless desolation?"

I trail my fingers over her racing pulse and her collarbone until I reach her erect nipple. I flick it with my nail and absorb her shudder. "A sexual dominant, who can make you forget whatever it is you're running from. At least for a while."

Her hand clenches around her phone, and for a moment, her face creases with utter fear and devastation. I bite my tongue to keep from demanding to know why.

"I... don't like being dominated. If we do this, my control will be my own."

I pull back and stare into her eyes. "Think about what happened on Saturday. And think about how much better it can be with me in charge. Are you really afraid of that much pleasure?"

I place a finger over her mouth when she starts to respond. "Before you say anything, let me make you another promise. Nothing I do will be against your will."

She swallows and nods. "Okay. How... how long is a while?"

I run my tongue over her lower lip and wonder if she's aware of how needy and pleading her tone turned just then. I suppress a groan when her mouth parts for me. "Until we reach our final destination in Greece, you'll be mine to fuck and use how I please, completely, without exception, with your pleasure and oblivion a guarantee. Nothing is off the table unless you use your safe word. Agreed?"

21

MASON

The mention of the safe word makes her grimace. "Do I have to have one?"

"Yes."

Her beautiful eyes gleam with a touch of rebellion. "Do I have to call you Master or Sir, too?"

I take her hand in mine and tug her out of the elevator. I don't respond until we're outside my suite. I cage her against the door and wrap one arm around her tiny waist.

She feels so fragile that I'm a little unnerved by how much strength she holds in her slight body.

"I would prefer it, but if you need some time to get used to the idea, I can wait."

One curved eyebrow lifts. "You think you can get me to do that in ten days?"

"Are you wet for me, Keely? Right at this moment, are your panties soaked at the thought that I'm going to be fucking you hard and possibly rough in the next half hour?"

Her breath hitches. "That wasn't what—"

"Answer me," I press, letting authority throb in my voice.

"I... Yes."

"What if I promise you that every time you call me Master, you'll get wetter, hotter? That your pleasure will triple with the knowledge that handing me that little control will guarantee bliss beyond your wildest dreams?"

"I'll say, it's a nice idea in theory, but logic says I have to believe what I'm saying in order for it to work."

I smile, and her lips part on a single, delicious exhale. "Then I look forward to putting the theory to the test."

I key in the code, and the door swings open behind her. When she stumbles, I catch her and walk her backward into the suite.

Her hands grip my arms and she stares at me. "Why do I get the feeling I've just walked into a clever trap?"

"Because you're an astute woman. A woman I've been dying to fuck again for days."

The moment my mouth touches hers, she moans. I kick the door shut and taste her deeper, harder, my hunger a force I can barely contain. My cock throbs painfully by the time I pull back.

I need to do this right.

I never actually thought of how much time we have together until she mentioned ten days. Now all I see is that damn neon clock, counting down again. I have a little over a week to appease the raging monster within, to find that jagged peace, which will carry me through the tormented wasteland of nightmarish days, weeks, and months that is now my life.

"Strip." I barely recognize my voice as I stop in the middle of the living room.

Her eyes widen. Apprehension and anticipation flit over her features.

My gaze skates over the curves I want to fuck and bruise. She's hot everywhere. Even her dainty little fingers...

I spot the damn cellphone still clutched in her hand, the death grip on it like she's welded to it.

"Put the goddamn phone down, Keely," I growl.

Her head snaps downward. "What? Oh..."

I stalk to her and hold out my hand. She regards me warily for a few seconds before she gives me the phone. My fingers curl over it, and a burning desire to know every last one of her secrets explodes through me. I could know them if I choose to, and for a heartbeat I weigh the risk/reward ratio.

Her tongue darts out and licks her lower lip and the rewards swing back in favor of carnal pleasure.

"I said *strip*. You make me ask you a third time, and this takes a turn you won't be ready for."

Her fingers flex, and she's torn between smart-mouthing me and doing as I ask. Her need wins, and one hand goes to the side zipper.

I hold my breath as she pulls it down. She's braless, and I can't make up my mind if that pleases me or pisses me off.

"You always go without a bra, kitten?" The urge to touch a finger to that hard, furling peak smashes through me, but I stay my ground.

"When I feel like it, yes."

"From now on, I tell you when to wear a bra and when to go without. Got it?"

Her mouth gapes, but knowledge flares in her eyes as she stares at me. Slowly, she nods. "Okay."

I shake my head. "*Okay* doesn't do it for me. Try again."

Her lashes quiver as she fights against narrowing them. "Yes, Mas— Mason." She chokes on the word she almost said.

I eat the smile threatening to explode and cup my cock, which *will* explode if I don't fuck this woman in the next three minutes.

Her gaze drops to where I'm stroking myself, and she quickly shimmies out of her dress and kicks it away. I pause to stare at her lush curves, caught between visions of demon-burying bliss and soul-shredding guilt. The opposing emotions threaten to tear me apart.

I fist my free hand and ground myself with deep breaths.

"Are... are you okay?" she asks hesitantly.

I want to laugh. I want to howl. I want to destroy myself. I want to destroy her. "No, I'm not." I release the first few buttons of my shirt and tug it over my head. "Slide your middle finger between your pussy lips, kitten. Show me how wet you are."

Heat flares over her cheeks. "I don't need to. I'm wet."

I pause. "Is that a *no*?"

Her face burns brighter, and in that moment, I want to adore her and punish her at the same time. The dichotomous feelings deepen when her thighs squirm against each other. "I promise I'm really wet, Mason. Do I have to touch myself?"

Mild shock unravels through me. "You don't like touching yourself?"

She mangles her lips and her lashes sweep down. "Not really. But I like it when you touch me." She lets loose a sultry smile and sways toward me.

"Are you trying to distract me, kitten? And did I say you could move?"

She freezes. "I..." A sigh passes over her lips. "I don't know how to play this game, Mason."

"Your first mistake is thinking this is a game. Do I look like I'm playing?"

Wide green eyes stare back at me. She catches a glimpse of the dark, turbulent arousal spiking through every emotion burning beneath my skin. Slowly, she shakes her head. "No."

"No, what?" I test her softly.

"No... sir." She pauses and swallows.

I let her response rest between us for a dozen heartbeats. "Touch yourself, Keely. Two fingers this time. Look at me when you do it. It'll please me."

Her left hand twitches, then slowly rises to rest on her hip. It stays there for an eternity before her fingers tiptoe into the thin strip of hair arrowing to her pussy. She squirms some more, and I see for myself how wet she is. My mouth floods with the hunger to taste her plump clit, but I wait, my temperate soaring with the need to devour her.

Her fingers slide between her legs, and she gasps. The sensitive skin around her nipples pebble as she glides her fingers back and forth. I take a careful step nearer and watch her eyes darken.

"Are you embarrassed?" I ask.

"No."

I circle her, stalking closer with each navigation. "Are you turned on?" I ask when fine trembles shake her body.

"Yes," she whispers raggedly.

"Show me how wet you are, baby."

She groans as she drags her fingers from between her legs and displays her wetness.

"Ah, fuck, baby. You want to see what it does to me?"

She swallows again. "Yes."

I wait a beat, and she inhales.

"Yes, sir."

"Does saying that demean you?"

"No, sir."

"Does it give you pleasure to say it?"

She starts to shake her head, but stops. "Not quite, but I know you like it, so I'm okay with it."

I show my pleasure at her truthful answer with a smile, and she gives me a tiny, need-laden one back.

"Good. Very good, kitten. Now get on your knees. Put one hand between your legs and the other behind your back."

She sinks to her knees without question, and my head pounds with the power filling my body. In that moment, my adoration of her exceeds any other emotion, and I have to breathe deep to get myself under control.

I take a few steps back and unzip my pants. I pull them and my boxers off and glance up to see her wetting her lips.

Her eagerness weakens my knees. "Are you touching yourself?"

"Yes, sir."

I catch her chin in my hand and bring my mouth to hers. "Slip your fingers inside and describe the feeling to me."

Her groan bathes my lips, and I kiss her hard and fast before I straighten. My quick study keeps her gaze on me as her fingers slide faster between her legs. Her trembles are now full body shudders, and her chest jerks with each breath.

"I'm slick and hot. I feel... I feel like a ball of electricity is concentrated between my legs, and if I move the wrong way, I'll explode."

"You're not allowed to explode. Not until I say so."

Her face contorts, but she jerks out a nod. "Yes, sir."

God.

I lock my knees to keep from lunging for her and ramming my cock deep inside her.

I grab the root of my dick and rest the tip against her mouth.

"I want you to suck on my cock while you picture me filling that tight little cunt. Visualize me stretching you until you imagine you can't take any more. Then think about me ramming those extra inches inside you, until your whole cunt is mine. Until I own every millimeter of you."

She groans again and the weight of arousal threatens to drag her eyelids closed.

"Open your mouth, kitten."

She opens her mouth and I slide in, all the way to the back of her throat. Desolation and rage slam into raw bliss, and I throw my head back. I have to take several deep breaths before I can speak. "Are you doing as I asked, kitten? Are you imagining me in your sweet pussy?" I grit out, my unreasonable fingers tightening in her hair as I seek the back of her throat.

"Hmm," she mumbles around my thick length. Her tongue flattens as she greedily sucks me down, and my balls tauten and ache with the agonizing pleasure spiking up my spine.

"Are you getting wetter?" I push harder, merciless in my wrenching desire to enslave her, to use her as an instrument of my temporary salvation. "I need you soaking. Because I want you to take all of me. Every single inch. Do you hear me?" I pull back when her eyes water and she gasps in several breaths.

"Yes... sir." Her voice contains the exact amount of obedience and deference that adds fuel to the fire licking through my blood.

I catch her chin in my hand as her tongue flicks over my head. "Fuck, Keely. You're either lying about not being good at this or you're one hell of a study."

"I'm a quick study, sir." She sucks me into her mouth in rapid hard pulls that make me grit my teeth against the urge to blow my load down her throat right here and now.

"You're fucking stunning is what you are." I return to fucking her mouth in long, fast thrusts. She holds steady like a champ and suction sounds fill the room. My control frays, unspooling faster than I can hang on to it. I squeeze my eyes shut to delay the inevitable, but it's no use. "God, baby, I'm coming."

She grunts her approval, and the vibration from the back of her throat flings me to the edge. I open my eyes and she's staring at me. The look in her eyes sharpens my pleasure with the added edge of fear. It's a look that says she sees me. All of me. The dark and the darker. The mangled and the desperate. She sees me. And she has me. If only for an instant, she has me.

A rough, wounded sound fills the room. A moment passes before I become aware that it's my grunt, my precursor to release. Pleasure I have no right to floods every cell, radiates through me in a futile cleansing, which I clutch with both hands and greedily consume. "Fuck. Oh, fuck. Keely!"

"Hmm," she groans. Her eyes widen as I explode and gush into her waiting mouth. The sight of her beautiful, flushed face and the hand working herself below triggers an even longer release. My lungs empty on harsh pants, and I can barely stand as she takes everything I have to give and swallows every drop.

I tremble and brace myself as guilt roars back. The stench and strength of it nearly knocks me off my feet. I battle through it and loosen my grasp on Keely's hair. My cock slips, wet and already wanting again, from between her swollen lips.

"Did I please you, sir?" she asks with a touch of smugness.

I stagger to the table and pick up her gift. "You did, kitten, which is why you get to open your gift before I fuck you."

She looks up at me with a question in her eyes. "What is it?"

"Get up, go into the bedroom and lie face up on the bed. Then you can open it."

The hand between her legs slows, then almost reluctantly leaves her slick wetness. She rises and sways for a second before she finds her feet. With her hair caught up and her neck bare, she's a long, graceful creature I can't look away from.

I follow her into the bedroom. When she kicks her shoes off and lies down, I place her gift on her stomach.

She looks from the box to me, uncertainty in her eyes. "I don't really like sex toys."

My gaze drops to the soaking wetness between her legs and my cock jerks to life once more. I kneel on the bed, grasp her knees and pull them apart to expose her pink flesh. "Can we agree that some things you believed you didn't like before we met need reassessing?"

A blush creeps across her face, and she tries to close her legs. I spread her wider and nod at the box. With pursed lips, she pulls apart the ribbon tying the box and opens the lid.

She lifts and examines the curved, almost transparent device attached to twin-gartered loops with breathless curiosity. "I haven't seen anything like this before," she murmurs.

"That's because it's a prototype." I lift her legs and place her feet on my chest. "You ready to put it on?"

"I don't know. Am I?" she asks nervously.

I caress her calves until her legs start to fall open. "Do you trust me with your body?"

Her gaze catches mine, and she knows why I've framed the question that way. She can trust me with her body, but she won't be wise to trust me with anything else. "Yes, sir."

"Then put it on."

A swallow moves her throat before she lifts one foot off my chest to tug the garter on. Once the second harness goes on, she tugs it until the large ladybug-shaped device rests on top of her pussy and frames her outer lips.

"It's a perfect fit. Hold still for a sec, kitten." I reach for the tiny button and flick it on.

She jerks off the bed, and her hands dive between her legs. "Oh, *fuck!*"

I capture her arms and stop her before she can pry my invention off. "No. Hold still," I say again.

Her head thrashes on the pillow. "I can't! Oh, God, it's... it's... Jesus, what the fuck *is* that?"

I press the device until it holds her tight. "Nothing but a little power-assisted suction. Relax. Let it do its work."

"Relax? God, Mason, I feel as if..." Her face flames and she grimaces with reluctant, decadent pleasure.

I lean over her and nip the corner of her mouth. "You feel as if a thousand mouths are sucking your clit?" I whisper.

"Yes! How is it doing that?"

I smile. "Trade secret. I can tell you, but then I'll have to fuck you until you forget."

A dirty smile curves through her pleasure. "Aren't you going to do that anyway?" She gasps through another wave of delight.

My mouth trails down her body, until I find a stiff nipple. I bite, then suckle, and I'm rewarded with a long, sexy purr. "I am, right after you thank me properly for my very thoughtful gift."

"Thank you, sir," she moans. Her fingers slide over my shoulders to fist the back of my head. The touch of unease that accompanies the subtle embrace threatens to unsettle me, but I push it away and concentrate on her pleasure. "Oh, God, that feels incredible."

I position my cock beneath the device. Her wet heat beckons me. "Let's make you feel even better, kitten."

I ram inside her and glory in her scream. My position pushes the device firmer against her pussy, and the residual electricity reverberates through my pelvis.

"*Oh*," she cries. Her whole body shakes, and I absorb each tremor, inside and out.

She tightens around me as I withdraw and push back in. Her

tightness blows my mind, and I'm at once grateful for her months of abstinence and insanely jealous of any other man who's come before me.

"Does it feel good, kitten?"

Her hips roll to meet my plunge and another moan erupts. "Yes, oh God, yes."

"Do you want more?" I demand harshly, pushing hard enough to make her wince.

Still, she nods eagerly. "Yes, sir. Please, sir."

A primitive roar fills my head and increases my thrusts. She's still not taking all of me, so I rear back and spread her wider and higher, until her knees touch her breasts. She's exposed completely, totally at my mercy, and power throbs from my balls to my brain. I fuck her harder, faster, denying her nothing, while taking everything. When her head bangs against the headboard, I pull her down and start over again.

"God, I can't take anymore!" she cries.

"You can. Take it, baby. Take it and come for me."

"Yes, please. Make me come, sir," she pants.

I reach between her legs and flick the button to mid-setting.

She screams instantly and tightens around my cock. I lean over her and capture her thrashing head. "Open your eyes."

Her lids pop open and her mouth gapes on a stunned, breathless O. She starts to unravel, and I glimpse a flash of fear and vulnerability as she cedes complete control to me.

"Mason," she whispers, right before huge convulsions seize her.

Her pleasure detonates mine, and I grunt as my semen floods her. We stare deep into each other's eyes, our gazes mirroring our lust-soiled turmoil.

I kiss her bruised mouth without disconnecting our gazes.

So I see when her wide-eyed stare whisper-screams: *What did you do?*

And I see my reply in her eyes: *I just fucked your shredded soul.*

22

KEELY

Our arrival in Palma de Mallorca saves me from further examining the depths to which I've sunk and the happy little freak I've become. For the last two days, I've barely left Mason's suite. I've been fucked in so many ways and so many times that I struggle to think of a time when an orgasm wasn't lurking at the back of my consciousness, ready to plough through me at the touch of Mason's hand. My cunt is Pavlov's Dog and Mason my tuning fork. He sets me off with a look across a room, a quirk of his eyebrow, his clever fingers dancing over a keyboard while he writes some insane code I have no hope of following.

I call him "sir" freely, with no inhibition or hesitation. The power I derive from seeing the effect that the address has on him is mind-boggling. The power he derives from having me claim him as my master staggers me.

I scoffed when he promised me I'd fall at his feet and stay there willingly. He proved me wrong in less than a day, and for the first time in my life, I'm happy to concede total defeat and hoist my white flag of surrender proudly.

After what I've been through, I promised myself never to

lower my guard or myself to a level of debasement. Little did I know that I'd find the most intense release and the most fulfilling sexual power on my knees.

There's also a feeling of vulnerability about possible addiction to a way of life I didn't contemplate this time last month. Mason Sinclair overwhelms me. He dominates me, takes me out of my mind like the best drug, and I crave him more with each order I follow, each bite of his nails in my hips, each plunge of his perfect cock that makes me forget my real life.

The moment distance is thrust upon me, however, the floodgates of fear and dread part, and I'm back in the bar, staring at my phone, reading that third email, instead of Mason's dirtier texts.

This one also came with a picture.

In the middle of the underground from somewhere in the Hollywood Hills, a black chair stood under a spotlight. White ropes dangled from it with careless artistry and sinister implications.

Someone has a record of what happened to me in that underground room in the east wing of the Los Angeles mansion six years ago. Someone who's bided their time until now.

For what purpose? Blackmail?

Since we set sail from Monaco, my phone has *blooped* with two further anonymous emails. The fourth and fifth pictures only show different angles of the same chair.

By now I'm in no doubt further emails will arrive. In my feeble attempt not to remain a victim, I responded with a 'Who are you, and what the fuck do you want?' after the third email.

My answer was a *System Delivery Error* fuck you in return.

If their aim is to torment me, they're succeeding. I'm torn between being supremely pissed off and cowering in a corner in a ball of shit and piss. Somewhere in the middle ground is Mason, and the pit of cheerful depravity I've hurled myself into.

In eight days, when I'm back in New York, I'll deal with this thing.

I dress in a black and white block dress and platform heels in preparation for taking the guests to their first venue of the evening.

Salamanca is Mallorca's most exclusive private club, and six of the guests are booked into the VIP rooms from eight till two in the morning. So far Mason has declined interacting with any Indigo Lounge sessions and a part of me is relieved. Enduring him 24/7, especially when I'm overcome with the need to blurt out my rigid fear, is wearing me down a little. Immersing myself in work, I hope, will bring the clarity I need.

If that fails, there's always Bethany. I smile a little at the thought of my best friend.

My feverishly-preparing-for-her-wedding best friend.

That slight feeling of resentment I first experienced in Montauk returns, and I feel like a little shit.

Blanking my mind, I'm tugging a brush through my newly washed and curled hair when knuckles rap on my suite door. I check my watch.

There's still half an hour before the three launches arrive to ferry the guests to the marina, and pre-departure cocktails don't start for another fifteen minutes.

I pick up my chandelier necklace and secure it as I walk to the door. My hand stills at my throat when I see Mason framed in the doorway.

"Mason? What are you doing here?"

We agreed to see each other when I returned from escorting the guests. As far as I'm aware, he planned to work on another top-secret invention in the room he secured within the bowels of the ship.

"Now, what way is that to greet me, kitten?" he asks softly.

The sound of his voice sends needy distress signals to my pussy, and I'm already getting wet by the time he steps forward and enters the room.

My pulse is jumping all over the place as I shut the door behind him. "I wasn't expecting you, that's all," I reply. I bristle silently at my defensive tone and look at him.

He's staring at me with an intensity that scares me a little, so I walk into my bedroom and pick up the matching earrings. Through the mirror on my dressing table, I see him fill my bedroom doorway. He's wearing an expensive black dress shirt, tailored trousers and a matching dinner jacket, and his hair is tamed a little from its usual touch of wildness.

So far, I've seen many facets of Mason Sinclair, which keep me enthralled—the mad genius, the sometimes cruel lover, the alpha dominant, the spiritually decayed man who keened his loss and rage in that room in Monte Carlo—but I've never seen him as this suave sophisticate. I don't know what to do with that, so I just let our gazes connect. Until even that becomes too much, and I lower my head.

"You were going to invent some bright and brilliant thing. And I was going to work. Wasn't that the plan?"

"Plans have changed. I'm coming with you tonight."

I shouldn't feel this delighted at the thought of his company. It speaks to an addiction I haven't entertained since my doomed crush on Leo Brummer. I'm getting attached and I don't know how to stop myself. So I try and play it cool by heading for where I placed my clutch and my tiny leather jacket on the bed earlier. He takes the jacket from me and helps me shrug it on, before he extracts a box from his back pocket.

My eyes widen when he holds it out to me. "What's that?"

"The bright and brilliant thing I was working on earlier."

"Another prototype? For me?" My addiction ratchets up another notch and my hands shake as I take the box from him.

To date, Mason has introduced me to six gadgets that haven't seen the light of a commercial market. To say I'm a convert from a staid no-sex-toys girl to a happy-nympho guinea pig is stating it mildly. Yet another thing that scares the shit out of me. While I finger the box, I tell myself perhaps I should be a little selfish and call Bethany. I really need clarity here.

"Can I open it later? We need to get going."

Mason's eyes narrow, but he nods.

I hurry out of the room and I'm halfway to the elevator by the time he reaches me. His fierce stare as we head to the top deck burns me alive. Mason has no compunction when it comes to watching me. In fact, when it comes to me, he has no compunctions, full stop. He stares for as long and as hard as he wants to. And sometimes he takes pleasure in watching me squirm. I'm at squirming point when the elevator slides open.

I stumble onto the wide, stunning, topmost deck of the *IL Indulgence* and immediately busy myself with the unnecessary task of ensuring each guest is happy. My job is that of grand overseer. I have hostesses assigned to each guest and I don't need to personally check on each one unless there's a problem. But I do anyway.

When it's time to board the launch, I feel a hand on the small of my back. I look up into Mason's set face. He's not happy. A different sort of panic bolts through me.

I sway against him, and he clamps his arm around me.

We stay pretty much glued together all the way to the private club. He comes with me when I go to check with the manager

that the burlesque performance is on schedule. He stays by my
side through dinner and the strip show that follows.

"How long is this thing going to last?" His voice is a
displeased rumble in my ear as we settle in our seats after
watching a nude fire-eater strut her stuff on stage.

"Technically, till two in the morning, but I'll stay as long as
I'm needed."

He grunts and his jaw clenches.

"Is there a problem, Mason?"

"There will be if that asshole keeps staring at you like that."

My head swings around and Titus Morton, heir to an energy
drinks empire and a known playboy, is staring at me while
sliding his hand up and down his girlfriend's bare arm.

I turn back to Mason. "Is that why you decided to come
tonight? Because of Titus?" A delicious tingle starts deep in my
belly. I'm momentarily struck dumb when I recognize it as pleasure. I'm ecstatic that Mason is jealous. And possessive.

I'm not sure whether I want to punch some rationality back
into my senses or dance in the rain of my new discovery.

"He was a prick when we were in Yale. From the looks of
him, he's only grown into a mega-sized prick," Mason snarls.

A quick glance at Titus shows the two men eyeing one
another with barely repressed animosity.

"I can handle myself, Mason. If that's the only reason you
came, you don't need to worry."

The moment the words leave my lips, I flinch.

"You want me to return to the yacht, knowing some asshole
is going to be hitting on you?"

"That asshole is one of the guests I'm charged with looking
after. It's my job to make sure he has a good time."

"And your job description includes being okay with guests
making passes at you?" His voice has grown lower, deeper. My

eyes connect with his and the look he sends me tells me he's deeply offended by my blasé attitude.

"I'm from Brooklyn, Mason. I've experienced worse."

His brows clamp. "Is that supposed to make me feel better?"

I flounder, unmoored in a sea of what-the-fuck-ness. "I don't know," I finally respond. "I don't know how I'm supposed to behave with you outside of the bedroom. I mean, what's your role here? You're not my boyfriend. You're not even my lover."

"What the fuck did you just say?"

His use of the swear word outside of the bedroom terrifies me even more than the rage clouding his face.

It takes a lot of effort to not cower. "Well, you're not really, are you? You're in charge of my orgasms, and that's pretty much it. So what do you care who hits on me?"

Dark hazel eyes flare with disbelief. "Repeat that," he challenges, his voice a living sword, poised above my head. "I want to hear those insane words fall from your lips again."

I bring my mouth to his ear and place my hand on his chest. "You. Are. Not. My. Lover. We're feral fuck parasites, taking what we need from each other for the next eight days. That's it. I refuse to be intimidated into hanging a label on it that doesn't exist."

I pull back, and he stares at me like I'm a rabid animal. I'm ashamed, because every word that has fallen from my lips is a lie. Or at least not the reality I desire. I want him to be my lover. I still want to be a feral fuck parasite, but a nicer one. I don't want our eight days to end. And most of all, I want a fat fuck of a label to hang on to, whatever dimension we're existing in.

When the look gets too intense, I jump up and run to the door.

He lunges after me, but a couple entering the room stops his progress long enough to give me the head start I need to make a dash for the ladies'.

I slam the door behind me and dump my clutch on the vanity before my shaking takes care of it for me.

Shudders race through me as I stare at my ashen reflection in the mirror. *What the fuck is wrong with me?*

My brain is eating itself with questions and cravings too terrifying to contemplate. Frantic, I dig through my purse and grab my phone. Bethany is about to get an earful.

She answers, and I suck in a breath, just as the washroom door crashes open. The other female occupant in the room gasps in outrage. "*¿Qué diablos es eso?*"

"*Salir. Ahora!*" Mason snarls.

"Hello?"

Bethany's voice flares from my phone, but I can't lift my hand to answer. My stomach twists as Mason locks the washroom door and strides to where I'm frozen. He plucks the phone from my hand.

"Bethany, how are you?" he asks in a perfectly reasonable voice that isn't in any way marred by the sadistic madness I see in his eyes.

I hear Bethany's spluttered response, followed by a garbled question.

"No, Keely is going to be indisposed for a while. I can guarantee that she will be alive by the time I'm finished with her, but everything else is distinctly debatable."

He hangs up, places my phone on the vanity next to my purse, then leans against the sink, arms crossed.

"Now, where were we, kitten?"

The latent danger in his voice shudders through me. "Nowhere. We were nowhere."

He snaps his fingers as if I didn't just speak. "That's right. You were saying I have no right to question if someone hits on you." His head tilts to the side. "Have I got that right?"

"Don't blow it out of proportion." I flap my hand in a *don't be ridiculous* way, then screech when he lunges for me and slams me back against the wall.

"Flippancy is your answer?" His eyes are narrowed, incisive.

The scent of sandalwood, muscle and man engulfs me. Wholly inappropriately, my knees start to weaken. "Mason—"

"Feral fuck parasites. I guess that explains your distance earlier," he broods.

I open my mouth, but no words emerge. He captures my chin in his hand, and I try not to let my panic show.

"You have something to say?"

I shrug. "To determine distance don't we have to know closeness?" I ask.

"And you don't think we're close, given that we're *fucking* parasites?"

My heart lurches at the dirty word again. He's beyond livid, and all I've done is hold a mirror up to our torrid little arrangement.

"I don't recall agreeing to a closeness that involves me spending every spare minute with you, or you getting bent out of shape over who does or doesn't make a pass at me," I reply, then exhale on a groan when my mistake stares me in the face.

"You don't *recall*?" he growls with veiled softness.

Danger tingles along my spine. The little happy freak inside me races to embrace it. "Mason..."

"You're deliberately goading me. Is that what's happening here? You want a *reaction* from me?"

I shake my head. "No." I want to say more to alleviate the situation, but a part of me realizes I *do* want a reaction.

When his hand goes to his belt, I exhale in a rush.

"You need a reminder, kitten?"

"Maybe," I respond shakily.

"The three reasons I gave you this morning and afternoon weren't enough?"

I shudder in recollection of the rough fucking I received at his hands a mere three hours ago. The two, which preceded it, were relatively tame, in consideration of the raw pounding from the middle of the night.

"I'm a little confused. Sir."

A muscle ticks in his jaw at the last word, but his expression doesn't alter. "You're confused. Well, allow me to provide some clarity." He steps back and reaches for his buckle. My heart jumps into my throat. I watch with sick fascination as his belt whistles from its loop as he yanks hard at it.

One hand spreads across my lower back, and he pushes me to the vanity.

Our gazes clash in the mirror and the charge that explodes between us steals my breath away. "Bend over and hold the edge. You let go, I start again. Understood?"

Dirty anticipation dissolves in liquid heat between my thighs. My happy freak squeals in delight, even as a part of me recoils at what I'm doing. What I'm letting happen.

"What's the matter, Keely? I thought silence doesn't work for you?" he sneers.

I clear my throat and force my voice to work. "I... Mason, please."

"Please, what?"

I shake my head as thoughts of denial and acquiescence clash in a battle to end all battles.

"We never got round to picking a safe word, did we, kitten?" he asks as he pushes me forward and snaps up the hem of my dress. "Now's your chance, baby. Go for it."

The cool air hitting my ass makes my brain freeze for a moment. The heat from his proximity helps me along, and I blurt the word that jumps into my head. "Fortis."

His brow slowly lifts, and one hand trails between my ass cheeks and up my spine to tangle in my hair. "You are that, my *brave* little kitten," he breathes in my ear.

The belt lands next to my right hand. From its coiled position, I can feel its warmth, and I experience an insane desire to caress it.

That thought flees my head as merciless fingers hook into my panties and rip them off. "Oh!"

Mason's fingers tighten in my hair. "No, kitten. You don't get to gasp your delight, or arch your back and moan. You answer *yes, sir*, or *no, sir*, or use your safe word. Are we clear?"

"Yes, sir."

He stares at me for an eternity, before he pockets my shredded pink lace panties. They look delicate and decadent, dangling from his precisely tailored pants. For some reason, I can't look away from them.

I jump when someone attempts to open the door, but Mason barely blinks. Coolly, he reaches for the belt and steps back.

"I said you would be mine until the yacht reaches its final destination. Do you remember?" he demands softly.

I swallow. "Yes, sir."

Smack.

The sting flames pure fire through my veins, spreading pleasure to my cunt and tears to my eyes. I eat my moan and shudder through the pain.

"I distinctly remember using the words 'completely without exception.' Did I not?"

"Yes, sir."

Smack.

"As an intelligent woman, did you think that meant I would be okay with other men hitting on you?"

I tremble at the naked fury in his voice. "N-no, sir."

Thwack. Thwack. Thwack.

The harder hits tell me that this is what enrages him most. My skin's on fire and tears pour down my face. My left knee buckles and smashes against the vanity.

"If you think of us as parasites, then so be it. But we will be parasites with no distance between us, in the bedroom or out of it. Do you understand?"

He's changing the terms of our agreement. "No, sir."

"No, you don't understand?"

"Yes, sir."

"It's simple, kitten. You'll be mine in *and* out of the bedroom, *completely*, or this is over."

I want a fuck load of things I can't have. Our initial agreement set boundaries that I could see, if not totally control. Agreeing to this will immerse me deeper into batshit craziness of oceanic proportions. His gaze holds mine, fierce and demanding. I feel the clock of my demise counting down.

"What's it to be, kitten?"

"Yes, sir."

Smack. I flinch. A hand slams repeatedly against the toilet door, followed by a demand in muffled Spanish.

"Will you forget again?"

"No, sir."

"Good. Do you want me to fuck you now?"

Every fiber in my body jumps at the low-rasped demand. "Yes, please, sir," I answer with a ferocity that speaks to my unbridled craving.

He drops his belt and pets my welted and flaming skin gently with one hand, while the other slides around my thigh to slip between my legs.

"Ah, my brave kitten." His voice drips with thick satisfaction. "So wet and fierce and so fucking gorgeous." He leans over me and aligns his rough cheek against mine. "Are you ready for your reward?"

My whole body trembles. "Yes, sir. Please, sir. Now."

He slams into me, the force of his possession mashing both my knees against the vanity. The hand in my hair moves to cup one breast. He yanks on the nipple as he pistons, hard and fast and devastating.

Within a dozen thrusts, I'm cresting toward the edge. I cry out, and he stops.

"*No!* Oh, God... Please, sir."

I'm ready to commit murder when he pulls out of me, but he yanks me about and sets my ass on top of the vanity. The cool surface soothes me, but the action of pulling myself forward and parting my thighs wide to receive him is tough on my ravaged skin. Yet I'll endure that, and worse, just to feel Mason deep inside me.

I gasp when he lifts me clean off the vanity and impales me on his cock.

I throw my arms around his neck, ready to die with happiness. "*Yes!* Thank you, sir."

"*Jesus.* You fucking destroy me," he growls against my ear as he plunges me up and down on his steely erection.

"I'm coming. Oh, I'm coming!" A hazy thought that I should be quiet fleets through my head, but it melts under the furnace of release surging through me.

"Do it, baby. Come with me," he commands, before he takes my mouth in a searing kiss.

I let go and let him catch me when my body loses all effort to remain upright. I lay my head on his chest and absorb the sound of his pounding heart.

We're still shuddering and twitching in each other's arms when three loud *bloops* from my phone announce incoming emails. I flinch and try to hide the premonition of doom that skates over my skin, but I fail miserably as I'm plunged into icy shockwaves teeming with dread and fear.

Mason's finger slides under my chin and tugs my head up. He scrutinizes my faces for several intense heartbeats before he turns to where the phone is lit up like a macabre Christmas ornament.

"What's going on, kitten?" he asks, his voice once again deceptively soft.

I shake my head, doubting my ability to form words just yet. Or ever.

"We're going to leave here right now and return to the yacht," he says with another slow, mind-bending kiss. His voice is almost conversational, but I'm not fooled by the steel framing his tone. "Once we're there, you're going to explain to me why you jump and look like your worst nightmare comes to life each time your email pings."

23

KEELY

I'm not going to tell him. Of course I'm not.

If anyone deserves to know what happened to me six years ago, what shaped my life, it should be Bethany. Maybe she doesn't know it, but while she's been leaning on me through the shit in her life, I've been leaning on her.

Her needing me has saved me more times than I can ever tell her. Because while I concentrated on her, helping her get over the super-douche ex who left her for another man, and the tribulations of dealing with Zach Savage's life before he met her, I've efficiently distanced myself from dealing with my own shit. Now she's found her rock-steady happy, she's more than strong enough to deal with whatever issues I bring to her.

So, by rights, she deserves first spot at my confession table.

But the moment we walk into Mason's suite, the weight of burden is suddenly too much to bear. I want relief from that weight. I want to ball it up and dump it, even if it's into a near stranger's lap. He might judge me, most likely condemn me. But I'll be selfishly lighter, less of a festering wound.

"Keely?"

His tone is a cattle prod that demands a reaction. I put my clutch down, minus my phone, which he has in his pocket, and turn. I raise my hand to push back my hair, and I smell him on me. He's imprinted on me as indelibly as the welts I can feel on my ass. He'll fade with time, just like the marks on my skin. But for now, he's a reality I can't ignore.

And I don't want to.

"You want me to tell you something I've never told another human being, not even the people who brought me into this world. Why?"

He watches me as he shrugs out of his jacket and drapes it slowly over the back of the sofa. "Because you've given me control over you, and you wouldn't have unless a part of you trusts me not to hurt you or use anything you say against you."

The naked, raw truth in that staggers me for a moment. "And am I right? Can I trust you?"

"To a point. We don't know each other well enough to demand unquestioning trust. We have it where it matters most, but you probably don't want to lose sight of the fact that a bastard lives beneath this skin. Trust me with what you need to unburden, and I promise I'll think long and hard before I let it influence our interaction any more than it's doing right now."

My mouth gapes for a moment, before I recover from that. "Can I have a second to think about that?"

He smiles and strides to where I'm standing. He cups my jaw and tilts my head up until I look into his eyes. "No. We promised each other the truth, Keely. I'll never waver from that, even if it's not what you want to hear."

"What if what I tell you isn't what you want to hear?"

His thumbs brush my cheek as hazel gold eyes probe mine, and I glimpse a wasteland of weary regret in his gaze before he blinks it away.

"Firstly, I've seen and done things that give me very little right to judge what other people do. Secondly, and this is very important, so listen closely." He pauses to suck my lower lip into his mouth. His tongue rolls over it, once, twice, before he releases me. The tingle he starts radiates throughout my body, and I lean closer to him. "I've never been surer in my life that nothing you tell me will diminish my need to fuck this stunning body, for as long and as often as it's available to me. And Keely...?"

"Yes?" I expel the word in a hushed whisper.

"The sooner you get to telling me, the sooner I can get to fucking you. I've been dying to take that ass again since you made me turn it raw and pink back at the club. The longer you make me wait, the harder I'll take you." He steps back, catches my hand and leads me to the sofa. "So, shall we get to it?"

Shall we get to it?

Five small words that lie between my protective fortress and the wrecking ball poised to bring it down.

My breath shudders out, and I decide that I'll start with the skinny version instead of the whole bloated, worm-infested carrion.

He sits and pats his lap. My ass still stings from my earlier punishment, so I crawl onto him with my knees on either side of his lean hips. His hands immediately settle on my waist, and he holds me in place. It's a perfect position for fucking, especially with me being minus panties and the fragrance of my come wafting up between us.

His nostrils flare and his eyes darken as he breathes in deep. The atmosphere becomes charged, but I know there will be no fucking until words are said and naked, ravaged souls—mine at least—are bared.

He captures my wrists and runs his mouth over my knuckles

as he stares at me. "Let's start with the emails. Who's sending them, and why?" he asks.

"I don't know who's sending them. But I know why. I'm... I think the end game is blackmail."

He freezes for a moment, then presses his mouth against my skin one last time before he lowers my hands to his chest. "The end game..."

"Yes."

"How long has this been going on?"

"A few weeks."

His thumbs massage my hip bones, and I melt into his touch. "And why would anyone want to blackmail you?" he asks softly.

"I don't know."

He stares at me, and this time I don't resent his silence. My answer demands elaboration, and I give it.

"What I mean is, I haven't done anything worth being black-mailed over." My mind screams at the un-wholeness of that answer, but I smother the rant. "Unless you call being at the wrong place at the wrong time a crime."

My words are flippant, nothing like the barbed wires of resis-tance digging into my soul, as memories, which I only allow to roam free in the dark apocalypse of my mind, break free into the light of day.

"Where and when was this?" Mason asks.

Reality drowns me.

I'm doing this. I'm really doing this.

I take a deep and useless breath as my gaze clouds and I'm back in that cold, horrid underground suite of rooms.

Ice drenches me until I can't feel the tips of my fingers. Maybe I react to the cold, or maybe I just look frozen. Peripher-ally, I feel Mason take my hands in his and warm them with his breath.

"Six years ago, I went to a party, hosted by someone I believed to be my friend. I had no idea what sort of party it was. I was young and wanted to fit in, and everyone was talking about the party to end all parties. I charmed my way into an invitation and on the day, I was driven from my campus at UCLA to a house somewhere in the Hollywood Hills. I have no idea whose house it was. I was taken to a part of the house named east wing on Friday night. I woke up in hospital on Monday morning."

Mason may have tensed. Or he may have sprouted a halo and turned into Angel Gabriel. I don't know because I'm sucked violently into the past.

24

KEELY

Six years ago

"*Omigod!* Leo, what the fuck is going on? Why is that girl screaming?"

I'm still holding my stinging cheek from the virtual slap from the TV bimbo. I look around, certain that if I search hard enough, I'll find the remote to turn this acid trip off.

Another scream rips through the room, this time from behind a black curtain positioned in a different section of the room. A flap opens as someone goes in and I catch a glimpse of another girl. This one is suspended from ropes tied to the ceiling. But there's a floodlight set up on a tripod over there too, showing her naked and severely contorted body, and the avid audience staring up at her.

My hammering heart climbs into my throat, and my hand falls uselessly to my side. As a teenager in a sex-centric world, I've on occasion thought of what an experience in a sex club would be like. Even as a nineteen-year-old virgin, I know this isn't it.

Morbid curiosity dampens my fear for a moment, and I stare at my surroundings.

In total, I count eight floodlights illuminating squared off areas the size of my living room back home. Besides the floodlights, there are no other lights. It doesn't stop my gaze from probing the dark, trying to make sense of what I'm witnessing.

It registers that Leo hasn't responded, and I start to turn.

Suddenly, my TV bimbo has gotten stronger and is yanking me by the arm down the dark middle of this amphitheater of fuck knows what to fuck knows where.

I start to fight, then realize it isn't my virtual nemesis, but Leo's hand shackling me. He's dragging me along faster than my unfamiliar stiletto-shod gait can keep up. I stumble and nearly trip, but I catch myself at the last minute and try to reverse my forward momentum into my first circle of hell.

"Leo, let go of my hand, please." I try to pry him off me, but he's strong. Way stronger than me. He has to be in order to do all but the most dangerous of his own action stunts during film shoots.

"I'm sorry, Keely," is all he says.

"What do you mean, you're sorry? Sorry for what?" My voice is high-pitched with pure panic as we pass yet another curtained-off square. Someone is moaning, and it's not the type of moan that proclaims pleasure.

It's the type of moan that says: *You're hurting me. I don't like it, but I'm at a point where I know I can do fuck all about it.*

The rise of excited voices in that section also tells me there's an audience lapping up whatever is being done to the individual beneath the spotlight.

"Please, Leo. You were right, I shouldn't have come. It's not too late. I... I can leave. Just let me go and I'll forget this ever happened. I won't tell anyone. You have my word." My words tumble over each other, and my heart tears from its moors and plunges into my stomach when I see where we're headed.

My eyesight has adjusted enough in the semi-darkness to see a last, unlit area at the back of the cavernous room. I can also pick out the dark, eager figures crowded around the parted curtain. They turn as Leo drags me forward.

"No!" I mean to roar the word like a fucking lioness, but it emerges as a whimper unworthy of a cockroach.

The ominous sound of a switch being thrown drenches the single chair in the middle of the room in blinding light. I see the black ropes snaking from the back of the chair and I spend a hot, insane little second wondering why they're not white like the others. Am I not worthy? Or am I worthy beyond my own comprehension?

The pause button on my nightmare releases and a scream kamikazes into my throat. Before I can let it rip, Leo's hand slams over my mouth.

"Whatever you do, Keely, don't scream. This will be over much quicker if you just go with the flow."

I lose all feeling in my knees, and my body drops like a stone. Leo catches me easily by the waist, and his other hand cups the back of my head and shoves me through the gap in the curtain. When I'm directly beneath the light, he releases me.

One calm part of me helpfully steps forward and offers flashes of my young life in a shockingly brief, but totally Oscar-worthy clip. I'm sure I hear ghostly applause as the other part stares at Leo, mummified in fear and shock.

"Why are you doing this?"

His head drops for several seconds, and I see that regret from earlier flash over his face. But he lifts his head and all I get is a blank, beautiful canvas.

"Take your clothes off, Keely."

"Fuck you," I say. The feeble power in my voice bolsters me a little. "Fuck you! Fuck you! *FUCK YOU!*"

"Dammit, Dorian. This again?"

I jerk at the bored, disembodied drawl. The murmurs from behind the curtain stop, and that scares me even more than anything that's gone on so far.

"That's fucking strike two. You know what happens should you commit a third foul," continues the voice.

Dorian/Leo shakes his head. "She wasn't supposed to be here."

"Did you not invite her?" the voice queries.

"Yes, I did, but—"

"And what do the rules say, Dorian?"

His jaw clenches tight for a minute, and terror slashes across my every nerve. "'One for all. Free for all.'"

"Prepare your guest, Dorian. If you can't calm her down, help will be provided. But remember, that'll be a third count against you."

The voice shuts off and a feed that sounds like a radio's echo sounds through the room before the voices rise again.

Leo raises his head and I see determination in his eyes. I shake my head as he advances toward me.

"No! God, please, no! Leo, stop this. You don't have to do this."

He reaches me and grabs my arms. "Dammit, Keely. Shut the fuck up!"

I fight with renewed strength. Whatever he's planning to do to me, I don't intend to make it easy for him.

"You weak, fucking pathetic asshole! Why did I think you were even worthy of one *second* of my time?" I snarl, my voice shaky with terror.

"That was your mistake, not mine." His fingers dig into me as he hauls me toward the chair.

I kick and scratch and spit. Some blows connect. Some hurt me more than they hurt him. My knee catches a sharp corner of the chair and it doesn't move. I realize it's bolted to the floor, and I fight harder. Leo's shirt rips beneath my frantic effort to escape my reality. The stench of blood and fear gags me as I'm thrown into the chair.

That's when my screams finally step up to the plate and put in the performance of a lifetime.

I'm hoarse by the time the first rope snakes around my calf.

The radio feed slices through the air again, and I hear a sigh. "That's it, Dorian, you're out. Space Cadets, step in and secure our guest," the voice says.

Leo freezes, then shuts his eyes for a sick little second. "I warned you, Keely. You should've listened."

25

MASON

Nothing will ever compare to the black rage that has lived in my soul since Toby died. I feed it, constantly and affectionately, to ensure it thrives. It has become the central nervous system that dictates each moment in my life.

Thus far, I've believed that I have no room in my life for anything else.

And yet, as I listen to the words falling from Keely's lips, an expanse shifts within me, a cavern widening itself to accommodate the sweet agony of new, undiscovered rage.

She stops suddenly and flinches.

I jerk back into myself and realize my fingers are digging into her hip. I let go, flex my fingers, but I don't feel right. This rage is different. It drills into me with a relentless single-mindedness that makes thinking an impossibility. I can't catch my breath, and it slowly dawns on me that I'm not as calm as I was when I set out to avenge my son's death.

My vision is blurred with red rain, and I can't tell whether I'm sitting or floating.

Warmth seeps into my cheeks. "Mason?"

Fear and apprehension infuse my name, and I battle to pull myself back from the edge. I blink and focus on her. Her beauty is compelling enough to ground me a little. Her hands on my face reel me in just that little bit more. Enough to formulate a single thought.

I place my hands over hers and shift one palm to kiss it, before I ask, "What happened after that?"

Anguish and despair contort her face and her shoulders slump.

"I don't know," she whispers raggedly. "I've never been able to remember. I woke up in the hospital three days later. According to the police, I was pumped full of sedatives and dumped somewhere on Mulholland Drive. A couple on a morning run found me and called the ambulance—"

"Stop." The black roar in my head makes saying the word difficult, but I need a break from the influx of rage eating me alive.

She purses her lips and nods, before her head drops to my shoulder. A tiny wounded sound pipes from her throat and slays me.

I surge to my feet with her in my arms. Her hands grip my nape and her breath washes my face as I stride with her to the bedroom. Silently, I undress her and carry her to the bathroom. She doesn't need a shower and neither do I. In fact, I like smelling myself on her to the point where I wouldn't care if she never showered after I fucked her.

But I need action, and while my preferred mode would be to fuck, I don't trust myself not to visit a sliver of my rage on her. Memories of what I did to Cassie in the year after I lost Toby filter through my mind and for the first time in forever, I experience a tinge of shame and regret.

I turn on the shower and guide Keely beneath the spray.

She hasn't said a word since I stopped her from speaking, and I feel slight panic that I may have shut a door I didn't intend to shut.

I smear gel over her body and wash her silky skin beneath the water. When she reaches out to brace her hands on my chest, I cage the flames leaping through my blood and force myself to continue.

"What's his full name? The guy who invited you to the party." My voice is a shiny scalpel, intent on honing the new rage inside me. To achieve that, I need names. Faces. Histories and vulnerabilities. Because I don't intend to stop until I've achieved the same results I did five years ago, right before I exiled myself to Roraima. "Tell me his real name," I urge calmly when I sense her reluctance.

Keely's beautiful green eyes flicker and her cheeks, already pale from recounting her ordeal, whiten a little bit more. I gentle my fingers, let them slide over her skin, when all I want to do is rip out throats and piss on severed heads.

"His name was Leo Brummer."

My fingers tense against her spine. "*Was?*"

She nods. "He was found in his apartment, overdosed on coke six months after that weekend."

The scalpel freezes midair. "He's *dead*?" The thought brings me no satisfaction whatsoever. In fact, I feel intensely aggrieved at the loss of prey.

She nods. "The detective who was handling my case called and told me." She laughs, but it's a bleak shadow of a sound that makes me want to bare my teeth. "I think he was convinced it'd bring me some sort of closure."

There is no closure. Not when something this precious is ripped from you.

I turn her away from me so she doesn't see my regret over

what she has to live with for the rest of her life. "Besides Brummer, was there anyone else there that you knew?"

A new tension tightens her spine. When she remains silent, I glide my hand to her nape and massage until she sighs. She knows without me having to insist that I'm waiting for an answer.

"My psychology professor was there that night."

I sense something more. "And?"

"And in relation to what happened to me, I can't say whether he was involved or not. Leo is the only one I can state with any accuracy who meant me any harm that night."

"Everyone in that godforsaken place meant you harm. You were taken there for the sole purpose of being taken against your will," I snap.

She flinches and I tug her into my arms. "Dammit. I'm sorry, kitten."

She rests her head against me for a minute, then she steps back and reaches for the soap. "My turn."

I allow her the mundane task of washing my body, and we leave the bathroom a few minutes later, clean but still tarnished with our dark pasts.

My arms open to her the moment we're in bed, and her readiness to crawl onto me helps me contain the rattling cages.

I slide my hands up and down her soft body, unable to get anywhere near enough to touching her. The distance I sensed in her earlier today is gone, for now. I bury my face in her hair and breathe deep.

When I sense her disinclination to further our talk, I want to respect her need for an end to the subject, but I can't let it go. Not yet.

"Tell me about your professor. Did he see you?"

Again, she tenses. "Yes. He was the one who took me down to

where Leo was. But I don't know whether he was involved personally."

I grip her hair and angle her face to mine. "You were drugged. How would you know?" Her eyes cloud over and I feel like a big shit. "Keely, I hate to state the obvious, but he knew you were there. He knew what would happen to you when you were taken to the east wing. And he still let it happen. Whether he was involved or not, he was culpable." And now on my list. "What was his name?"

"Elliot Harding."

The way she says his name makes my senses burn. "What aren't you telling me, Keely?"

She blinks a few times before she says, "During my first semester, I thought Harding was coming on to me. He would ask me to stay after class, or ask me to come to his office. He always had a legitimate reason and he didn't do anything sleazy, like stand too close or leer down my top. But... something in his eyes made me feel uneasy, like a subliminal promise of filth and pain that felt a little too, I don't know... raw?"

"Kitten, let's dispense with the graphics, okay?"

Her eyes widen at the violence in my voice and she swallows. "Okay. Well... anyway... I confronted him about it one day."

"And?"

"Let's just say, by the time I left his office, I felt like a piece of fossilized shit. He didn't raise his voice, or threaten me in any way. But I knew if I dared to repeat my suspicions to anyone else, I would be finished."

"But you were right to trust your instincts and confront him then."

The look she gives me is full of self-recrimination. "I was right. But what good does that do me now? Deep down, I knew going into that basement would end badly. But I went anyway.

For god's sake, would you ride an elevator with a guy who calls himself *Moriarty*?"

"Yes. Because I'm better than Sherlock." My joke falls flat when the corners of her mouth turn down.

"I wasn't. I lost three days of my life because I ignored my instincts."

I flip us over so she's lying beneath me and slide my fingers into her hair until she has no choice but to look at me. "This is why you tried to throw yourself in the ocean," I seethe. "You think killing yourself is the answer?"

Her mouth quivers before she firms it. "Since there's only one way to answer that definitively and I'm still alive, I guess I don't know."

I kiss her hard, and roughly, trying to infuse her with fuck knows what. All I know is that I can't let her think ending her life is okay. Never mind that I may have contemplated the same path. Never mind that I forsook that path because living was a far better punishment than dying.

I kiss her until she moans, and her nails dig into my back in a plea for either oxygen or fucking. I don't grant either. Not until she's out of her frantic mind.

Then I flip us back around, tuck her into my side, and pull the covers over her body.

"Go to sleep, kitten."

She exhales in astonishment. "Mason. You can't leave me like this."

"I need you to have something to look forward to tomorrow. Even if it's only the prospect of being fucked to within an inch of your life."

I snap my fingers in a timed sequence and the room darkens.

Her arm jerks around me, then her hand heads south to grip

my rock-hard cock. Her body undulates against mine and I thicken in her hand.

"God... Mason, please. I need you." Her voice quivers with her need and I almost waver.

"I'm not in a good place right now, baby. Let's get some sleep. I promise I'll give you double of everything you need in the morning."

Although my whole body is on a razor's edge of need, I infuse enough steel in my voice for her to heed my request. She strokes me a couple more times, before her hand reluctantly returns to curl against my chest.

Sleep isn't on my churning horizon anytime soon, but I fake it until she settles, soft and pliant around me, and her breathing deepens.

In the darkness, I let my furious growl loose.

The name Elliot Harding pounds through my brain until it fuses into my neural pathways.

"Seven, switch to silent computronic mode," I murmur. A green light blinks from the device on my dresser to signal compliance. "Commence full search. Subject: Elliot Harding. Professor. UCLA, California. Full history—financial, medical, academic. Current location. Cross reference with Leo Brummer, same parameters including next of kin. Also search for dwellings with extensive underground development in Hollywood Hills, California. Specific dates of interest, first half of 2009. First report by zero six hundred."

The green light blinks three times to signal message received.

I exhale and tangle my legs with Keely's. She murmurs softly in her sleep, and I'm about to pull her even closer, bask in her warmth, when another device lights up, this one right next to me on the bedside table.

Cassie's name is backlit in blue neon on my phone and the tiny sense of peace I felt a moment ago vanishes. I let it buzz, not trusting myself to be civil to a woman whose only sin against me is the blue blood that runs through her veins.

I was indifferent to Cassandra McCarthy long before I married her for the sake of consolidating our families' financial power. Unfortunately, it took three years of mind-fucking cruelty for me to recognize that I was punishing her for being a carbon copy of my mother.

But more than detesting her for taking what I doled out like a meek, pearls-draped, upper-class lamb, I detest her for giving me the son I grew to love more than I ever believed I was capable of loving another human being. She tore open a heart I didn't want to believe I possessed and filled it with hopes and dreams, magic and endless possibility, for a senselessly brief time.

The day I lost Toby was the day I came within an inch of killing my ex-wife.

I divorced her the day after I buried my son, for her own sake as well as mine.

That compulsion hasn't abated.

She knows better than to contact me. So I know she has a good reason for contacting me now.

I wait for the beep that tells me she's left a message. It never arrives. I place the phone back on the bedside table. Three calls in one day. Three calls with no messages.

My ex-wife has either grown brass balls.

Or something is very wrong.

26

KEELY

I'm not sure what wakes me. All I know is that I'm lighter than a cirrus cloud and soaring just as high, even though I'm weighted down by a heavy limb.

Mason's scent hits my nostrils and memory rushes back.

I told him. Another human knows what happened to me six years ago.

I wait for my stomach to turn, for the hot poker of shame to stab me in the heart, because let's face it, the Sodom-sized hell visited upon me wouldn't have happened if I wasn't following the dictates of my pussy. The bundle of nerves between my legs has altered my reality for all time, and for as long as I live, I'll have to bear the consequences of that, so yeah... shame.

I wait for it to drown me.

Nothing happens. I'm still floating. A little heavier than I was a moment ago, but I'm a happy, shame-free cloud.

A happy, shame-free, *horny* cloud.

Slowly, I open my eyes. The room is dawn-dark, so I know we haven't been asleep longer than three hours. I turn my head and watch a softly snoring Mason. He's lying on his side, as if he fell asleep watching me. The thought tightens my chest, and I dance away from the warning light flickering on inside me.

He was a handy confessor. More than that, he received my burden with no outward judgment.

For that, he deserves a reward. And I know just the thing.

I lean closer and touch his eyebrow. He shifts, but his eyes remain closed, so I kiss the corner of his mouth, linger on his sensual upper lip before I trail kisses along his jaw to his ear. He stirs beneath me, and I know he's awake.

"'You are the one I am lit for. Come with your rod that twists and is a serpent,'" I whisper the line from "To a Dark Moses" in his ear.

His jaw moves and I can tell without looking that he's smiling.

"You wake me with talk of rods and serpents. Either you're a celestial being come to deliver the end of days, or you're a little horny. Which is it, kitten?"

I rub my aching breasts against his chest and revel in the quiver that rushes through my belly. "Hmm, the second one. And I'm more than a little horny."

"You want me to do something about that, baby?" he croons into my ear.

"Yes, please."

One hand spreads over my back and pulls me deeper into his body. The rod of his cock prods hard into my belly. "Yes, please, what?"

"Please, sir. Make the ache go away."

His hand moves from my back to my hair and captures a sheaf in a punishing hold. He pulls me by the hair until my face hangs over his, and we stare deep into each other's eyes. "Ask me again," he commands tightly.

"I want you. So badly I hurt everywhere. Fuck me, sir. Please fuck me and make the pain go away."

He shuts his eyes for a second. "*Christ*. You know how perfect you could be?"

Could be? Something fragile cracks open and oozes fuck knows what inside me. "No, I don't, because perfection is an illusion."

His mouth twists without regret. "That it is. But fucking you isn't."

My senses leap a mile high. "No. Yes. Do it, please."

His fist clenches until my scalp burns. "Fuck, I get so damn hard when you beg."

I groan, and my eager hand slips down his hot torso to delve beneath the cover. He captures my wrist before I reach my goal.

"Did I say you could touch me, kitten?"

So that's the game we're playing? Okay. I slowly circle my lips with my wet tongue and try to look suitably contrite, while impatience and need burn me alive. "I'm sorry, sir. Permission to stroke your cock, sir."

"Permission denied." He lets go of me and slaps his hand against the headboard. "Get up here," he instructs and lunges out of bed.

I raise myself on my elbows, alone and adrift in my confusion.

Like everything on the *IL Indulgence*, the furniture design is elegantly simple, but luxuriously comfortable. There's nothing about the steel headboard that promises me relief from the increasing ball of agony between my legs.

"Umm... why?"

"Keely," he warns.

"I'm sorry... sir. I just don't understand how the headboard will give me what I need."

My mind zeroes in on what *will*, and I groan helplessly.

A smile splits his face that catches at my heartstrings. "You don't trust me to give you what you need?"

"I do, but..." The plaintive note in my voice irritates me, but this is what he's reduced me to. I clear my throat. "I don't want it to be dragged out. Sir."

He thinks for a minute, and his gaze gentles. "It won't be. Not this time. I'll make you come in under three minutes. Does that work for you?"

I nod eagerly.

"Then get up on your knees and hold tight to the headboard."

I comply with pathetically wanton enthusiasm. When he walks backward to the dresser, I hold my breath. I watch him open the drawer and pull out a familiar box. It's the one he gave me yesterday that I never got round to opening.

Anticipation tingles up my spine as I track his return.

When he climbs onto the bed behind me, it takes supreme effort not to reach for him. But I've learned that compliance brings quicker gratification than defying my dominant lover.

"A little old-fashioned, but effective nonetheless." He flips the box lid open and pulls out a long silver chain with a knot in the middle and pegs at each end.

My nipples tighten just from the sight of the clamps. My Pavlova-tuned cunt ripples and dampens in delight.

I can barely breathe when Mason unhooks the knot and ties the chain around my waist. The opposing textures of cold metal against my hot skin chases goosebumps over my body.

When the metal drapes over my hip, he holds one clamp to my lips. "Make this wet for me."

Keeping my gaze on his, I suck the peg into my mouth and swirl my tongue around it. A faint flush darts over his cheekbones and feminine power fills me, even though I know it won't be mine for long.

It vanishes the moment both clamps are wet and he crouches behind me. "Your nipples are so perfect for this," he whispers. "Hell, your whole body is perfect for however I choose to fuck it."

"Does that please you, sir?" I'm amazed at how easily the word falls from my lips now. I may not know the ins and outs of being a true submissive, but this is a learning curve I'm okay with.

"It pleases me, kitten. Very, very much." His tongue trails up the side of my neck and I tremble hard.

I cry out as the teeth of the clamp pinch my sensitive bud. Pleasure follows and my pussy grows wetter. By the time Mason places the second clamp on my other nipple, I'm halfway to coming. I look down at myself, and the sight of the silver dangling from my breasts and across my body nearly sends me over the edge.

"See how beautiful you are?"

I shake my head. "I'm not beautiful."

His hand glides down my spine to grip my ass cheek, hard. "Are you disagreeing with me?"

"Umm... no, sir."

"What, then?"

"I've always thought I'm okay to look at, maybe even pretty. Beautiful isn't... quite me."

He pauses his ministrations. "So you are disagreeing with me."

My eyes squeeze shut, and I curse silently with frustration. "Maybe a little. Mason, please."

He slaps my ass hard. Pain and pleasure spiral in opposite directions. "You're forgetting yourself, kitten."

"I'm sorry, sir."

"You're beautiful. Say it," Mason growls.

I feel a little ridiculous for starting this argument, but I'm caught in it now, and the quickest way I can get the orgasm I crave is to give in. "I'm beautiful," I mumble.

That half-assed attempt earns me another smack. "You want to try saying it like you believe it?"

"I'm beautiful," I say louder.

"Again."

"I'm beautiful!"

The mattress shifts and I look down to see his head between my knees. I almost come right there as his dark gold eyes and strong hands worship my body.

"You're beautiful," he rasps. His tongue licks up one inner thigh and down the other. "You're so fucking beautiful." He flicks my clit and stars burst before my vision.

"I'm beautiful," I repeat, daring to believe it a little.

He cradles my ass in his hands and brings me down hard on his mouth. I loved the device Mason clamped on my pussy the first time we fucked on the yacht, but it's nothing compared to the skill and texture of his mouth and tongue on my cunt. And when he hooks his fingers and pulls on the chain attached to my nipples, I'm a ball of pure sensation, cannoning down the slope toward bliss.

"Oh, *God!*"

My orgasm bursts on me before I'm ready, but I ride it with sheer abandon. When convulsions rip through me, I roll my hips in rough, ecstatic undulations. Mason lets me fuck his mouth until my shudders die down, then he rearranges me over his body.

He plunges into my clenching sheath while I'm still twitching, and the fireworks erupt again.

He fucks me like he owns me, which I guess he does until we part, and I hang on for dear life.

We're both bathed in sticky sweat and come by the time the sun rises. I can barely move, and all I do is purr as he pets me into sleepy bliss.

From our brief time together, I know Mason Sinclair isn't a heart and flowers guy. So when he pushes back my hair and raises my head so he can look in my eyes, I'm prepared for a rasped command, or punishment for an overlooked slight. What I get instead strangles my breath in my throat.

"You're fucking beautiful, kitten. *Nothing* that happened to you was your fault. Wanting to explore your sexuality is nothing to be ashamed about. I know there's more to what happened to you." My residual pleasure takes a nosedive, but he shakes his head. "I won't force you to tell me. But what I know is more than enough to make me pissed off that you think you don't have anything to live for."

My gaze drops.

"Look at me, Keely," he demands.

I reluctantly comply.

"You're beautiful. And you have a hell of a fucking lot to live for. If nothing else, to prove to the bastards who violated you that you're not broken."

"How can I, when I don't know who they are?"

A shadow shifts through his eyes, a molten rage that he tries to hide. But I see it, because that rage lives within me too. Rage for what was done to me. Helpless rage that I can't fight faceless ghosts.

"You may not know who they are. But they obviously know you or they wouldn't be trying to pull you down. Do you want to give them that satisfaction?"

I shake my head.

"Then promise me you won't try to pull that shit you did in Montauk, or anything similar, again."

"Mason—"

"No. Promise me!" His face hardens, and although he's beneath me, his dominance overpowers me.

I swallow, and nod. "I promise."

Hazel eyes probe mine for a full minute before he brings me in for a long, wet kiss.

"Good. Now we can begin the day properly."

I draw in a shaky breath. "I have to work, Mason."

"Not until this afternoon. And not until I've fed you and introduced you to some other carnal delights."

Despite my scrambling emotions, my blood quickens. "Oh? What have you in mind for me, sir?"

A wicked smile spreads across his face. "Pancakes and waffles. Then a visit to the lower deck."

* * *

Four hours later, I'm dressed in a sexy little sundress, Mason in a dark T-shirt and jeans, and we're sitting on a wide balcony, eating breakfast. When his phone buzzes, it's face up, so I can't miss the name that pops up.

Cassie. His ex-wife. The blueberries I'm chewing turn a little sour.

I look from the phone to his face when he continues to ignore it.

"I can give you privacy if you want to answer it?"

He stuffs half a waffle in his mouth and stares at me across the white-lined table. "No."

"No, you're not going to answer it, or no, you don't need privacy?"

"No to both."

"Okay." We eat in silence, until the silence becomes too loud. "Why?"

He sighs. "Because I was married to her. Which unfortunately grants her a little insight into which buttons of mine to press for the desired response. When I'm within contactable distance, she finds ways to push those buttons. And I'm wired to respond in a certain way. One that never bodes well for either of us."

"So by ignoring her..."

"I'm saving one of us the need to check into a facility at the end of the month for emotional distress." A hard, wry smile curves his mouth, and I lose my appetite. "See? I'm turning over a new leaf."

"Why not uproot the whole tree and lose her number?"

He gives me a sad smile. "I'm a sadist?"

"You asking or you telling?" I quip.

"Crap, I'm losing my powers if you can't tell."

I reel a little as I stare at him. The intense, brooding man I met in Montauk is still very much present, but I dare to imagine I see another side to Mason Sinclair, one that entices gentler creatures, like his ex-wife to their doom. But what if it's a side that's genuine? And needs bringing out more? By me?

I shake my head at my insane line of thinking. "Seriously, why leave her dangling?"

All laughter fades from his face, and he links his hands over his stomach. "Because we'll always share an unbreakable connection."

My heart pounds, its roar filling in my ears. I bite my tongue until it bleeds, then I ask anyway. "Your son?"

Emotions flit over his face, before it settles on a poisonous sadness that rakes white-hot coals across my ravaged soul. "My son."

Before I know it, I'm standing. Rounding the table to slide into his lap. He doesn't move his hands to accommodate me, and I know I'm risking a hell of a lot by pushing where I may not be wanted. But the compulsion is stronger than I can handle.

I tuck my head into the crook of his shoulder and cup his rock-hard jaw. "Tell me about him."

"No, kitten."

"Please, Mason. Tell me."

He shakes his head and tension spears from his body into mine. I'm glad it locks us together, because now there's no escaping me.

"Thinking of it doesn't put me in a good place. Telling it will make it worse."

The warning is clear. But I've kicked danger in the nuts before. I didn't come out well, but the kicking felt good. "I can take it."

He laughs, and the sound is a cruel, sadistic one. "I seriously doubt that."

I raise my head, anger fighting with compassion. "You can't praise my courage in one breath and belittle it in the next. Tell me if you want to, or don't, but don't be cruel about it."

I start to rise, but his arms shackle my hips. I'm thrown back against him and my hand falls on his chest. His heart pounds beneath my open palm, and I raise my gaze to see the seething self-flagellation in his eyes.

"It's not a good story," he says, his voice a mangled pain-filled rumble. "It's a very, very bad one."

"I know. Tell me anyway."

He shuts his eyes and drops his forehead to the top of my head. He's going to refuse. I know he is. A part of me doesn't blame him. Another part of me refuses to stay in the dark. "Tell me his name." He asked the same of me in the dark of night. I've earned this little right.

"Toby." The sound is ripped from his throat. "His name was Toby Callum Sinclair."

I absorb that and curl into his chest. His heart continues to pound with the weight of mournful memory, and I keep myself wrapped close about him, this man whose pain calls to me like an addict to narcotics.

We stay like that and seconds turn to minutes. To an hour.

Above us, seagulls caw in the sky, a reminder of where we are. I look up at him and his eyes are closed, but his breathing is rough, harsh. He's caught in a blizzard of savage memory, and I put him there.

I cup his frozen jaw. "Mason, I'm sorry."

He gives a broken groan. My arms slide around his neck, and I hold him tighter. Another shudder rips through him. He groans again, and tears squeeze through his shut eyes and tremble on his lashes.

"He was five when he was taken. Just five fucking years old," he whispers.

27

KEELY

I freeze. "Taken?"

He remains silent, his eyes still squeezed shut.

My mind tries to grapple with the many interpretations of what he's saying. In the end, I blurt out, "How was he taken? Who took him, Mason?"

A hard swallow moves his throat. "I did some work for the government when I was in college. It was all top-secret shit... Writing code for satellites that helped win some obscure war I had zero interest in. A few years later, they came back, asking for my help again."

His jaw is so tight, I'm surprised it hasn't cracked, and for a moment, I'm afraid that's as much as he can say. But then his lips part with a savage twist and he continues.

"They offered me a fuck load of money to alter one of my security algorithms, but I refused." Again, he pauses, but this time whatever dam has held him back seems to have cracked open and the words spill from him in a flood of heat and pain I feel ripping through his rigid body.

"They waited a few years, then offered more money. Cassie

and I were married by then. And Toby... God, my son would never want for anything. What the hell did I need more money for? But now I was interested in the world he would grow up in. If altering a simple code could help catch a few bad guys, then I was in."

He sighs and it sounds like his soul is squeezing from his lungs in a tormented rasp. "They wanted me to work in a lab somewhere in the bowels of some faceless building in the middle of nowhere. I said, *Hell no*. I'm Mason Sinclair the Third. If they want *my* program, they have to do things my way, which includes not taking me away from my son for weeks on end."

I want to move, to stroke his agonized face. To kiss his tormented lips. But I'm frozen, afraid if I move it will tip the balance and he'll stop his soul-bleeding confession. So instead, I feel the heavy beat of his heart and try to ignore the racing of my own.

"We tussled over that a bit and reached an agreeable arrangement. They would send a junior analyst to live with me and learn the code in case I became compromised." He stops and shakes his head. "I said yes."

He shudders and his grip shifts, releasing my frozen state. "And this analyst... he just... took your son?"

"He was great with Toby." His voice rumbles on, an arid recounting. "They got on like a house on fire. I never suspected a thing. Peterson was living with us for a couple of months. The day I... That day, he offered to take Toby for ice cream. He'd done it a bunch of times before. I was in the middle of writing code. I barely looked up to say goodbye to my son. I didn't even realize what the time was until Cassie came home and asked me where Toby was."

Mason finally opens his eyes and I see the black, irredeemable despair that fills them. "It was one in the morning. My son had been missing for over eleven hours, and I had my head buried up the ass of some goddamn coding."

Just like he asked me to stop talking when the crush of words became too much, I want the words falling from his lips to shrivel up and die. I don't want the image of that beautiful boy on the cinema screen in Monte Carlo to alter in any way. But then I remember the sound Mason made when he watched his son's image. The sound of a defeated soul preparing itself for the seventh circle of hell. It's that sound, and my impossibly arrogant need to free him from it, that makes me speak now. "What did you do?"

"The usual—calls to the police, followed by calls to heads of every law enforcement department, threatening to kill each and every one of them if they didn't dedicate every single resource to finding my son. The less brave ones promised me jail time once Toby was found. I threatened some more, even managed to get a few incompetent assholes fired." He exhales and I swear I see the flames of hell leap in his eyes when he looks at me. "Seven days, Keely. He had Toby for seven days."

The vice around my chest strangles my lungs. "You found him?"

His mouth compresses into a blade. "I was building Seven as a side project at the time. I altered her parameters and programmed her for the sole purpose of finding Toby. She pinpointed a mile radius of his location on the seventh day, to some farm in Virginia. But... we were too late."

Oh God. I pull him tighter into my warmth, but he's statue-still and chilled despite the sunshine surrounding us. "Mason." I say his name, not to prompt him into any sort of action or response, but to let him know I'm there. "Mason. Mason."

I give in to the urge to kiss his cheek and feel the blood flow beneath his skin. I'm encouraged that there's life beneath the petrified sorrow and rage. I trail my mouth to the corner of his mouth and kiss his frozen lips. I don't get a response, but I'm not dissuaded.

"Mason."

He jerks his head back when I try to deepen the kiss. I recognize his need to purge, and I place my head on his chest again, my thoughts calmed a little by the rhythmic beat of his heart.

"He took him, Keely. Right from underneath my nose. So you see, you're not the only one who was fooled into ignoring the warning signs. I've had a long time to think about those signs."

My fingers glide into the hair at his nape in a gesture of inadequate comfort. "What signs?"

"Peterson was a schizophrenic. He hid his condition with medication while under scrutiny at his job. If I'd known about it, I would have been more cautious, but instead I dismissed his sometimes erratic behavior as embarrassment because he wasn't learning the code fast enough. Truth is, he stopped taking his meds. By the time I found him two months later—"

My head snaps up. "You found him?"

Mason's gaze connects with mine. The raw barbarity stops my breath, but it's nothing like the sadistic smile that curves his mouth. "Yes, I found him."

"On your own?"

"Yes."

My throat has gone desert-dry, but I try to swallow anyway. "What did you do?"

His eyes are so dark they're almost black. Every single moment of danger—latent or otherwise—which I've felt since meeting Mason fuses into that moment. That look. And although I know it's not directed at me, my insides still congeal with fear.

"I made him pay," is all he says before he surges to his feet with me still in his arms.

His phone starts to ring again, and he turns away from it.

"Mason."

He strides through the room to the door before he sets me on my feet. "It's noon. We have an appointment downstairs," he replies, his voice a sharp blade, punctuating the air. He yanks open the door and pulls me after him.

"Wait!"

He slams to a stop and crowds me into the wall. "*I can take it* —those were your words to me. True or false?" His hot breath washes over my face as he bends his knees and looks into my eyes.

"True," I exhale.

"Good. I'm going to hold you to that."

Our trip down the elevator to the lower deck is conducted in a cracked silence, foaming with sex and despair, rage, and tortured sorrow. Mason doesn't hide his erratic breathing. The sound fills the small enclosure, fills my every pore, until I'm breathing in synchrony with him. His head turns and his gaze meets mine.

"Mason," I murmur.

Something shifts in his eyes, but it quickly disappears.

The doors part, and we're confronted by Titus Morton. He has two scantily clad women hanging off each arm, and his black silk shirt is secured by a single button. His gaze swings from Mason to me and proceeds to crawl over my body.

The raw snarl from Mason's throat snaps everyone's attention to him.

"This is your last warning, Morton. You keep your fucking eyes to yourself when you see us coming—"

"Or what?" the pudgy man stupidly challenges.

Mason lunges forward and wraps his hand around Titus' neck. The girls dart out of the way to keep from being flattened by the seething mountain that is Mason Sinclair. "Or I'll introduce you to scuba diving without a tank."

Titus' eyes bulge, then he throws out his hands in a quick gesture of surrender. "Hey, it's cool, Sinclair. I just thought since we both fish in the same pool, you wouldn't mind, you know... sharing—"

He never sees the hand coming. But the agony of a possible broken nose, and the blood spurting onto his chest, certainly registers as Mason calmly steps back.

"What the fuck!" Titus screams, clutching his nose with both hands.

"We've never had, and never will have, anything in common. Keep out of my sight, or the next time we're this close, you lose more than a little nasal cartilage."

Mason calmly turns to me and holds out his hand. "Come."

I slip mine into his without question, and we're walking down the hall as if the past two minutes never happened. I'm a little ashamed that the raw exhibition of Mason's jealousy has me all hot and wet, so I keep my head down, my body tucked close to Mason's and drag my free hand up and down his arm.

"Kitten?"

"Yeah?"

"Are you breathing like that because you're afraid, or because you're turned on?" he rasps in a strangled voice as he reaches the last door along the corridor and throws it open.

I see where he's brought me, and my nostrils quiver on a weak breath. "Can I be a little of both?"

"I prefer a seventy-thirty ratio in favor of being turned on."

He puts his hand on the small of my back and pushes me into the spanking room.

"Why thirty?" I ask.

The door slams behind me, and he keys in the code that locks it. A moment later, he's standing behind me; a tower of white-hot heat that I imagine can melt my clothes off. "It's a perfect balance that keeps your blood pumping. I want it pumping long and hard for me."

I bow my hips backward and rub my ass against his thickening crotch. "Consider it done."

He circles to stand in front of me. Dark hazel eyes examine me with intense contemplation. "Hmm... just like that?"

I want to say soft words that will show him how much I feel connected to him through our pain. But Mason isn't in the mood for soft, and the only connection that speaks the loudest is sex.

Nevertheless, I put my hand on his chest and luxuriate in the hard, warm muscles rolling beneath my fingers. "Our agreement was for you to fuck and use me as you please. I know I'll get what I need from you in return. So why argue the point?"

With his gaze locked on mine, he curls a hand over my hip and drags me into his body. "You remember when I said you could be perfect?"

How could I forget that damning compliment? "I remember."

"You just graduated to near-perfection." He licks the corner of my mouth and I purr. "My kitten. Purr for me again."

I make the sound, and he groans.

"You're so getting fucked, baby. Take your dress off."

I slip it over my head and fling it away. As per his instructions, I haven't bothered with a bra this morning, so I stand in only my black French panties and await my master's pleasure.

My heart catches when he strides toward the spanking equivalent of a jungle gym. High handlebars mean the spankee will be hanging at least a foot off the floor while being spanked. I like Mason's hand on my ass when I'm naughty or defiant, but I don't think I'm ready for that. I breathe a sigh of relief when he walks past it. My relief turns to tension when he slides the familiar three-sided partition from an enclosed wall panel.

A visceral reaction punches through me. "Mason, no."

He freezes. "Say that again, kitten?" he asks with veiled softness.

"I won't be put in that thing."

He turns and faces me across the room. "Because...?"

Resentment fires higher. "Are you kidding me? I watched you pleasure another woman in it. Fine, you were just testing the equipment, but she still got off by your hand. I'm not getting into it. You can use any other gadget in this room. But not that one."

His head tilts a little. "Come here, Keely."

I make a growling sound in my throat as anger and jealousy twist inside me. It colors my hurt and defiance, and he sees it. He lets go of the equipment and returns to me.

"I don't care what the punishment is, Mason. I'm drawing the line."

His answer is to tug his T-shirt off, fling it across the room and send his shoes and socks to join it. I gape when he continues undressing until he's gloriously naked.

Then he closes the gap between us, surrounds me with his warm, intoxicating heat, and cups my cheeks. "You keep striding towards perfection, and I just might have to alter our arrangement again."

Astonishment punches a hole in my chest. "What? You're not mad?"

"That you're ready to defy me because just the thought of sharing something I *didn't* give another woman makes you crazy?" His thumbs slide over my heated skin. "Kitten, I just punched a guy in the *fucking* face because he looked at you," he breathes.

28

KEELY

Despite the howling eddies of loss and rage that still grips us, I can't help it; I smile. "You're swearing."

"Your bad habits are rubbing off on me."

I sway into him. "What else can I rub off on you?"

"Your trust. A little bit of it right now will please me."

The lighter mood evaporates, and we're back to raw intensity. "Mason..."

"Come with me, baby."

The plea in his voice is what tips me over the edge. I take the hand he holds out, and I pray that whatever is going to happen in that partition, it'll be over quickly so I don't lose my shit.

We reach the corner of the room, and I stop. "That's..."

"The first prototype I used last week. This one"—he points to the newer, shinier black one in front of me—"has never been used."

My eyes widen. "Oh."

"Yeah," he says with a wry twist of his mouth.

I'm a touch ashamed of my little display now, but not enough to not be seriously turned on and seriously disturbed that he's as viciously possessive of me as I'm becoming of him.

I'm astute enough to know that doesn't bode well for me, emotions-wise, so I focus on the gadget in front of me and decide to save the ponder-and-prod of what's happening to me for later.

"What is it, exactly?" I ask.

Mason shrugs. "I don't have a name for it yet, but it's pretty much every sex toy you want it to be."

My brows spike as I stare at the plain partitioning. "How is that possible?"

He presses his finger to a raised rectangular button and the center partition starts to vibrate. I look close and see that while the two sides are only a few inches thick, the center partition is almost twelve inches thick. Mason presses another button and a thin front layer slides back.

The membrane-like gel shimmers, and I reach out and touch it. "It's warm. Oh," I gasp as the lifelike skin molds and clings to my fingers.

"It's something I developed a few years ago. I call it Memory Membrane. It retains dimensions and produces a sequence of programmed movements when required. Step up against it. I'll demonstrate."

I step onto the black square in front of the partition, and a wall of soft heat bathes my front. Mason slides one hand down my back as he presses a few buttons in the panel. An outline begins to form. I recognize Mason's body shape in about ten seconds, then my mouth drops open when it begins to turn three-dimensional. In about half a minute, I have a body double of my lover in front of me, complete with abs, pecs, and that thick cock I've become addicted to in such a short time.

"Fuck, I think I'm going to come right now," I say to the living, breathing one behind me.

"That's the idea, baby," he responds gruffly.

I hear the darkness in his voice, and I'm reminded of what he confessed a short while ago. I glance at him over my shoulder and see the turbulence jumping in his eyes.

Keeping my gaze on his, I step closer to the Mason-like outline and run my hand from its chest to thigh. Real-life Mason's cock jumps as he watches my hand.

"Is it nuts to be so goddamn turned on and fucking jealous at the same time?" he rasps.

I wonder if he realizes he's swearing again as I slide my palm down to the thick, very lifelike cock in front of me. "Show me what else it can do," I encourage.

He drags his attention from my slowly cock-pumping hand and presses another button. Arms extend out and hover just above my waist.

"Wow. I so want to fuck that big brain of yours right now."

"That's what I'm counting on."

Again, I hear the edge in his voice, and I shudder. We may have been heading down here anyway, but the parameters have changed for him from *need-to-fuck* to *need-to-fuck-hard-enough-to-forget.*

I recognize that need for oblivion, the need to fling oneself over the edge and hope the world helps you crash out of existence.

So I turn and face Mason. I wrap both hands around his cock and plead, "Use me. However you want. For as long as you want."

Relief and gratitude leap in his eyes, and I almost want to cry.

His throat moves as he swallows. "Kitten."

He cups my skull and slants his mouth over mine. The barely leashed violence in his kiss jacks up my animal arousal, but the human part of me that wants to nourish and care whimpers with concern.

My mind contorts around everything Mason didn't say during his confession. What did he do to the man who took his son? Was he alive? Was he dead?

I don't really care. Whatever retribution he received won't have been enough in my book. But I'm more concerned about the effect it's left on my lover. I'm even more concerned about what it will mean for us when he finds out what I did.

I realize I'm thinking beyond today, about future revelations and judgments. Future pleas for understanding and forgiveness. I try to check myself from ways to make my case and keep whatever place I have in Mason's life, but what's the fucking use?

The circumstances of our meeting set an irreversible path I know I'll see to its conclusion.

Acceptance seeps through me, and I release the chains of *what ifs*.

Something in me must have transmitted that decision to him because Mason pulls back and stares at me. "Keely?"

I feel a thousand times more naked and exposed than I am in this moment, but I embrace the vibrant danger and feel alive for the first time in a very long time. "I want you, Mason. Beyond today. Beyond tomorrow. Maybe saying that makes me vulnerable, but I don't care. I want you." My voice threatens to break when his eyes widen. "*I want you,*" I whisper-scream.

He says nothing. Just lowers his head until his forehead rests against mine. We stare into each other's eyes for an eternity. Then his breath explodes in a shuddering exhale.

"Whatever you have to give, I'll take it."

My heart leaps with sharp joy and deadly dread. Because I know I'll probably give more than is wise. And he'll leave me less of a shell than I was before.

But for now, I'm in. All the fucking way.

I kiss him. Teeth-mashing hard. The way I know turns him on.

He growls and goes deeper, until I taste blood mingled with our saliva.

My pussy throbs and I open my legs, ready to rub it on whatever body surface I can find.

But Mason catches my restless leg behind the knee and raises it. Before I can fathom what's going on, another cock is rubbing between my legs, it's velvety abrasion just what I need. I pull away from the kiss and look down at the artificial intelligence, rubbing its cock head so expertly between my legs. "My God, that's..." Words fail me and I raise my gaze to Mason's intensely aroused scrutiny.

"You like that?"

"I *love* that," I groan.

He nods and pushes another button. The arms move into a low embrace position. He carefully places my bent knees over one arm and grabs me by the waist. "Put your other leg over."

I obey, and a moment later, I'm wide open for both him and the outline behind me.

The idea of two Masons continues to blow my mind as the warmth against my back molds and shapes until I'm snug and horny, awaiting my lover's next pleasure.

Mason crouches before me and blows on my pussy.

I shudder as sensation pulls me under. When his tongue flicks my clit, I grip his hair and moan. He eats me until the first orgasm hits, hard and long.

I'm still convulsing when he stands and rubs my juices, which coat his lips, all over mine. "You ever been double penetrated, baby?" he growls when we're done licking my taste from each other. "For your sake, I hope the answer is no."

Since I have no idea what happened to me that weekend six years ago, I reply, "No."

He grunts his satisfaction, then steps away from me. The look in his eyes when he sees me cradled in the arms of his invention, wide open and ready to be fucked, staggers me.

He reaches out and circles my nipple with his forefinger, before he trails it down to my navel and up in a fiery V to my other nipple. "You're so beautiful."

"Mason," I moan.

He looks into my eyes with his turbulent golden ones. "I'll fuck you up, Keely."

I swallow. "You've already fucked me up. Now just fuck me. Please. Fuck me like you stole me."

It seems that's all he needs to go to town on me. Lube appears from somewhere and my asshole is prepped and ready to go in minutes.

The moment I'm filled from behind, Mason thrusts brutally into me.

Time ceases to have meaning as pleasure and pain grab me with vicious teeth and mangles coherency into a savage death.

Mason calls me *kitten*, and *Keely*, and *baby*, as he fucks me, long and hard, raw and rough. My orgasms feed into one another, and the more I come, the more Mason demands of me. With each release, I sense him quieten, the flames of hell in his eyes banking down to searing embers.

When he collapses into me, slick with sweat and sticky with my come, I drop my head to his shoulder.

We stay like that, contented and broken, until I hear a tiny beep next to my head.

"The quick brown fox jumps over the lazy god."

"What?" I enquire hazily.

"Say it."

"Why?"

When he doesn't respond, I lift my head. He's staring at me, but there's no sign of mind-fuckery in his eyes. It's a tiny thing, but I see the request to trust him.

"Okay, but isn't it 'the quick brown fox jumps over the lazy *dog*'?"

A smile caresses his lips, and he presses a couple of buttons. "Doesn't matter. It's done."

I glance at the panel, then back to his face. "What's done?"

"The recording of your speech pattern. Now you can use your *Keelinator* however you please."

"My...? Are you serious?"

He nods. "I'll have it shipped to your place in New York. We can give it a second christening when it arrives."

My heart lurches over the implications of what he's just said.

"Does that mean I'll see you after the IL trip?" I ask, feeling reckless.

"It means I'm officially hooked on you, and very much want to see you for however long I can before the inevitable shit circus descends. But I have an ulterior motive for this bribe."

"Oh?"

His thumb caresses my lower lip, and the way he's *not* looking into my eyes shocks me into thinking he's a little nervous about something.

"I have a thing at the White House at the end of the month. Come with me."

I stare at him. "It may be my just-fucked buzz deafening me, but I could've sworn you just said you have a thing at the White House?"

He stays silent, but the corners of his eyes crinkle in amusement.

My eyes widen. "*The* White House?"

"Yes."

"Permission to swear, please, sir?"

His eyes darken. "Just this once."

"Holy Mother of Fucking Fucks!"

He grimaces, but his eyes twinkle. "Is that a yes?" I hear a touch of vulnerability in his voice, and I stop joking. The work Mason did for the government may have added to his billions and given him power and prestige. But it'd also taken his son. Whatever reason is summoning him to attend, it can't be easy for him to face the head of the nation under those circumstances.

"I'm waiting for an answer, kitten."

I shake my head, still in a daze. "I don't know. Are you messing with me?"

"Why would I?"

"Because... *hello*? It's the *White House*. Also, I'd think you'd say no, given the circumstances."

His nostrils flare before he shrugs, but I know there's nothing carefree about the gesture. "There are only so many times you can say no to the commander in chief before it becomes a problem."

I chew on that for a minute. "And you want to go with me? Are you sure?"

"I'm sure. Let me buy you a dress, a few trinkets, a pair of fuck-me shoes, and use you shamelessly as the buffer between myself and every asshole government bureaucrat whose throat I want to rip out?" There's a little light, and a lot of darkness, in that statement, and my heart bleeds for him.

"Well, when you put it like that..." I let my voice drift.

"No lies, Keely. You okay with that?" he asks.

I suck in a deep breath. And smile. "I'm okay with that."

29

KEELY

The next four days race by.

Mason disappears into whatever area he's commandeered in the bowels of the yacht to work when he has to. He never tells me what he's working on, and I don't ask.

He, on the other hand, questions me about that Friday night six years ago. Sometimes, he's subtle. Other times he demands to know every single detail. I hate myself for withholding that final part of the jagged jigsaw, but I tell myself there's no need for him to know. I also know he's gathering the information I give him. Most likely to find who's behind the emails. I let him. My past will inevitably rise up and slap me in the face. But for now, I'm living in the present.

I also don't ask why he keeps ignoring Cassie's phone calls. They've graduated from three or four a day to almost hourly now. He always checks to see whether she's left a message. She never does.

The question of what the hell her deal is looms larger and larger in my mind, but I refuse to give it voice. I want nothing to take up extra room in the *Mason & Keely Temporary Bliss Shuttle*.

Our routine is simple. *Fuck. Eat. Fuck. Sleep. Fuck. Debate about the world and about nothing. Fuck.*

A couple of times, he's ventured out to meet me for dinner or drinks on the boat or at whatever venue I happen to be escorting my guests. After that time at the club in Mallorca, I've learned not to flirt when he's around.

Titus-Asshole-Morton, however, hasn't learned his lesson. His nose wasn't broken after all—much to my regret—and his leers have taken a dirty angle, especially when Mason isn't around.

I wondered what he meant when he referred to him and Mason as fishing from the same pool.

Well, I found my answer when I stepped into the elevator after a long afternoon of thermal baths and cocktails at Vulcano, Sicily.

The hostess I scheduled to take the guests came down with food poisoning, so I was left with no choice but to step in and head the trip. The healthy mud bath wasn't too bad, but the constant bickering of Titus' pets gave me a piercing headache.

Finding the man himself, lounging against the wall of the elevator, doesn't improve my mood. I stab for the lower deck and do my best to ignore him.

Of course, he's obnoxious enough to disregard my pointed signal and moves into my eye line.

"Enjoy your day of rolling around in the mud?" he jibes. "I'm more than willing to dirty you some more if you want?" he adds with a chuckle.

I turn and stare into his pale blue eyes. "I don't want, asshole. And I see your nose is still bent out of shape. Maybe you want me to bend it some more, finish what Mason started?"

Cold rage fills his eyes. "I paid a fuck load of money for this trip. I was promised an experience that's so far been severely lacking. Isn't this gig supposed to be a free-for-all? And as for Sinclair, I don't know what his fucking problem is. We've both fucked the same girls from Hani's stable. He suddenly doesn't want to share, that's fine." His sleazy gaze slithers over me, and I'm glad I'm wearing the kimono-like gown that covers me from neck to feet. "You're not super-hot, but I see the appeal. Sinclair got a free pass the last time. If he so much as points a finger at me, my lawyers will turn him into chump."

The elevator door opens. I walk through it, then turn and cock my head invitingly. "He's right this way. Care to come and tell him all of that bullshit in person?"

Fear crawls through his eyes, but he snaps, "Not worth my time. I have somewhere else to be." He stabs the button for the floor below repeatedly until the door starts to shut.

I smile. "Enjoy your evening, you fucking coward."

Outraged anger is the last thing I see before I turn and head down the hallway. At the door, I pause and take a deep breath.

I tell myself I'm a modern woman, that I'm okay with which-ever way Mason chose to get his rocks off before he met me.

But... I'm not okay being confused for a member of Hani's stable, whoever the hell she is.

I jump when the door is yanked open. "You plan to stand there all night?" Mason glares at me.

He wasn't happy when I abandoned our lunch and fuck plans to go on the excursion. Clearly, his mood hasn't improved in my absence.

I walk past him into the room, careful to avoid his gaze in case he sees my agitation, but he grabs my wrist and pulls me into a rough hug.

"You were supposed to be back an hour ago," he gripes as he buries his face in the crook of my neck.

"Sorry, the mixologist who accompanied us was a little too good at his job. Either that or serving decadent cocktails while indulging in an ancient mud bath is something no woman can get enough of."

"Hmm," he grunts, his mouth sliding to my collarbone. "Did you have a mud bath, too? Is that why you're wearing this dirty, delightful stink I want to roll around in?"

I tilt my head to give him better access, all the while trying to get my brain to erase Titus Morton's words. "The sulphur's supposed to be good for my skin."

"*I'm* good for your skin," he growls softly. "You want me to demonstrate?"

I open my mouth to say yes. Instead, different words emerge. "Who's Hani?"

Mason tenses against me, then lifts his head. "Who told you her name?"

I stare back at him. "Does it matter? Apparently, I'm good enough to be one of the many girls from her stable."

His features harden from granite to titanium. "Morton." The word is a death sentence.

I shiver but plow on. "I have to ask, Mason. Is this information public knowledge?"

His eyes narrow. "Why?"

My shoulders lift in a shrug that feels as if it's weighted by the world. "I just want a heads up if anyone who sees me with you will automatically think I'm a prostitute."

"They wouldn't dare."

"Umm... sorry, but they kinda already did."

"I'll deal with Morton."

I place a hand on his chest and shake my head. "No need, I already did. He's probably thick enough to try something again, but I can handle him."

Mason watches me, trying to gauge my mood. His phone starts to ring and relief punches through me.

Of course, I realize a moment later, it's probably Cassie. And he's not going to answer it.

"I'm going to take a shower," I say.

He frowns. "Keely—"

"You're right. I stink. And I'm starving. You mind ordering me some food?"

Still watching me, he nods.

"Thanks. I'd love a juicy Indulgence burger. The chef tops the meat with a mean mango salsa I can't get enough of. Oh, and I want an extra-large portion of fries with it, please."

One brow lifts. "Anything else?"

"No, that should about cover it. See you in a few."

I bolt for the bathroom and jump into the shower. Despite having used the spa facilities on board the yacht when I returned, I scrub myself again from head to toe.

Two truths smack me in the face as I'm drying myself.

The first is, I don't care what anyone who sees me with Mason labels me as. All I want is to be with him.

I also possess a rampantly alive and kicking fountain of jealousy and possessiveness. Enough to equal or even surpass Zach Savage's. I want to throat-punch each and every woman that Mason has ever fucked.

The first observation fills me with even more dread. The second I accept with weary resignation. I wasn't joking when I told Mason I was already fucked up. Learning this new dimension of myself only adds to my unique quirkiness.

I'm chuckling cruelly at myself as I leave Mason's bedroom, wearing nothing but a short silk robe. When I hear voices, I think it's the restaurant's concierge, delivering my food.

My feet slam to a halt when I enter the living room. "*Bethany?*"

She turns and smiles when she sees me. "There you are! Was thinking I might need to barge in there and pull you out of that shower."

She reaches me and tugs me into a hug. Beyond her shoulder, I see Zach talking to Mason.

A sense of déjà vu fills me. The last time I was in this position was in Zach and Bethany's kitchen in Montauk. Now, as then, I'm filled with turmoil and dread. It's strange to think so much, and so little, has changed since that day.

Bethany pulls back and stares into my face. I see the concern and anxiety in her blue eyes, and my heart catches.

"What's wrong?" I ask.

Her eyes widen. "Nothing. *I'm* fine. But I was about to ask you the same question."

A knock on the door stops further conversation. I let the bellboy in and direct him where to leave the trolley.

The moment he leaves, Bethany grabs my hand and clutches it tight. "We need to talk. Can we go to your suite?" There's tension in her body, and I notice that she's not doing her usual *devour-Zach-from-across-the-room* routine.

In fact, her body is precisely and deliberately turned away from the two men on the balcony.

"Bethany, what the hell's going on?"

She shuts her eyes for a fortifying second, before she stares sadly at me. "I promised Zach I wouldn't say anything. He'll kill me if he knows I'm even thinking about it. But—"

"Stop *fucking* with me, girl, and spill." Whispering the dirty word brings a ridiculous swell of shame, as if I'm betraying Mason.

Compelled by his name ricocheting though my mind, my

gaze finds his. He's staring right back at me, intense speculation narrowing his eyes.

"Not here," Bethany pleads.

I drag my gaze from Mason's and nod. Plastering a fake smile on my face, I stride to the trolley and grip the handle.

"Hey, we're going over to my suite to catch up on wedding stuff," I lie to Mason without looking him in the eye. "I'll see you later."

He jerks straight from the cross-legged, cross-armed position he adopted while talking to Zach. I wonder whether he'll stop me from leaving. I wonder what I'll do if he does.

"Keely."

Heart hammering, I turn. He comes to me and catches my face in his hands. His kiss is hard, but brief. Hazel eyes probe mine for a heart-stopping second before he releases me.

"Hurry back."

I swallow and nod. "Okay."

Bethany holds the door open, and I wheel the trolley through like a bank robber hightailing it out of a heist.

I don't know why I'm in a hurry to hear what my best friend has to say.

Because I do know that whatever it is will bat my fucked-up-ness into the next century.

30

MASON

I stare at the door Keely just walked out of and calmly acknowledge that the feeling spreading its way through my bloodstream is panic.

Not the crash and burn type that leaves just as quickly as it arrives. This is the slow, insidious type that taunts you with its possibilities and ability to grow extra appendages to fuck you with.

It started with the left-field question about Hani. Then grew when I realized how the thought of her interaction with Morton made me feel.

The little shit doesn't have a spine worth crushing, and I'm sure Keely can hold her own more than adequately. And yet none of that matters. The protectiveness that welled up in my chest, and which is still present, beacons a chaotic sequence that's been building since I told her about Toby. Since she let me purge on her.

I recall a conversation with the tribal priest in Roraima. He told me I'll never find peace for the chaos that reigns in my heart. I informed him that peace is the last thing I wish for, or want. He told me he would pray that my chaos never quietens.

My chaos isn't quietening. It's mutating into something less virulent and less murky, which makes me see through the dense jungles of pain and rage.

She's looked into my eyes and witnessed what I've done. Or at least she suspects. She hasn't called me a monster despite knowing what lives in my soul.

I'm not sure if the open acceptance is better or worse. All I know is I crave her beyond imagining, whether she's trapped beneath me, giving me what I need, or out of my sight.

The Hani issue isn't a problem.

The thought that it might keep Keely from me is. Keely is all I need.

"Have you heard a fucking word I've said since Keely walked out that door?"

I inhale my irritation and turn to Zach. "So besides bringing your fiancée to help clusterfuck my evening, and then soiling my eardrums with goddamn *small talk*, why are you here?" I ask Zach.

He lifts his beer and takes a long pull. "My staff alerted me that I have a Titus-Morton-shaped problem that needs to be dealt with. Know anything about that?"

"Yeah, the guy's an asshole. He'll be a lifeless asshole when I get my hands around his pussy neck."

"You see, talk like that is why I thought I'd better come and check on my investment before you turn my yacht into a killing field or start throwing guests overboard."

"Great, I suggest you go take care of your problems and let me deal with mine."

"I think it might be too late, buddy," he mutters.

I glance sharply at Zach. "Care to shed some light on that declaration?"

A hard, almost regretful smile twists his lips. "My soon-to-be wife—if she ever stops nitpicking every motherfucking detail of this damned wedding and gets round to actually marrying me—and your... What is she to you, exactly?"

My teeth smash together. "Get to the damn point, Savage."

Zach shrugs, unconcerned by the seething volatility raking through me. "My Peaches and your Keely are close. Closer than you or I will be comfortable with, if you two survive the shitstorm that's coming long enough to become a thing."

The roar of the chaos increases, and panic deadens my limbs. "What shitstorm? What the hell are you talking about?"

"Keely called last week, after you dumped her."

"I *didn't* dump her." I can barely speak through the poison tearing through my bloodstream. "What did she say when she called?"

"She wanted to know whether there were any bare-assed skeletons in your closet."

"*What?*"

"You can freak out in your own time when you're chasing rats the size of lions in that shit of a jungle you're so crazy about. Right now, shut the fuck up and listen, because I know one of two things is going to happen in the next five minutes. Right now, my Peaches is spilling her sweet little heart to her best friend—despite promising me she won't—about what happened to Peterson after you got your hands on him."

"*Mother of Christ!*" I charge for the door, but Zach gets there first.

I knock his hand away, intent on chasing down Keely, but he shakes his head. "It's too late, man. By now she knows."

"How? And how the fuck did your woman find out?"

Zach's eyes gleam. "This is where I'm supposed to say I don't have any secrets from the woman who holds every beat of my useless heart in her fucking hands, or some shit. And yeah, it's true. But the unvarnished truth is, she was freaked out with worry about her friend. I couldn't have that. So I asked a guy I know to look into things."

I shake my head. "Bullshit. I covered my tracks better than 'a guy I know to look into things' standards."

Zach crosses his arms and leans back against the door. "Let's agree to disagree on how good we are at what we do. Does Keely know you're investigating what happened to her six years ago?"

My hand drops from the door in a dead weight. "Shit! How the fuck do you know that?" I spike my fingers through my hair, certain in the knowledge that if there was any hope of salvaging anything from the first piece of shit news, it's just gone out the window with the second.

"She's important to Bethany, which makes her important to me. And before you throw a tantrum, Bethany doesn't know about the investigation, or what Keely went through."

My head snaps up. "She doesn't?"

"No, and I'm going to make damn sure my little firecracker doesn't find out from me. But do me a favor. Tell Keely. Trust me, things have a way of coming out whether you want them to or not."

I thrust my hands into my pockets to keep from putting my fist into the wall. "I don't intend to let the person or *persons* who violated her get away with it. But yeah, thanks for the hearts and roses and forgiveness sermon," I snarl.

Zach bares his teeth. "Any time, pal. That code you wrote me ten years ago for tracking my stock made me a bundle and stopped my companies from tanking during the '08 fuck storm. And I won't divulge which one, but one of the toys you invented for me makes my Peaches a very happy woman. I figured the least I could do was give you a little man-to-man heads up that your life's about take on epic clusterfuck proportions. As for letting anyone get away with it, I'll go after them myself if you don't."

Our gazes meet, and an understanding passes between us. I nod, then pace in tight circles, noting wryly that Zach is still guarding the door. I can't hear myself think over the roar in my ears. I want to see Keely, but I don't know how I'll react if she walks away from me.

I stop in my tracks as steel blades of irony slide between my ribs. I've been walking away from everyone who comes within caring distance all my life. Now, by attempting to care for Keely, and bringing her the justice she deserves, I've risked her walking away from me.

I see Zach turn sharply toward the door, and I lunge past him and yank it open.

When I see Daniel, instead of the woman whose importance has crept beneath the black noise of my life, I bite back a growl. "What do you want?"

The young guard looks from me to Zach, senses the volatile landmine before him, and hurries to speak. "We've a call to the captain's office for you, Mr. Sinclair."

I shake my head. "Take a message."

Daniel grimaces. "That's just it. She won't leave a message, except to say it's urgent."

"*Who* won't?" I snap, although I know who he means before he replies.

"She said her name is Cassie McCarthy."

"For the love of Christ," I growl under my breath.

"Problems?" Zach enquires.

I veer toward him. "No."

She isn't in trouble—financially or health-wise. I've made sure to keep an eye on her and my mother since my father died three years ago. Seven is also programmed to alert me if anything happens. Besides those parameters for keeping an eye on them, I consider myself free from obligation to Cassie and my mother.

"My ex-wife's definition of urgent and mine vastly differ."

"Are you sure?"

I spin around at the softly worded question.

Keely is framed in the doorway, her beautiful face pale and drawn. That air of fragility I saw in Montauk is back, and the eyes that track me as I close the gap between us are a dark, haunted green.

"What?" I ask, forgetting what she said as I'm confronted by the feeling I've only ever felt once before in my life. Hopelessness.

"I said are you sure your definition of urgent and hers are that different?"

I shake my head in confusion. I reach out to touch her hand, but she jerks away.

I ball my hand into a fist and lower it to my thigh. "What are you talking about?"

She dismisses Daniel with a nod and walks into the room. I vaguely register Bethany enter and cross to her fiancé's side. Or that they exchange a whispered argument before Zach leads her out.

"Cassie called me."

That jars in a way that unnerves me even more. "Why would she do that? She doesn't know you."

A frigid little smile touches her mouth. "Stop underestimating the people around you, Mason. You're not the only one who knows how to track another human being."

I search her eyes in a last, desperately futile attempt to save what's coming. Not so long ago, I proudly boasted that I have nothing worth salvaging and therefore nothing to live for. Now everything I've flung away in my grief and murderous despair comes flooding back. I feel my heart beat, my lungs fill, my soul raise its head and condemn me for abandoning it.

"You know," I rasp through lips that want to beg for every single act of cruelty I've ever perpetuated.

Ravaged green eyes meet mine. "That when you caught up with Peterson, you kidnapped him and kept him locked in a cage for ninety days with just enough food and water to keep him alive? Yes, I know." Her voice shakes with echoes of her own tortured past, and I die a million agonizing deaths in the face of her pain.

"Keely..." I grab her hands, but they're cold and almost lifeless. I rub them between mine, but she just stares at me.

"Did you torture him?"

The poison in my blood bleeds into my stomach and sickens it. "Don't ask me that."

"I'm asking, Mason. You can choose to answer truthfully, or you can lie."

Bile rises higher and I swallow several times before I can speak. "I wanted answers. I couldn't accept that his illness was the sole reason he took my son."

"And did you? Get your answers? Or do you go back to the mental institution he was sent to, once a year, to demand more answers?"

"You already know the answer to that, or you wouldn't know what to ask." My fingers scramble up to cup her shoulders, and I compel her to look at me. "But I can't explain to you the hell of living with this every day, of knowing it's my fault my son is no longer with me. Not until you have a child of your own."

She shakes her head. "You're wrong. I do know," she murmurs hollowly.

I feel a little hope when her hand lifts toward me. But it hangs between us, then drops as her face convulses and a dry sob rips from her throat.

"Baby, please, if you know... if you have any inkling of what I feel, then don't write me off. Tell me what I can do to fix this. I know you think I'm a monster—"

Her teary laughter cuts me off. "Trust me, I know what real monsters look like. Actually, no I don't." Her self-flagellation flays me. I move to tug her into my arms, but she pulls away and folds her arms around her middle. "I don't know what my monsters look like, and I've never wanted to know. What sort of person does that make me?"

I hesitate, then attempt to save the life I can see slipping away from me. "There's no right or wrong way to deal with what happened to you. You wanted to put what happened to you behind you. But... if you ever want answers, I can help."

"Oh, you mean Seven hasn't come up with any yet?" she asks with a voice devoid of emotion.

Blackness encroaches, and I scramble to stay above the void threatening to swallow me up. "Shit." I stop to regroup. "She found a property in the Hollywood Hills area that matches what you described, but the house was pulled down and rebuilt three years ago. She'll carry on looking, if you want."

"I don't want."

Shock spikes through me. "What? Why not?"

"Did you stop to think there might be another reason why I wouldn't want to know what happened to me? Why I wouldn't want justice for myself?"

The bleak echoes in her voice have deepened, shadowing her beautiful face, shrouding her precious body. I scramble harder to follow what she's saying. "Why wouldn't you want justice?"

She shakes her head in deep mournful twists. "You seem to think I hate you for all the things you've done. I don't."

I know I'm not safe, that the ground beneath my feet is shifting and cracking, ready to swallow me whole should I misstep. But I move toward her anyway.

"If you don't hate me, then why are we fighting?"

"We're not fighting. It's just the ugliness, which we both know lives beneath the surface, coming up."

"No, this is me. All me. Kitten, you have nothing to feel ugly about. You're beautiful."

"*No!*"

I reel at the tears filling her eyes. I reach out for her and my hands are shaking. She evades my grasp, and the soul I thought I didn't possess shrivels at the stark emptiness I see in her eyes. "I'm not. Please... I'm not," she repeats. "I'm so, so far from beautiful that... Oh, *God!*"

She releases a God-awful sound and crumples before my eyes. I catch her before she falls. She moans and tries to get away from me. I hold on tighter, tuck her face against my shoulder for far more selfish reasons than the comfort I freely offer her. When she's in my arms, I can dare to believe that there will be a way back for me.

I run my fingers through her hair and plead, "Keely, baby, please. Tell me what's going on."

She sobs quietly for another minute. Then she raises her wet, guilt-ravaged face to mine. "What you said just now, about me not knowing the hell of losing a child..."

I frown and try to backtrack. "Yes?"

"I said you were wrong. I wasn't being empathetic. I was being factual. I *know* how it feels to lose a child."

The naked agony shrieking from her is the final string of code that connects the dots. Visions of her on the beach at Montauk and in the shower afterward; the outbursts that guaranteed she would get punished. Her certainty that she didn't have anything to live for. The facts whizz through my brain at top speed as she staggers away from me.

I follow, needing to tell her she can lean on me if she wants. We can be battered, broken halves of a jagged whole. But she's staring at me with those big, guilt-soaked eyes again, and the force of her pain is so visceral it paralyzes me.

"You loved your son, Mason. Enough to find answers. I gave birth to mine and gave him away without a single question or protest minutes later. Which one of us is a monster now?"

Shock rains on me and I watch her drag herself to the door. I can't lift a finger to stop her. The depths of what was done to her are too much for me to fathom.

So I stand still. And I drown.

Her hand trembles as she turns the handle. Then her back tenses.

"Oh, by the way, the message Cassie left? She wants you to call her back asap. Her exact words were, 'Tell him the head of the institute wants to know which way to go concerning Max Peterson.'"

31

KEELY

Six days later

"Thank fuck that's over!" Bethany flops into the club seat next to me on Zach's private plane and secures her seatbelt over her Zac Posen dress and matching shoes combo. "Don't get me wrong, I love the Indigo Lounge and everything Zach's built. But no matter how extensively you vet them, the guests are *always* an unknown variable. Case in point—Fake Rack Olga the Ogre for me last year, and Tetanus Titus with you this trip." She stops and giggles, then purses her adorable lips. "Hmm, I think if we put our heads together, we can come up with some idea of a personality yardstick to measure them with. Or beat the crap out of them if they misbehave. What you do you think, Keels?"

I drag my frozen heart and aching body out of its icy morass and force my head to bob up and down. "Yeah, sure. Whatever."

Fuck. Moving my mouth hurts and my eyes water when I blink. Every second for the past week, I've wanted to lie down and die. From the moment I revealed the true depths of my rotten soul to Mason, and saw the frozen shock in his eyes, I've been a piece of toxic driftwood, bobbing toward a great and final plunge into nothingness.

Except the nothingness hasn't ever arrived.

Instead, tidal surges of pain keep me afloat, and while the occasional twisting current pulls me under, it's never enough to do away with me.

Bethany has put her wedding preparations on hold to make me her personal project. I'm sure Zach hates the very mention of my name by now. All week, I've secretly hoped he would do something about it. Hire a team of hitmen to take me out so he can have his Bethany back. Instead, the big pussy indulged his fiancée, who in turn has stood by me, held my hand when tears defied me and dared to fall.

Her heart broke for me when I finally told her what I went through at nineteen, and I fought her to stop her getting Zach on the case when I told her about the emails. We cried in each other's arms when I told her about the child I gave birth to, then gave away.

She grabs my hand now and squeezes it tight as the plane taxies and surges into the sky. Her face is a tableau of sadness and worry. "What can I do, Keels? I can't stand seeing you like this."

For a hot little second, I hate her for not throwing me off the edge of a cliff when our positions were reversed and I was smugly confident I knew what she was going through.

"You should've told me to go fuck myself when I tossed out relationship advice to you last year," I murmur around a throat that refuses to work properly.

She smiles. "Are you telling me to go fuck myself now?"

I try to grip her hand, but my fingers are too weak, so I let them go slack again. "Of course not. What I'm saying is you haven't judged me once this week, whereas I was Judgey

McBitch when you were going through that stuff with Zach last year. I whined about you not telling me straight away, when I'd kept my own shit from you for years. Then I was an ass to Zach for daring to want you back after he hurt you."

"No, Keely. You listened when I needed you to, and you encouraged me to take a chance with Zach. I don't know what'll happen with Mason—"

"Nothing will happen!" Even the sound of his name is like a blowtorch to my skin. "You didn't see his face, B. For God's sake, he... he lost his child. I gave mine away—"

"After you were violated so horrifically, you spent months in hospital." Her fingers twist through mine and I see her heartache for me. "Perfectly healthy, well-adjusted women take that option every day. No one can judge you for that. No one has *a right* to. And if Mason thinks he can, well... he can fuck right off. There, I can be bitchy about him in return."

A drop of liquid falls onto my white jumpsuit, and I realize I'm crying. Bethany's face twists, and she swipes her fingers over my wet cheeks.

"Dammit. Sorry, B. I don't mean to... I can't... God, it hurts so fucking much!"

As soon as the seatbelt sign goes off, she unbuckles hers and pulls me into a tight, deep hug. The next minute, I'm bawling my eyes out, each sob ripping me to pieces all over again.

"I'm sorry," she croons over and over in my ears.

I love Bethany, but in that moment I wish for other arms around me. I yearn for the stronger arms of the man I've fallen in love with despite all the signs pointing to it being the biggest mistake of all.

I was so stoned with shame and self-recrimination when I stumbled out of Mason's suite, it never occurred to me that it would be the last time I'd see him.

Now, I wish I'd taken one last look at his face. Stayed a minute longer in his arms when he pulled me close.

Delayed my confession by another day?

I suck in a tortured breath. I would have ended up here, like this, wishing my every breath would be my last.

You have a hell of a fucking lot to live for!

Pain lances through me when I hear Mason's voice. God, I bet he wishes he'd known the depths of my sins before he made that assumption.

More tears flow when that thought flares through my mind.

"Oh God, Keels. Tell me what to do," Bethany begs.

I take pity on her and pull myself together. For one thing, if I return her to Zach as stressed as she is right now, he'll serve my head on a silver platter. While that thought is palatable right now, the situation will stress Bethany out even more.

"You want to help me?"

She nods. "Whatever you need."

"Get the stewardess to rustle up some Dom P. I'll go clean up and we can get pissed in style. Yeah?" I croak.

She looks uncertain for a few seconds, then she nods. "Okay. Let's do it."

* * *

The limo drops us off at my place when Bethany refuses to go home until she's sure I'll be okay.

She knows better than anyone that I won't be okay for a long time, so I don't bother putting up a protest.

I lean disconsolately against the wall while she grabs my mail. She hands it to me as we enter the elevator. After I shut my front door, I toss the mail on my console table. A couple of envelopes slip off and drop to the floor.

I bend to pick them up and see the unmistakable seal marking the back of a heavy, rectangular envelope.

My blood runs hot, then cold, then freezing. I make a sound that probably isn't human, and Bethany hurries to my side.

"What's wrong?"

My fingers tremble as I clutch the envelope. "Omigod, it came. It actually came."

Bethany gasps. "What did you say?"

I repeat it and turn the envelope over, staring at it incredulously. I assumed that all arrangements we made before our relationship's fiery demise were null and void.

But I hold in my hands physical proof that I was mistaken. I want to lift the pristine white paper to my nose and sniff hard to see if Mason's scent clings to it. Of course, the likelihood that he doesn't send out his own invitations is quite high. Plus, this invitation probably came straight from the White House—

"My God."

I look up and Bethany's wiping a tear away from the corner of her eye while grinning like a freaky circus clown.

"What?" I demand.

"What you said kinda freaks me out a little. That was my first thought too, when I saw Zach's Indigo Lounge envelope."

I let out a defeated sigh. "Baby girl—"

"No." She grabs my hand in hers. "It's my turn to help you, and we're doing things *my* way. Open the envelope."

My whole body shakes as I slide my finger carefully beneath the gold crest. I lift the flap and cautiously remove the invitation. I see my name next to Mason's and my heart squeezes hard enough to make me dizzy.

"Shit! Don't fucking pass out on me," Bethany cries.

We walk arm in arm to the living room and collapse on the

sofa. I lie there, wide open and defenseless against the waves of pain as Bethany talks about designer fittings and makeovers.

"No," I croak when it all becomes too much.

"What do you mean, no?"

"I'm not going."

"Yes, you are. It's the fucking White House. Refusal could be treasonous."

I manage a weak snort, which fails miserably.

When she launches into another shopping list of things I need to get me ready, I sigh. "Mason said he'd send me a dress. And shoes. And *trinkets*." I attempt another snort. It works this time, and suddenly I can't stop. I laugh and cry and snort until I'm a giant wrecking ball of hysteria, rolling around on my living room floor.

But as quickly as the mania begins, it ends, and I curl my knees to my chest and hug my heartache close. I don't know how long I lie there or when I give in and let sleep claim me.

When I wake, there's a blanket over me and a pillow beneath my head. Bethany is on the floor next to me, with a steaming bowl in one hand and the remote in the other.

My gaze meets hers, and she gives me a heartbreaking little smile. I nod and shuffle my broken body upright. I take the bowl of chicken soup from her, and she clicks on the first episode of *Game of Thrones*.

I drink my soup. And let the carnage onscreen wash over me.

And I wonder if the rock of agony in my stomach will ever leave me.

* * *

The dress arrives two days later. I refuse to open the Valentino bag and shoe box when Bethany shows it to me. I ignore her huff as she goes to hang it in my closet.

The diamonds arrive two days before the Friday event. This time, I'm alone at my apartment, having finally convinced Bethany that I can take care of myself and Jeigerhamster, my pet hamster, and that I'm going to Washington D.C.

My hands shake—I wonder if I'll ever stop shaking—as I carefully pry open the Harry Winston velvet box. I gasp at the sheer amount of diamonds on display and swiftly shut the box again.

But my fingers curl around the velvet exterior, and I stumble to the living room. The reality that Mason has sent the items, despite how we left each other, confuses me. It also fans a tiny flame of hope for a life that I know I shouldn't build on.

He left the yacht the same day I walked out of his suite, and despite having my phone number, he hasn't been in touch.

My heart lurches when it occurs to me, he could've made the dress and necklace arrangements the day I said yes and never got round to cancelling them.

I throw the box on the coffee table and pace my living room, torn between calling him and just turning up in D.C.

I pull out my phone and finger the buttons. My breath strangles with yearning at the thought of hearing his voice, but it's the chance to see his face again, even if it is for one last time, that makes me put the phone down.

I'm going to D.C. And if there's the smallest chance that I can see and talk to Mason again, I'll take it.

* * *

Do not pass out. Do not fucking pass out.

I recite the words to myself as I lift the hem of my black

sleeveless gown and quicken my steps. I'm ushered into the State Dining Room, where the Industry Innovators dinner is being held.

An accident on the Brooklyn Bridge held up the limo taking me to Teterboro Airport, and even the efficiency of travelling by private jet couldn't save me from being late to the dinner.

"Right this way, Miss Benson."

I follow the usher as we weave through tables holding seated guests. I keep my flame-hot embarrassed face down and pin a smile on my lips when I'm shown to the last empty seat in the room.

An elderly woman smiles at me and I smile back. "I'm so sorry for being late. There was a pile up on the Brook—"

The words strangle in my throat when I look up into a pixie-like face and a pair of eyes I've only seen once before in a photo.

Cassie Sinclair, Mason's ex-wife, is staring back at me with unabashed curiosity and an almost pitying smile on her lightly glossed mouth.

Shock lodges in my chest as I glance one along and encounter Mason's dark, intense hazel eyes. He looks a picture of perfect and suave health, while I know my face is an unpleasant caricature of gold-fish-in-death-throes.

I can't move. Or breathe. Or think beyond the fact that Mason has come to the dinner with his ex-wife!

Bile rises in my gut and settles at the back of my throat.

When the woman next to me addresses me, I nod and clasp my shaking hand in my lap.

Drinks are served. I gulp down fine white wine without a thought to taste or vintage. I respond to small talk with monosyllables and I don't ever look back across the table.

The moment the announcement is made for a twenty-five-minute mingle before the awards ceremony starts, I jump from the chair and head for the door.

An usher steps in front of me, a solid wall of courteous muscle. "May I help you, ma'am?"

"Yes, I need to leave."

"I'm sorry, guests are required to stay until the ceremony is over."

Panic claws up my spine. "I can't wait that long."

"Is it an emergency?"

"Yes," I say, then I remember I'm standing in the White House. "No."

He frowns. "Which is it, ma'am?"

The thought of being denied escape fills me with horror. "Please, I really... really need to leave. I think I may be coming down with something."

Concern streaks through his frown. "Okay. Come with me."

Relief pours through me. I'm walking down what I think is the west corridor when an arm slides around my waist.

"Where the hell do you think you're going?" Mason blazes in my ear.

"Get your fucking arm off me," I whisper-scream.

The usher stops and turns. "Is everything all right?"

"Yes—"

"No, my girlfriend's recovering from the flu. She just needs somewhere quiet to catch her breath. Can we go somewhere?"

"Of course, Mr. Sinclair. If you'll follow me."

I glance at Mason and see the warning in his eyes. I want to throw the mother of all tantrums, but I'm in the fucking White House, so I bite my tongue and follow the usher.

"This should do it, I hope. Can I get you two anything? A glass of water?"

"No, thanks. She just needs a minute."

I keep my head down so the usher doesn't see how livid I am. The moment he shuts the door behind him, my head jerks up.

"Your *girlfriend*? You can say that with a straight face when your ex-wife, *the woman you came here with,* is just down the corridor?"

Mason strides toward me, looking far too dashing in his tuxedo. "Calm down, Keely—"

"Do not tell me to calm down! Play your cruel games with her all you want, but I will not let you drag me into this."

"Are you finished?"

"No, I fucking well am not! Why did you do it? For some sort of cheap thrill?" I exhale shakily, feeling pain from head to toe. "Actually, don't answer that. I don't want to know. All I want is to get out of here."

"No."

"What the fuck do you mean *no*?"

His eyes gleam at the torrent of swearing, and I cock my eyebrow at him. "I mean you won't leave this room until you hear me out. We have twenty minutes. Shall we talk first, or get your punishment out of the way?"

My face flames in anger, but my heart flip-flops like a foolish thing in my chest. "Lay a hand on me and I'll kick your fucking ass."

He nods solemnly. "Talk first then."

"Yeah, talk to yourself. Leave me the fuck out of it. I'm leaving." I reach for the door handle. His hand captures mine a second later.

He crowds me with a wall of heat and muscle, and I helplessly breathe him in, inhaling the scent I've missed more than I want to admit.

"I didn't bring Cassie *instead* of you. I brought Cassie so she could meet the woman I'm in love with," he says next to my ear.

I gasp, then sway against the door as dizziness hits me.

"Dammit, are you okay?" Concern colors his voice.

"I'm fine."

"You don't *look* fine."

Cursing, he grabs me by the waist and lifts me from the door.

"Mason, put me down."

He ignores me. Heat ripples through me when he sits and pulls me into his lap.

"I tell you I'm in love with you, and the first thing you do is pass out?"

"You're not in love with me." The pain that grips me when I say it makes me groan. "You can't be."

"Why the hell not?"

My heart tears wide open as I stare at him. "You know what I did. I gave my child away because I couldn't cope. It wasn't his fault, Mason. And yet, I couldn't stand the sight of him when he was put in my arms." I shudder in remembrance. "He screamed so loud I thought I harmed him."

"Baby, don't do this to yourself."

"Why not? You know what I felt when he was taken away?"

He remains silent.

"Relief. I was *glad* he was gone."

"If you truly were, would you be suffering as you are now? Would you not have gone on with your life, never giving him another thought? Instead, you've spent the last six years ripping yourself apart about it."

He inhales, and I wonder if I'm imagining his chest shake beneath my shoulder.

One hand captures my chin and tilts my face up to his. His heart-stopping features explode across my brain, and I'm dizzy all over again. I want to touch him so bad that I curl my hands into fists to stop myself from reaching for him.

"What? You don't want me to tell you how I feel because it's not what you want to hear? Or because you don't love me back?" His eyes are alive with heat. And frantic with apprehension. Deep with an emotion I don't want to acknowledge, in case it's a dream.

"Mason..."

"You know me, better than anyone on this earth. I've suffered a great loss and repaid it with acts that will stain my soul for eternity. There's a man locked up in a mental institution who will never be whole again because of what I did to him. I have to live with that." His head drops forward, and his forehead rests against my cheek. "I left the yacht and stayed away from you because I knew it was wrong of me to ask you to live with it too. But I can't do it, baby. I know what hell feels like. Being without you has been beyond any pain I could've imagined. I can't go through life not knowing if there might be the sliver of hope that you'll say yes. That you'll let me love you and worship you, that you'll let me pay for what I did by allowing me to devote my life to you."

He lifts his head, and I see the sheen of tears in his eyes.

I shiver uncontrollably.

His face twists. "You can't, can you?"

"Mason—"

"It's okay." His arm convulses around me. "I'll let you go in a minute. Just... let me hold you for one last time."

"Mason..."

"Please, kitten. Just one minute."

I stay silent, let him hold me, let myself drown in the heat and joy and completeness of being with the other half of my soul.

When the minute is up, he groans. "God, what the fuck am I going to do?" His voice bleeds naked anguish.

"I love you, so you don't have to do anything," I murmur.

"What?" Disbelief echoes through his voice.

"I love you," I say again. "If you can accept me and what I did—"

"You have nothing to be agonized about. I'll drill that into you for the rest of your life if I have to."

"Oh, Mason."

"Tell me you love me again."

"Tell me first what Cassie's doing here."

He hears my irked tone and smiles. "I've had a lot of time lately to... mend fences. Cassie wanted to meet the woman responsible for making me human again."

"Fine, but did she have to sit next to you? And why the fuck didn't you warn me she was going to be here?"

"That seat was yours. She took it when I thought you weren't coming. When we go back in, you'll be next to me, where you belong. Now tell me you love me again."

Of all the emotions churning through me, only one floats to the surface and I know it's the truth that I've tried to resist since meeting this man. But saying it again, now, sets me flying higher than I ever thought I deserved to be. And it feels good. Deliriously good. "I love you, Mason."

He groans and kisses me with a fervor that warms my frozen heart. I slide my arms around his neck, and he surges to his feet. He walks forward without breaking the kiss. It's only when he sets me down that I look about the room.

"Where are we?"

He spins me around and slams me back against him. "Lincoln's Bedroom."

I gasp and reassess the elaborate furnishings. Sure enough, the room I've seen in books is laid out before me. I reach out to touch the antique bed cover and feel Mason's hand lifting the hem of my gown.

My heart kicks up a thousand notches. "What're you doing?"

"Delivering your punishment, of course," he rasps in my ear.

I bite my lip to stop the groan of bliss that spirals through me. He gathers the cloth in one hand and pushes me forward with the other. My tiny thong is no barrier for what's coming, and I gasp as the first smack lights up my ass and spreads through my body.

"Oh God!"

Smack.

"You knew this was coming, didn't you, kitten?"

"Yes."

Smack.

"Yes, what?"

Smack. Smack. Smack.

"Yes, sir. I love you."

He groans. "God, I wasn't going to fuck you now... Was going to take my time with you later, show you how much I've missed you, how much I love you. But your ass... I need you, baby." He's panting, and I hear his zipper open.

Love and fire, electricity and joy, light up my veins. "Mason, what if we get caught?"

"Then we'll be the happiest jail birds in history." He pulls my thong to one side and slides, thick, hot, and delicious, inside me. "Now shut up and let me love you. I have an award to collect."

EPILOGUE
KEELY

"Are you ready?" Mason asks, his smile lighting up my heart, my soul, my world.

But I can't smile in return. "I'm too nervous. What if I mess it up?"

"You won't. It's just a meeting. We don't have to take it further if you don't want to."

I look out the window of our SUV at the sun-dappled office building in Maryland, where our search has brought us. It's been a year of incredible highs and a few heartbreaking lows.

When another email arrived shortly after my return to New York, this time with a photo of me tied up in the chair, and a ransom demand for one million dollars, Mason put his foot down.

He called in favors, and investigations were launched. The search took three months, but the blackmailer was found.

Richard Donner, a fellow UCLA freshman, confessed to sneaking in a camera and taking the pictures of me, before raping me. He was tried and convicted. Despite his confession, he wasn't able to shed light on whether there were any other violators.

Professor Harding was also brought in for questioning, and arrested for several counts of sexual harassment.

Although I've found a little closure now, the deep dredging up of my past hasn't been pleasant.

But Mason has stood by me throughout. And with a line drawn under the events of six years ago, I'm ready to move on to the next step: finding out if the child I gave birth to is happy.

Mason and I talked about it, but ultimately I've decided it will be better, if there ever comes a time that we meet face to face, to leave my child in the dark about his conception. I don't know if I'll ever be able to have a connection with him, but for now I'm leaving the door open to possibilities.

My hand glides over the small swell of my belly, and the smile that's been missing bursts from my soul.

Our little girl is scheduled for arrival at Christmas, and my heart can scarcely contain the love I feel for the new life growing inside of me.

I look up, and the love of my life is staring at me with utter adoration.

He picks up my left hand and kisses my knuckle just above where my diamond and platinum wedding rings rest.

"Happy thoughts, Mrs. Sinclair?" He quirks his brow at me.

"Happy thoughts. Always."

* * *

Mason

"Come on. Let's go do this thing."

I round the car and open the door for my new wife. She smiles and slips her hand into mine as we head for the Child Protective Services office. Her skin glows in the mid-morning sunshine and I want to stare, and keep staring, at her for the rest of my life.

She's beautiful.

And mine.

When further revelations of her past surfaced and threatened to send me back down a dark and tortuous road, her strength held me together.

And when thoughts of becoming a parent again terrified me, she talked me down.

Neither of us are bright-side people, but with Keely by my side, I greet each new day with a positive perspective. Especially if the day starts with one of us initiating a session of the mind-melting sex that drew us together in the first place.

"Careful there, Rusty, you're leering with intent."

I laugh, not minding the name so much now since it's a reminder of how we met and what we've been through.

"Ah, sorry, Officer. Please go ahead and arrest me now. I intend to be a repeat offender."

Her unfettered laughter lifts my soul and infuses me with so much happiness, I can barely catch my breath. I pull her close and I don't let go. I hold her as she weeps softly through being informed by the social worker that her first child is happy and healthy, and living a fulfilled life with adoptive parents who love him.

I hold her when we re-emerge into the sunshine and both our phones ping.

"You think the Savages have anything better to do than check up on us?" I gripe without malice.

She laughs. "Nope. They know today's a big day for us. Bet

they're waiting by the phone, ready to call the moment we respond." She lifts her phone, but I stay her hand.

"Leave it for one second, kitten."

Her eyes gleam at the pet name, and her hand slides around my neck. "Are you going to make it worth my while, sir?"

I kiss her, long and deeply, in the middle of a car park in Maryland, and I'm filled with a sense of homecoming so strong, my head spins.

"Kitten, you rescued me and made my life worth something other than the hellish wasteland I turned it in to. You nourish my soul with your love and trust." My hand caresses her belly. "I can't wait to love and cherish our child the way I love and cherish you. I love you, Keely. So much."

Happy tears fill her eyes and I brush them away.

"I love you too, Mason. Always."

* * *

MORE FROM ZARA COX

Another book from Zara Cox, *The Mastermind*, is available to order now here:

www.mybook.to/MastermindBackAd

ABOUT THE AUTHOR

Zara Cox is the writer of spicy contemporary romance, she writes intense, spicy billionaire romances for Boldwood, including the Indigo Lounge series.

Sign up to Zara Cox's mailing list for news, competitions and updates on future books.

Follow Zara on social media here:

facebook.com/zara.cox.98
x.com/zcoxbooks
instagram.com/zaracoxwriter
bookbub.com/authors/zara-cox

ALSO BY ZARA COX

Boldwood
EVER AFTER

x♡x♡

JOIN BOLDWOOD'S
**ROMANCE
COMMUNITY**
FOR SWEET AND
SPICY BOOK RECS
WITH ALL YOUR
FAVOURITE
TROPES!

SIGN UP TO OUR
NEWSLETTER

HTTPS://BIT.LY/BOLDWOODEVERAFTER

Boldwood

Boldwood Books is an award-winning fiction publishing company seeking out the best stories from around the world.

Find out more at www.boldwoodbooks.com

Join our reader community for brilliant books, competitions and offers!

Follow us
@BoldwoodBooks
@TheBoldBookClub

Sign up to our weekly deals newsletter

https://bit.ly/BoldwoodBNewsletter